To :

BAGGY PANTS AND BOOTEES

lovely to
meet you. Happy
reading !

BAGGY PANTS AND BOOTEES

MARILYN CHAPMAN

Published by
Amelia Press

First published in Great Britain in 2014

Copyright © MARILYN CHAPMAN 2014

Amelia Press
Great Britain

Printed and bound in Great Britain
ISBN: 978-0-9929749-0-9

DEDICATION

This book is dedicated to my late father Harry Brown. Without him, and the endless patience of my family, Baggy Pants and Bootees would never have been written.

CHAPTER 1
Yorkshire, 1968

Sophie stared at the dog-eared photograph of a naked pin-up randomly sellotaped to the wall above her head. 'The Horticultural Society's annual show *is* very important to the *Harcot Weekly Tribune*, I can assure you, Mrs Potts,' she said, cupping the phone between her chin and her shoulder. She shifted position in the telephone booth, knocking her knees against the overflowing ashtray which teetered briefly on the shelf before depositing its foul smelling contents into her lap.

'Yes I *am* new here, as it happens,' she tried to keep the impatience out of her voice, 'but I can assure you that I do know what I'm doing. Well, two weeks, actually, but you'd be surprised what you can learn about a place in –' She stopped abruptly as the line went dead.

Slamming the phone back down on its cradle, Sophie brushed the cigarette ends off her lap and pushed her way out of the booth. She had deliberately worn trousers to blend into the testosterone-filled newsroom that passed for her place of work these days.

'How are you doing, young Soph?' The news editor's voice boomed across the office. 'Getting the hang of things?'

'Great, thanks,' she smiled back sweetly. 'I'm sure Marje Proops would be proud of me.'

She sat down at her desk, sandwiched between the teleprinter and a rickety stationery cupboard that was always empty, fed some copy paper into her typewriter and began to hammer on the keys.

'Here we go – tap tap tap – it's that damn woodpecker again.'

This came from Joe Suchins, a tall, blonde-haired lad who had recently been promoted from theatre critic to junior sub editor and now regarded himself as superior to everyone.

'If you are referring to my typing, I can assure you, Joe, that my copy is more accurate than yours already. The speed, I agree, needs improving but believe me I intend to keep practising.'

'Aren't there some women's things you should be doing? Knitting patterns, wedding reports, cookery? I'm sure Cynthia would be happy to have an assistant.'

Cynthia was a freelance who contributed syndicated pieces on 'topics of interest to women'.

'For the last time, I am not here to do the women's page. I am a trainee reporter, indentured to the North Riding Group of Newspapers for the next three years with every intention of becoming a fully-fledged member of the National Union of

Journalists –'

'Okay, okay, don't get that pretty little head of yours in a tizzy. Now make me a mug of tea will you, there's a good girl?'

Sophie averted her eyes and carried on typing. She had a right to be here along with everyone else. Maybe she shouldn't have forged a reference from the managing editor of the *News of the World*, but how else was she supposed to have got the job? Besides, if he'd known how keen she was, he'd surely have agreed to write the letter anyway. She pushed her glasses up on to the bridge of her nose and tried to concentrate. Strictly speaking she didn't need the wretched things, but they gave her the air of sophistication it was difficult for a female reporter with blonde hair and green eyes to otherwise achieve.

She gazed blankly at the eight mismatched desks and chairs that served the entire editorial staff of the *Weekly Tribune*. Luckily her fellow hacks were never in all at the same time or the oxygen levels would have plummeted to zero.

What had made her think that newspaper life would be so different? As an only child growing up in Lancashire without a father, she had pictured herself in many heroic roles, such as first-ever female leader of the Labour party or manager of Manchester United FC. But when the lights were turned out and she couldn't sleep, the names of famous journalists came into mind: John Pilger, Alistair Cooke, Germaine Greer – now they knew how to make a real impact. She'd read books all her life, but it was newspapers, tabloid, broadsheet, English or foreign that fascinated her most.

The sound of the editor's voice brought Sophie back to the

present. Albert Moulton was strictly of the old school; a kindly man who smoked a pipe and always kept a copy of *The Grammatical Rules of the Harcot Weekly Tribune* at his side. He was aggrieved, she knew, at being 'fobbed off with a young girl', and hadn't the slightest idea why a member of the opposite sex would ever want to get involved in the news. Kindly he might be, but when he was cross everyone within earshot stood to attention, stopped inventing their weekly expenses and started working.

'*Sophia – Sophia.*'

'Coming, Mr Moulton.' She stood up and headed for the inner sanctum.

The editor sat in his office, tapping an empty pipe on the wall behind him. 'This piece about the stolen tent – have you interviewed the owner?'

'Well, no, Mr Moulton, they didn't appear to be on the telephone so...'

'Of course they weren't. No one in Winton Street has a phone. They're very lucky if they have a TV.' He threw her half-subbed story on to the crowded desk. 'Now get down there immediately and find out what really happened. You're not going to learn anything if you stop around here.'

'Yes, Mr Moulton.' Judging by the enthusiasm of her colleagues, he certainly had a point.

'And being a stranger to these parts, I presume you have a map?'

'Yes, of course, Mr Moulton.'

'Then why are you still here?'

Sophie grabbed her coat and ran down the three flights of stairs, past the front counter with its ancient wooden switchboard and out of the latched front door. She rounded the corner sharply and climbed into an ancient Austin A40 – her only mode of transport. Seconds later the car spluttered into life, belching black smoke from the exhaust as she set off down the road. She had forgotten her map, but could soon find the whereabouts of Winton Street down at the police station. Anyway, it made sense to keep in with the local bobbies. Turning the corner, she parked opposite the hundred-year-old magistrates' courts taking care to avoid the double yellow lines.

'Quick, Alan, there's a nice piece of crumpet here,' the duty policeman whispered loudly, adjusting his tie as she approached the counter. 'Can I help you, Miss?'

'Yes please.' She smiled sweetly. 'I'm the new reporter from the *Weekly Tribune*. Are you any good at directions?'

'Well, now, I can direct you into the back office to meet my partners in crime.

We could make a brew and discuss how we can help you in your new role.' He winked. 'What do you say?'

It was gone eleven o'clock when Sophie finished work. After leaving the police station, she had called at Winton Street, re-written the tent piece and grabbed a stale sandwich. She'd spent most of the evening covering a play by the Harcot drama group, returning to the office to send the copy through on the teleprinter for the following day's *Evening Standard*. It was her third night job that week but she was determined not to complain. News editor Patrick Porchester, a swarthy man in his late thirties, clearly had an axe to grind and she wasn't going to give him any more ammunition.

'Let's get one thing straight,' he'd said at the beginning of her second week in the job. 'You want to be a reporter? Then act like a man, think like a man, and you might just make it. If you don't like the rules, there's a little secretarial job going right now at head office. I'll give you the number – I'll even give you a reference if you like. Just don't give me any more crap.'

To hell with patronising Patrick. If he thought he could scare her, he'd chosen the wrong girl.

Sophie locked up the office, trying to remember where she'd left her car. Five minutes later she jumped into the front seat and turned the key in the ignition. Nothing happened. She tried again but the engine turned over without as much as a spark. She pulled out the choke till the ancient saloon was filled with fumes, swore under her breath and retreated back on to the pavement.

Aiming a kick at the car bumper, she headed towards the nearest bus stop. Granted , forty quid was a bargain – even for an old banger – so what did she expect? She glanced up as the heavens opened then pulled her hood over her head and broke into a run.

The Ford Zodiac appeared out of the dark, screeching to a halt within inches of her life. Visions of the following night's headlines floated in front of her eyes. *Cub reporter killed after three weeks with Tribune.*

'Sorry about that.' The driver grinned as he lowered the window. 'It's Sophie, isn't it – the new recruit? I thought I recognised you. I'm Steve Sibson, a photographer from head office. Want a lift?'

'Well, seeing as I'm lucky to be alive, I might as well say yes.' Sophie clambered in begrudgingly out of the rain. 'Do you usually try to run down your colleagues?'

Steve had a mass of brown hair and a cheeky grin that she found strangely disconcerting. 'Not if I can help it. Though it has crossed my mind once or twice. So, what's the hurry?'

'Firstly, although I'm not sure it's any of your business, my car wouldn't start. Secondly, in case you hadn't noticed, it's pouring with rain and I've already had one bath today.'

'Okay, okay, don't be so touchy. Just trying to be friendly. Where would you like me to drop you off?'

'Home seems a good a place as any – do you know Sedgley Street?'

'Of course. My ex-wife lives there with our three sons.' He burst out laughing. 'Only kidding. Do you smoke?'

Sophie shook her head as he roared off down the road, watching as he removed a cigarette from the packet with practised ease and held it between his lips. 'Can you light it with one hand as well?' she asked.

'Actually, I was hoping you were going to offer.' He passed her the lighter without taking his eyes off the road. 'When you're ready, of course.'

They drove for several minutes in silence, Steve drawing the smoke deep into his lungs. She peered at him out of the corner of her eye like an inquisitive child.

'Sedgley Street, Miss – all in one piece and no fare to pay. ' He doffed an imaginary cap. 'You could always invite me in for a cup of coffee.'

'I could *not*, Mr Sibson,' she said sharply, trying to hide her amusement. 'And as for payment, have you any idea how much a trainee reporter actually earns?'

'A fiver a week, so I've heard.' He winked and leapt out of the car, opening the passenger door with a bow.

'Well, Mr Know-it-all,' she accepted his outstretched hand. 'It's thank you and good night.'

'Goodnight. Maybe I'll see you tomorrow?'

She let herself into the building and walked up the stairs to her flat. Somehow she felt sure he would.

Over the next few days Sophie had little time to dwell on Steve Sibson. The harder she worked the more she reckoned a three-headed lion would be more welcome at the *Tribune* than a female reporter. Her hours seemed longer than the others' and her night jobs so frequent that all she seemed to do was sleep and work. But she loved the adrenaline rush, and the thrill of seeing her copy in print somehow made up for it all.

'Shouldn't you be gone now, Sophie?' Patrick's stern face loomed in front of her. 'You're down for a working lunch.'

Glancing at the clock, she grabbed her bag and notebook and ran down the stairs.

Seconds later, Steve's Zodiac careered into the office car

BAGGY PANTS AND BOOTEES

park. 'Sophie – where have you been? Not trying to avoid me, I hope?'

'Only your advances, Mr Sibson. And you're not supposed to park here. The editor says it's only for visitors.'

'I am a visitor,' Steve winked. 'I've come to visit *you*. Now how about meeting me for a drink tonight?'

'I'm far too busy for a drink.' She did her best to look disdainful. 'Patrick Porchester has me working from dawn till dusk.'

'After dusk's fine with me,' he grinned. 'Come on, Sophie, I'm only kidding. Strictly a business meeting. Sounds like you need someone to show you the ropes.'

'I'll manage the ropes, thanks all the same. Besides, I wouldn't dream of interrupting your social life. Now I must dash. My car's parked miles away and the meeting starts at twelve.'

'Where are you off to?'

'Harcot Rotary Club. The famous Jed Corcoran is giving a talk.'

'In that case, hop in. I'm going there myself.'

Sophie hesitated. She was already late and her car had been acting up again this morning. 'Okay, it's a deal. As long as you promise not to knock over any pedestrians.' She jumped into the passenger seat and held on tight to the door handle. 'Right, Stirling Moss, I'm ready.'

Steve drove sedately over the crescent, increasing his speed as they approached the main road. 'Have you been to a Rotary meeting before?'

'No,' she glanced across at him. 'To be honest, I'd never even heard of them till today, but I'd like to meet Jed Corcoran. He's one of my favourite singers.'

'He'd probably like to meet you too,' Steve said, swerving into the hotel car park.

'What do you mean by that?'

'Rotary's men-only. Didn't Patrick say?'

Sophie got out of the car and slammed the door behind her, ignoring the laughter that echoed in her ears. She pulled back her shoulders and thrust her chest forward. It would take more than a room full of men to frighten her away.

CHAPTER 2

'Mail's on your desk,' Joe grinned as Sophie walked into the newsroom. '*You're* getting popular all of a sudden.'

There were two envelopes: the first, from the secretary of the Harcot Women's Help League, requesting coverage of a sponsored shuttlecock competition. Sophie sighed. The second, marked "private and confidential", had come on the delivery van that made daily visits from head office to the *Evening Standard*'s sister papers all over the county.

The note inside was simple: *How's the car? Let me know when you'd like another spin in mine. Your Partner-in-Crime, Steve X*

Sophie cringed at the memory of Jed Corcoran's chauvinist speech. Fortunately he'd seen the funny side when Sophie first appeared, making her the butt of one or two harmless jokes. She'd then had to sit through an excruciating hour of risqué humour and endless sidelong glances before being officially proclaimed 'one of the boys'.

'I wouldn't get involved with sexy Steve if I were you,' Joe said, peering over her shoulder. 'He's the office Romeo.'

'Are you still here?' she looked up, her face indignant.

'Nothing's private at the *Tribune*, Soph.' Joe tapped his nose. 'This is a newspaper office. I'd remember that, if I were you.'

Sophie screwed the note into a ball and threw it at the waste paper bin. She'd more important things to worry about than Steve Sibson. The editor had asked her to write a one-off feature for next week's *Tribune* and this could be her chance to prove herself.

'We're not used to having young blood about here,' he'd announced, as if finally noticing she was on the payroll. 'So come up with something new and fresh. And give it a woman's angle. No more than a thousand words, mind. This isn't the *Daily Telegraph*.'

He laughed out loud before she had a chance to reply, and then carried on puffing on his pipe.

The feature had taken her ages to write, though she'd done most of the research at home. She'd gleaned ideas from one or two liberal-minded women's magazines, and she reckoned she'd pitched it just right. She could see the heading now with her by-line at the top of the page...

'*Sophieee...*' The editor's booming voice interrupted her reverie.

She put on her studious-looking glasses and entered the inner sanctum.

'What's this?' Alfred Moulton was staring at the desk, his

face a strange shade of purple.

'It's the feature you asked me to write.'

'Yes, I gather that, but I asked for a *women's* feature, remember.'

'And that's exactly what it is, Mr Moulton, if you don't mind me saying – a subject of real interest to the female population.'

'Real interest?' He held the offending copy up in the air. 'This is just poppycock. Whoever heard of equality for women?'

'You'd be surprised actually, Mr Moulton. Lots of women these days object to being treated like second class citizens.'

The editor put on his spectacles and began to read in a deadpan voice: '*Most would-be employers think women will give up work before they finish their training...* What sort of message is that?'

'It's a topical one, actually. If you carry on reading you'll understand what I mean.'

Arthur Moulton took out a leather pouch and began to stuff its contents into the top of his pipe. 'This is a small town, Miss Wainwright. The women here are interested in serious matters, like bringing up their families, how to prepare nutritious food, raising funds for charity, that sort of thing. The fact that Victorian women had to choose between husband and career is simply not relevant to their lives. Did you look at the ideas I left for you?'

She managed a nod. 'I did, thank you. But Mrs Thistlethwaite has postponed the jam-making competition as she hurt her left hand playing bowls, and the mayoress is too busy taking part in the sponsored walk from here to Clegborough to see me at the moment.'

The purple hue on the old man's cheeks deepened. 'I'm sorry, Miss Wainwright, but I can't publish an article about bra-burning. The Women's Institute would be up in arms. So I'm taking you off this assignment, I'm afraid. Be a good girl and go through the archives in the attic, will you? We need some copy for the Harcot History column.'

'From now on you're in charge of the weekly calls.' Joe's oversized mouth spread into a grin.

'So what do I have to do?' Sophie eyed him suspiciously.

'Every Monday morning you ring the police, the fire station, and the local churches – you can have my contacts book – and try to get some leads.'

'The churches?' she interrupted. 'What's the point in that?'

'Not a lot,' Joe yawned. 'The last time I spoke to the Vicar of Harcot he'd fallen asleep in the pulpit. That's the nearest to news you're likely to get.'

'Thanks, Jo,' she said, scowling. 'I'll let you know when I get a scoop.'

'You do that, Soph. Can't stop now, it's our lineage meeting at ten. I've got a crackin' story for tomorrow's *Daily Mirror*.'

Sophie hadn't a clue how her colleagues managed to make extra money from the nationals during working hours, but now wasn't the time to ask. Flipping through the well-thumbed pages of Joe's book, she found the fire station number. She could ring it, she supposed, but what was the point? One quick blaze and the whole town would know about it straight away. The police weren't much better. There hadn't been a criminal in Harcot for the last twenty years, unless you counted the underwear thief who returned his swag to the washing lines the morning after. Anyway, the lads at the station kept her posted if anything happened. Sighing, she picked up the phone.

After fifteen minutes and almost as many clergy, boredom set in. One more call and she'd move on to something more productive.

'Hello – is that Reverend Sloane? My name's Sophie Wainwright. I'm calling from the *Harcot Tribune*. I was wondering if you had any news for us this week?'

'No, my dear, nothing's happened, I'm afraid.' The voice at the other end sounded despondent. 'Nothing at all, in fact. There were only seven of us at evensong last night. It's getting worse every week.'

'I'm sorry to hear that,' Sophie said doing her best to sound interested. 'How many people do you usually have?'

'Fifty or sixty at least – and more on a fine day. But ever since that TV programme on a Sunday night, the congregation's dwindled to nothing.'

Sophie started to listen. 'Which programme is that, Canon Jones?'

'You know, the one set after the Great War – about life in a stately home.'

'*The Starlight Saga*?'

'That's the one. Starts at six thirty. The whole country's watching from what I can gather. Never seen it myself.'

'But how do you know it's the programme that's keeping them away?'

'The parishioners have told me themselves, I'm afraid. Some of them come to matins instead. Very apologetic, of course. I just hope the Good Lord understands.'

Sophie stifled a giggle. 'So what do you intend to do about the problem?'

'I've written to the BBC, dear girl. What else could I do? I've asked them to move the series back to eight o' clock. Not an unreasonable request. And it should do the trick, don't you think?'

'I think that's a very good idea.' Sophie was scribbling fast. 'Do you mind if we use the story in the paper?'

'Mind? Not at all, my dear. Anything that brings back the congregation is quite acceptable to me.'

'Perhaps I could see a copy of the letter?' She held her breath. 'The one you sent to the BBC?'

'I've got my original draft, if that's any help. A few crossings out, but I'm sure you'll get the gist. Call in any time.'

'Thank you, Vicar. I'll be round in ten minutes.'

Grabbing her notebook, Sophie ran down the stairs, colliding head on with Steve as she reached the door.

'Frigidaire – why the hurry?' He dusted himself down. 'I was hoping to have a word.'

'I've no time now, sorry,' she brushed past him. 'Got a great lead to follow.'

'Pity. I was going to ask you to lunch.' He gestured to his Zodiac on the car park, the engine still turning over. 'Not to worry. Can I give you a lift?'

'I've had enough of your lifts.' She turned to go. 'And please don't compare me to a fridge. I happen to have a very warm heart underneath.'

'So what are you up to?' Steve persisted, jumping in the car and reversing noisily into the road. 'Murder? Felony? It must be a pretty big scoop.'

Raising her hand into the air, she grinned. 'I'm off to the vicarage.'

The following morning brought the first of the winter frosts. As she turned the corner, Sophie saw that her car, which she'd parked at the back of the flats, resembled an ice sculpture. Returning a few minutes later with a kettle, she poured boiling water over the car windscreen, got into the driver's seat and tried the ignition. Nothing happened. She pulled out the choke until it almost flooded the carburettor. Still nothing. Finally, she gave up and made her way to the bus stop. She was used to walking these days and, besides, she could do with some time to think.

Crossing the road, Sophie half expected Steve to appear out of nowhere in his Zodiac. She'd heard he was dating a girl from head office, so maybe that would keep him out of her hair for a while. She had more important things to consider than the office Romeo.

Since the day she'd met Jed Corcoran, Sophie had been

working on an idea. The crooner was currently in York topping the bill at a popular local venue. Unlike most current heart throbs he took his wife with him on every tour. How did *she* feel about the young girls who followed her husband around?

Sophie had got on well with the Rotary club chairman, who'd given her his card after the talk. Maybe she could persuade him to give her the Corcorans' number?

Half an hour later she settled herself down in the booth and put on her best telephone voice. 'Good afternoon. Is that Mrs Corcoran?'

'No – it's her private secretary. Who is it?'

'It's Sophie Wainwright from the *Evening Standard*. I met her husband at Rotary the other day.'

'Hold the line. I'll see if she's free.'

Sophie held her breath.

'Jane Corcoran speaking?'

'Hello, Mrs Corcoran. My name's Sophie. I'm sorry to trouble you, but I met your husband at the Rotary club last week and –'

A peel of laughter echoed down the line. 'Of course, Sophie. Jed said it was one of the best talks he'd ever given. Tough cookie is what he called you. How can I help?'

'I work for the *Harcot Weekly Tribune*, part of the News Group. The paper can be a bit dull at times, so I'm trying to liven it up. I wondered if you would give me an interview, you know, about what it's like being married to a pop star?'

'Mmm. I don't usually do interviews to be honest, I leave

that to Jed. Unless...' she hesitated. 'Would I be able to see a draft before it's printed?'

'I'm *sure* that could be arranged, Mrs Corcoran.' Sophie wasn't sure at all, but she needed this feature badly.

'Okay – it's a deal.' The other woman's voice interrupted her thoughts. 'It might be quite fun. I'll put you back on to my secretary and you can arrange a date.'

Sophie slammed down the phone and hit the air with her fist.

By the time she caught the bus back home she was in a good mood. Climbing on to the top deck she caught sight of a newspaper hoarding. "Evening Standard Special: Sunday TV drama empties Churches". A broad grin stretched across her face. That should silence her critics for a while.

Sophie almost forgot about the office Christmas party, which was held in the middle of November to avoid the festive rush. She'd known about it for weeks and now the day had arrived.

'You've got to go,' Val on switchboard had insisted the previous night. 'It's a sort of initiation. You won't *really* belong to the news team till you've been to one of these.'

'You make it sound like an obstacle course.' Sophie scowled. 'I'll only go if you'll come with me.'

'Oh I can't possibly do that.'

'Why not?'

'It's for editorial staff, only. Paid-up members of the NUJ to be exact.'

'That's good. I'm a probationary member, so I'm sure I

won't count.'

'Let me explain.' Val lowered her voice. It's "them and us" in editorial at the best of times, as you well know. It's bad enough being female but if you duck out of this, believe me, they'll make your life a misery.'

'You think they haven't already?' Sophie grinned. 'Oh, what the hell. I've had lunch with Jed Corcoran and half the male population of Harcot so I reckon I can manage a few drunken reporters. Thanks for the advice, Val, and wish me luck.'

Now, glancing at the clock, she had just a few hours until the party started and no idea what to wear. She rifled through her wardrobe for the only two formal dresses she owned, dismissing them both as unsuitable. The black catsuit she tried on next was straight out of *The Avengers,* but she'd had enough of wearing trousers all day. Finally, stuffed in a carrier bag under the bed, she found an emerald green suede miniskirt bought in the Lewis sale and soon forgotten. A black skinny-rib polo neck and her matching knee length boots would complete the look. Smiling to herself, she ran a bath, oblivious for once to the groaning gas geyser, and sank into the soapy water.

By the time the taxi dropped her off, Sophie was almost looking forward to the evening. She'd spent too much time working lately and not enough time enjoying herself. The club door, lit by a garish neon sign, opened straight on to the road with a wide row of steps leading to the first floor. She could hear the loud thud of music above.

As she entered the dimly lit room, a girl in a bright red mini dress appeared like magic.

'Hi – I'm Julie, the editor's secretary. I thought I'd introduce myself, seeing as there's so few females here tonight.' The girl was at least five feet ten with heavily backcombed bleached blonde hair, a low cut top and extremely long legs.

'Pleased to meet you. I'm Sophie, new recruit on the *Tribune*. Have you been to one of these before?'

'Oh yes, I have. As a matter of fact, I organise them. The editor won't be here till later, but he likes to know what's been going on. Can I get you a drink? There's free punch over there.'

'Don't worry; I can get one myself, thanks all the same. Nice to meet –' Sophie stopped mid-sentence as Julie let out a loud yelp.

'Steeeeve, you're here at last... *Do* come and meet Sophie.' Julie had linked arms with none other than Steve Sibson who was frantically attempting a conspiratorial wink.

'We've met, actually,' Sophie said drily.

'A few times, actually,' Steve nodded. 'Miss Wainwright shares my passion for vintage cars.'

'I didn't know you liked old cars.' Julie stared at Steve, a frown forming on her perfectly made-up face.

'There's a lot you don't know about me,' he winked, 'like I'm going to be the next David Bailey.'

'And I'm the next Marje Proops,' Sophie retorted.

'You've got the spectacles, Frigidaire, that's a good start.' Steve's mouth stretched into a nervous grin

'Frigidaire?' exclaimed Julie before Sophie could think of a reply. 'Am I missing something?'

'No, but I will be if I don't have a pint very soon. So if you don't mind, ladies, I'll leave you to it.' With that he winked and disappeared.

'I didn't realise you knew Steve,' the other girl said, her eyes glazing over. 'Gorgeous, isn't he?'

'*Gorgeous,*' she nodded in agreement, trying to keep the sarcasm out of her voice.

It was almost midnight when Steve stumbled towards her, waving a beer glass in each hand.

'Ah Shofee. I'f found you at lasht. I've brought ush both a drink.'

'That's very kind of you,' she tried hard not to laugh, 'but I don't usually drink beer.'

'Oh, go on.' He handed her a glass. 'It'll warm the cockles of your hearth. So whath did you think of the editorth speech?'

'It seemed very short.' Sophie shook her head. 'Maybe he had another engagement?'

'Oh no - he doth it deberit, debilerath, you know, on purpoth, so he doesn't have to stay and see the staff get pithed.'

Sophie smiled despite herself. 'I gather you're pretty inebriated yourself?'

'I can't thay long words when I'm pithed and in any case, ith you who ith pretty, not me.'

'Well, thank you, Mr Sibson. I'll take that as a compliment.'

'Good, becuth thath what ith meant to be.'

'Would you like some black coffee?'

'I'd like toothay I love you Shofee. Do you love me tooth?'
Before she could answer, Steve swayed ever so gently and collapsed in a heap at her feet.

CHAPTER 3

The phone was ringing when Sophie got back to the office. 'Editorial,' she said, grabbing the receiver. The place was deserted.

'There's a call for you.' Val sounded harassed. 'The woman's rung four times already.'

'Did she give her name?'

'She wouldn't, I'm afraid. Anyway, I'm putting her through – can't hold on any longer.' There was a click on the line then the sound of breathing.

'Is that you, Sophie'?

'Speaking. Can I help?'

'It's me. Your mother.'

'Frances?' She sank into the chair, her heart pounding. 'How on earth did you find me?'

'I just did. I need to see you.'

'What is it?' Sophie lowered her voice at the sound of footsteps clattering up the stairs. 'Is something wrong?'

'I'll explain when I see you. Just say you'll come.'

'Why now, Frances, why now after all this time?'

'Because there's something really important I need to tell you.' The older woman's breathing was laboured now. 'Something I should have told you years ago.'

'Have you been drinking again? Tell me – have you?'

'Never mind that. I'm still in Blackpool. I'll give you my address. Just come.'

Sophie replaced the receiver, a tight band of fear gripping her chest. Almost eight years had passed since Frances had thrown her out. Eight years with not a single word between them. The day she left was forever etched in her memory. It was her sixteenth birthday and she'd arranged a night out at the Tower Ballroom with a few friends. Sophie spent ages getting ready, curling her hair, doing her make-up and fixing her new false eye lashes. Finally, in the blue dress and low heels, bought from a jumble sale, she knocked on her mother's bedroom door. Frances had been drinking. The room was strewn with empty bottles and her mother lay sprawled over the eiderdown.

'What do you want?' Frances spat out the words.

Sophie did a twirl, a false smile pinned on her face. 'What do you think? I'm going out on the town.'

'You look like a whore, get out of my sight.'

'But Mum, what's wrong? What have I done?'

'I told you never to call me that. You should've died. You're no daughter of mine.'

Bile burnt the back of Sophie's throat. 'Just look at you,

you're disgusting. You're drunk and not –'

Just then, Frances grabbed an empty bottle and lifted it over her head.

'Well, what are you waiting for?' Sophie yelled. 'Go on – throw it. You've done it enough times before!'

The glass split into a thousand shards as the door banged shut behind her. When Sophie returned it was gone midnight. The front door was bolted, and her every last belonging strewn haphazardly across the pavement. She never heard from her mother again.

Now, dashing blindly down the stairs, Sophie bumped into Charlie the odd-job man, who was carrying a tray of hot drinks.

'Steady on, girl,' he said, frowning at the pools of liquid, 'I haven't got nine lives.'

'I'll take that,' she said impulsively. 'There's hardly anyone up there.'

Climbing slowly back to the office, she set the tray down on her desk, grabbed the biggest mug and knocked on the door of the inner sanctuary.

'I've brought you your tea, Mr Moulton.'

The editor looked up. 'That's very kind of you, Sophie. Where's Charlie today?'

'He's – well – he's just taking a delivery.' Sophie hovered by the door.

'Is there anything else?' He peered at her over the top of his spectacles.

'I was just wondering if I might have some time off to –'

'Time off?' The old man's voice rose like a foghorn. *'Time off?* How long have you been with us exactly, Miss Wainwright?'

She bit her bottom lip. 'Three months, Mr Moulton.'

'Three months? Ah, that explains it. You need a holiday. Time for a trip to the Tropics, eh?'

'Not exactly, no. It's my mother, you see, she's...' Sophie hesitated.

What was she exactly? Mad, drunk, trying to ruin her only daughter's life? None of these sounded appropriate. 'She's ill, actually – and I wondered if I could possibly take two days off, well, you know, *after* the weekend, which would give me three, maybe four days in all.' She knew she was waffling but she couldn't help it.

'Granted.' Alfred Moulton's eyes returned to his copy.

'I'm sorry, what did you say?'

'You can have your two days. But I want twice as much work from you before you go. Understood?'

She was just about to reply when he started talking again. 'Have you ever done an obituary?'

Sophie shook her head.

'Alderman Alfred Acton. Ex-mayor. Not expected to last more than twenty-four hours. Well go on girl – what are you waiting for?'

Sophie swung the old A40 into the sprawling car park, her forthcoming trip to Blackpool temporarily forgotten. She'd been summoned to head office by the *Standard*'s news editor and that could only mean one thing: Wally Thompson was after her blood.

Since the ex-mayor's obituary appeared, the *Evening Standard* had been swamped with complaints. A typo had found its way into the unfortunate man's name and now his whole family were threatening to sue. She should have checked the piece more thoroughly, granted, but she *did* have a lot on her mind. Anyway, it wasn't her fault the old man had popped off on a light news day and ended up on the front page.

She entered the door of the city centre building, the smell of newsprint assaulting her nostrils. Walking along the narrow corridor, she gazed longingly through the open door at the hustle and bustle of the news room, before knocking firmly on the news editor's door.

'Come in.'

'Hello, Mr Thompson. I'm Sophie Wainwright. I'm very pleased to meet you.'

The man's eyes narrowed to two small slits peering out from a shiny bald head. 'So *you* are Moulton's prodigy.'

'I'm not sure he'd put it quite like that...' her voice tailed away.

'I don't care how he'd put it.' Wally Thompson was standing now, thumbs looped over his leather braces, a murderous look on his red face. An inch or two taller than Sophie at most, he rocked up and down on his stacked heels. 'One thing you'll learn, young lady, and you'll learn it fast. You should never be pleased to see me. You're here because you messed up and you *messed up badly.*'

'Yes, Mr Thompson.'

'Alderman *Action,* as you called him, was very well known in this town, I'll have you know. *You* managed to make him a laughing stock.'

'Yes Mr Thompson.' She shifted her feet, squirming under his gaze.

'*Yes Mr Thompson,*' he mocked. 'Is that all you've got to say for yourself?'

'I'm sorry for my mistake, of course, but I'm sorry the sub editor didn't see it either.'

The news editor's face creased with rage. 'Never mind the sub. This is *you* we're talking about. *You* made the mistake and I hold you personally responsible. If you ever do anything like this again you're out – is that understood?'

'Yes, sir, of course, sir.' She turned rapidly on her heels.

'Just a minute, young lady. Was it you who wrote the piece on the empty churches?'

'Yes, as a matter of fact it was.' She held her breath.

'Pity,' he looked at her with disdain. 'Remember this – you're only as good as your last mistake. Now get out of here before I sack you on the spot.'

Sophie dashed out of Thompson's office and headed for the photographers' room, her pride decidedly dented. She had a package to deliver to Steve and it would give her an opportunity to see the 'office Romeo' in situ. When her knock got no reply, she put her head round the door. At the far end of the room a sullen-looking man was studying a strip of negatives.

'Is Steve in?' she asked brightly.

'Was a minute ago.' The man didn't look up. 'Probably in the dark room. Can you wait?'

'No, it's fine. Would you just give him these?' She pulled a brown envelope from her bag.

Before she had a chance to leave, Steve appeared from a door at the other end of the room, grinning. 'If it isn't our Sophie! What are you doing here?'

'I came to see Mr Thompson.'

'And I thought you'd come to see me.'

'I was summoned here, to be precise, after dropping a clanger... '

'Is that all?' He pulled out a packet of Embassy and searched the cluttered desk for his lighter. 'Everyone's done it at some time or another.'

'...on the front page of the *Evening Standard*.'

'Ah,' he grimaced. 'It's called initiation. Tomo frightens the hell out of you and you never mess up again.'

'Is that supposed to make me feel better?' He was really irritating her now.

'No, but it's the truth.' He sat down at his desk. 'So, how are they treating you back at the ranch?'

She peered at him disdainfully from under her lashes. 'Moulton thinks my church scoop was just a lucky break and Joe's no longer speaking to me.'

'Well that could be an advantage.' Steve winked. 'But you didn't steal the story, did you? You got it fair and square.

Serves him right – he's always offloading stuff on to you.' He gestured round the room. 'What do you think of our humble abode?'

'It's a bit old fashioned, from where I'm standing.' She glanced at the familiar mismatched furniture. 'I thought it might be, well, a bit posher than the *Tribune*.'

'Even David Bailey had humble beginnings.' Steve lit a cigarette. 'It can take a while for genius to show through, especially when good looks get in the way.'

'And you would know, of course.' Sophie smiled. She was still trying to fathom why he attracted so many women. 'And now I must be off.'

Just then the phone shrilled on Steve's desk.

'Photographers.' He covered the mouthpiece with his hand. *'Stay a bit longer, Frigidaire.'*

She shook her head.

'Hi Tina – good to hear from you.' A broad smile spread over Steve's face.

'I'm busy right now. Can I call you back?'

'Please don't let *me* interrupt you.' Sophie headed for the door.

'Okay, okay.' He nudged the phone back into its cradle. 'It's not what you think, you know. But even if it was, it's not a crime, as far as I'm aware, to have girlfriends.'

'It depends how many you have.' She glared at him. She'd had enough hassle for one day.

'Well, actually –'

'No thanks, I don't want to know.'

Shrugging, he picked up the envelope from his desk. 'What's this?'

'Nothing, really. Mr Moulton doesn't like your proofs.' She smiled sweetly. 'So he's sent them all back.'

'Excuse me?' The rain crept down the back of Sophie's neck forming a pool below her shoulder blades.

'Can I help you, Miss?' The guy with red hair and blue tracksuit was chewing gum whilst keeping a watchful eye on the other end of the pitch.

'I'm Sophie Wainwright from the *Weekly Tribune*.' She removed her mud-splattered spectacles. 'I'm here to do a match report.'

'*Offside*,' yelled Red Hair at the top of his voice, glancing at the rain-drenched creature in front of him. 'What do you know about football?' He raised his sodden eyebrows in amusement.

'*About as much as you know about women, apparently,*' she muttered under her breath.

'Sorry – I didn't catch that.'

'I'm hoping you'll teach me, Mr er –' She pulled a copy of the offside rule out of her pocket.

'Davies. Terry Davies,' he proffered his hand. 'Did Joe Suggins put you up to this?'

'Actually, it was my news editor.' She pursed her lips. 'I think it's meant to be a form of punishment.'

'Well, we can't argue with Patrick, can we now?' he grinned. 'That there at the end of the pitch is the goal. If you need to know anything else, just give me a shout.'

'Hold on – have you got –?' her voice was lost in the roar of the twelve-strong crowd as he raced across the pitch.

'Meet me in the clubroom after, Sophie Wainwright,' he shouted back, 'and I'll tell you who won.'

'Why so glum, Frigidaire? You look as if you lost half a crown and found sixpence.'

Sophie turned swiftly to see Steve standing on the touchline beside her, covered in waterproofs from head to toe.

'You again! It's a wonder you have time to develop those photographs.' She shook her head disdainfully, 'Or do you send them off in a job lot to Kodak?'

'Ooh, we are sarcastic today. It's not my fault I keep bumping into you. I don't write the diary, you know, I just follow it. Anyway, what are you doing at a soccer match? I thought you were away this weekend.'

'Porchester's got it in for me. He said we were short-staffed. I'm leaving first thing in the morning.'

Steve took her hand, his face crumpling into a frown 'You're a hard woman, Sophie Wainwright. The poor man's probably terrified of you, just like the rest of us.'

Sophie laughed, despite the rain. 'Do you ever manage to stay serious for more than two minutes?'

Me – serious? What's the point? I leave that to Harold Wilson. Anyway – how's Harcot's answer to the *Daily Herald*? Any more scoops in the pipeline?'

'Don't mention scoops. Mouldy Moulton reckons my TV story was a fluke and wants me to take over the women's page.

I'd be cheaper than Cynthia apparently. So, it seems I'm judging the Miss Harcot competition at the summer gala next weekend.' She raised her wet lashes. 'What do I know about beauty competitions?'

'You could knock them all into a cocked hat with your looks, Sophie. It wouldn't surprise me if that's why the lads give you such a hard time.' Steve's smile widened. 'That and your obsession with equality.'

At that moment an idea flashed through her mind. 'So, what do you know about football then, Steve?'

'I was in the school soccer team, if that's any help.'

'Then say you'll do me a match report – *pleeease*?' She tried her hardest to sound desperate.

A wide grin spread over his face. 'Only if you'll come for a drink with me tonight. There's something I need to tell you.'

She wiped her arm over her rain-soaked face. Come to think of it, she *was* desperate. 'Only if you stop calling me Frigidaire.'

'Okay – it's a deal.'

CHAPTER 4

'So – what do your folks do?' Steve asked amiably. They were sitting in the snug of an eighteenth-century tavern several miles out of town.

'I'm an only child and I never knew my father.' The words came out before she could stop them. 'I haven't seen my mother since I was a teenager.'

'That must be tough.' He took a gulp of his beer. 'I had a bit of a bum childhood as it happens. My father was, well, unreliable. In and out of prison most of the time from what I can remember. Petty thieving, that sort of thing, but it made my poor mother's life hell. I don't think Dad ever said an honest word in his whole life.'

Sophie nodded, unfazed by his apparent confession. Maybe Steve had exaggerated the whole thing to make her feel better? She made a mental note not to drink on an empty stomach in future. Out loud she said, 'No wonder you've got such a sense of humour. I hope you haven't inherited your dad's light fingers.'

'Don't worry,' he held up his hands. 'I promise I'll keep them to myself.'

'Good. And now – you said you had something to tell me?'

'Yes, well, the thing is, I owe you an apology.'

She raised her eyes. 'What for?'

'For trying to chat you up. For not seeing beyond the blonde hair and the er... well, anyway. I wanted to ask you if we could start again.'

'I'm not sure we started anything in the first place, Steve. The reason I'm here in Yorkshire is to learn about newspapers. I'm not interested in men.'

'*Now* you tell me,' he winked.

'You know very well what I mean. You're a nice guy and you make me laugh, but that's about it. I don't need to join the fan club.' Sophie sipped her lager. She'd deliberately worn jeans and an old shirt so this didn't count as a date. She'd rinsed her rain soaked hair, and then piled it up on top of her head. A bit of green shadow to match her eyes and that was it.

'Do you want to tell me about your mum?' He was looking at her earnestly now.

'There's not a lot to tell, really. Having me was a bit of a shock, to put it mildly, especially as she wanted a boy. I think she blamed me for the way things went wrong in her life.' Sophie stopped mid-sentence. Why on earth was she telling him all this?

'And?' He was looking at her intently now.

'As a matter of fact I'm going to Blackpool tomorrow to see

her. She's er, not well, so she's asked to see me.'

'Not serious, I hope?'

'No. I should have gone today but Patrick made me work – so here I am.'

'We'd better make the most of it then. What can I do to cheer you up?'

'You can get me another lager, but I'm paying.' She proffered a ten shilling note.

'Another lager? Good job I'm driving. You girls can't be trusted behind the wheel when you've had a few drinks.'

'And you can, I *suppose*?' She eyed him furiously. 'I bet you invented that story about your thieving father just to get some sympathy.'

He flinched as if he'd been bitten by a rattlesnake. 'I've got the newspaper cuttings at home if you'd like to see them. They're filed in chronological order, photos included. He looked a bit like me, my dad, when he was young, though not as handsome, of course.'

'Thanks for the offer, but another time, perhaps? I think I'll just stick to the drink.'

She watched as he headed for the bar, head back, walking with a swagger, nodding good-naturedly here and there to people he knew. To think she'd almost been tempted to tell him the truth about her past. Hearing from her mother again had obviously stirred up all her emotions. Anyway, she knew better than to listen to some well-practised chat-up lines, even from someone with such devastatingly deep blue eyes. No, the last thing she needed right now was to get involved with Steve.

CHAPTER 5

'Miss Wainwright?'

'Yes?' Sophie yawned. The policeman looked younger than she did.

'Sorry to trouble you so early on a Sunday morning. May I come in?'

'Sorry, yes – it's just that I don't remember seeing you at the station. I'm not on call today, I'm afraid.' She glanced at her watch. 'I can give you the number of someone who is.'

'It's not work, I'm afraid.' He coughed nervously. 'My name's Constable Richards. I'm from –'

'Not work?' Something made her shiver. 'Then what – ?'

'I think you should sit down first.'

'Oh don't be ridiculous. We're not on *Z Cars* now.'

'It's about your mother.'

'My mother?'

'Yes. I'm afraid Mrs Wainwright was involved in an accident this afternoon.'

'An accident? Is she dead?' The words came out in a strangled screech.

'No, but she is in a coma. The prognosis is not good.'

Sophie sank into the chair. 'What happened?'

'It seems she had some sort of seizure and fell down the stairs.'

'But I spoke to her only the other day. I'm going to see her this weekend – she had something she wanted to –'

The constable hovered awkwardly in front of her. 'Can I get you a glass of water?'

'Is this your first time?'

'I'm sorry, Miss?'

'An accident –you know. Telling the relatives?'

'Oh, um, yes, it is, as a matter of fact.' His face reddened. 'Sorry if I'm not –'

'If you don't mind, I think I'd rather be on my own.'

'Of course.' He busied himself with his notebook. 'Is there anyone I can contact for you?'

'No thank you.' She got up and undid the latch. 'No one at all.'

Sophie drummed her fingers as she waited for an answer. 'Steve – it's me, Sophie. Can you speak?'

'It's seven o'clock on Sunday morning.' He yawned loudly. 'Is something wrong?'

'My mother's collapsed – the police have just been round. She fell down the stairs and now she's in a coma.'

'My God, that's awful. Do you want me to come over?'

Yes, no – I'm not really sure. I've got to get down there fast. I just needed to tell someone. I could have phoned Val but I don't want everyone knowing.'

'Don't worry about that now. I could take you to the station. Just for some moral support.'

'Would you?' She hesitated.

'I'll be there in twenty minutes.'

'It's my fault, I should have gone sooner,' Sophie said as they drove through the empty streets. 'Frances – that's what I call her – tripped down the stairs on her own in the dark and it was hours before a neighbour found her.'

'That hardly means you're to blame, does it? ' Steve looked puzzled.

'She called me at work the other day. She sounded really upset. I've no idea how she found my number but I should have gone straight away.'

'It's not that easy though, is it? Not with Moulton on your case.'

'You're right, I suppose. But she said she wanted to tell me something, something very important. Now I might never know.'

'What do you mean? You're not making sense.' Steve swung the car into the station car park. 'Look Sophie. I've no idea what's going on, but don't deal with this on your own. I can help, if you'll let me. Why don't you let me drive you there?'

She opened the passenger door. 'Thanks. I know you mean it, but I have to do this on my own.'

'Just give me a chance, Sophie?' He jumped out and ran round the car, forcing her to look at him. 'I'm not asking for commitment. I'm not even sure if I know what the word means. I just –'

'Not now please, Steve, I've got to go. Just square it with Moulton for me, will you?'

He placed his hand on her shoulder and squeezed it gently. 'Good luck.'

She could still feel his fingers burning into her skin long after he had disappeared.

The smell of disinfectant hit Sophie the minute she entered the hospital. Pushing her way through the double wooden doors, she walked slowly along the drab corridors, searching for the ward where her mother lay unconscious. She could have asked one of the nurses who strode by, white caps pointing to the sky, but what was the point? The moment would arrive soon enough.

Ward eight housed the seriously ill patients, who were lying in rows of identical metal beds, their eyes tightly shut, as if they'd already gone from the world. Fortunately Frances had been put in a side ward.

'We've put screens round Mrs Wainwright's bed,' the middle-aged matron lowered her voice, 'so that she won't be disturbed. Feel free to talk to your mother. Just say whatever comes into your head.'

'Thank you,' Sophie nodded. 'But I don't understand. Surely she won't be able to hear me?'

'Possibly not, my dear. We still don't know if the unconscious mind can absorb information, but the sound of your voice might just trigger some memories.' With that the older woman pulled back the screen and disappeared.

Frances Wainwright lay completely still, her face as pale as the starched white pillows underneath. The years had etched lines into her skin, like un-named lanes on a map of the English countryside, and her dark hair was now marbled with grey.

Sophie took hold of her mother's hand, gently stroking the semi-translucent skin.

'I'm sorry,' she whispered. 'I should have come on the day you called. But when you're better, you can tell me everything you wanted to say. I've got a job now, Frances, on a newspaper in Yorkshire. Me, a reporter, can you imagine that? The place is full of men – ten to be exact – and they've never seen a woman doing their job before. Most of them treat me like the hired help but there's one – not a reporter but a photographer at head office – who's sort of got my interests at heart. Actually, he acts as if he's God's gift to women, but most of it's only for show. To be honest I find him very attractive, in an irritating sort of way. Please keep this a secret, won't you, just between you and me.'

Letting go of her mother's hand, Sophie blushed furiously. What had got into her? Here she was having fanciful thoughts about Steve that she'd never admit to anyone. Why didn't she say what she really meant? After so many years she just couldn't find the right words. Sophie stood up and smoothed the creases from her skirt. 'Please don't leave me, will you, Mum? Don't give up without a fight.' There - she had done it – she had finally used the word Mum.

'What's the prognosis, doctor? Is there any hope of recovery?'

'It's hard to say, Miss Wainwright.' The doctor sat behind his desk, hands clasped in front of him. 'Your mother's injuries are, well, complicated. We think she had some sort of seizure and that's why she fell.'

'Seizure? She's only forty-three. Surely she's strong enough to survive?'

'Mrs Wainwright's injuries are further complicated by the fact that she is an alcoholic – I presume you knew that?'

Sophie shifted in her seat. 'She's been drinking since I was a child. We had some sort of fallout a few years ago and, well, we hadn't seen each other for a while. I suppose I hoped she'd stopped...' her voice tailed away.

'Well, she hadn't, I'm afraid.' He shot her a disapproving look. 'The alcohol has damaged her liver. We will have to do more tests, of course. But in the meantime we must keep her sedated.'

'I'll have to go back to Yorkshire soon. I've only just started a new job and there's –'

'Does she have any other relatives?'

'No – my, er, father died before I was born and I'm an only child.'

'I see. Then I suggest you speak to the hospital almoner. Whatever happens to your mother in the future, she won't be able to manage on her own.'

Sophie's heart plummeted. That was the last thing she wanted to hear. 'Thank you for your honesty, doctor,' she replied, uncertain of what else to say. She would go to her mother's flat, sort out some of her things and come back in the morning. Maybe things would seem clearer after a night's sleep.

Sophie pushed her way through the flat door, the smell of alcohol and cigarettes assaulting her lungs. Papers and unopened letters were strewn across the hallway, some recent, some dating back several months. After climbing the stairs she walked through the rooms of her mother's dingy flat, flinging open windows and clearing the debris as she went. Nicotine clung to the walls, like smears of sticky brown treacle; the kitchen sink was piled high with unwashed crockery and ashtrays overflowed with cigarette ends.

In the living room, yellowing blankets were strewn along one wall as if someone had used them as a makeshift bed. Over the mantelpiece a photograph had been removed from the chimney breast leaving a square of murky green wallpaper. And then there were the bottles; endless wine and spirit bottles, some overturned on the table and sideboard, others partially hidden in cupboards and drawers, but all of them empty.

Across the entrance hall the bedroom drawers had been wrenched out of the cabinets, their contents strewn over the floor, like the aftermath of a burglary. The wardrobe doors were hanging open, hangers bunched crazily at one end while unwashed clothes were piled high underneath. Sophie wanted to wretch, her stomach churning at the sight. How long had Frances been living like this? She pulled out a handkerchief and wiped the sweat from her brow. Amongst the debris she spotted an old biscuit tin lying untouched.

Sophie sank down on to the matted carpet, suddenly oblivious to the stench, and lifted the tin onto her lap. Very gently she removed the lid. There were several newspaper cuttings, yellow with age, depicting the Coventry Blitz, each with a date written in ink at the top. One showed Coventry Cathedral before the war, another with the building reduced to a smoking ruin. Others showed rows of once-neat houses and gardens transformed overnight into a battlefield. Underneath she found a faded photo of a couple in their late thirties, holding hands in the sunshine and smiling at the camera. Turning it over, she saw the words "MUMMY AND DADDY - KILLED IN THEIR OWN HOME" scribbled on the back. Sophie held the photograph for several moments, swallowing back a surge of emotion.

Forcing herself to finish searching for clues she found an old regulation notebook and a faded envelope that looked as if it hadn't been touched for years. As she held it to the light, the envelope slipped through her fingers, a scrap of something peeping out as it fell to the floor. She bent down, pulled open the flap, and tipped the contents into the palm of her hand: a piece of faded blue silk and a newborn baby's bootee. The tears fell now without constraint. The bootee was hers, surely?

But why, if Frances despised her, had she kept it for so long? And what had happened to the other one?

At last Sophie stood up, the forgotten notebook still clutched under her arm. Her heartbeat quickened at the sight of the familiar handwriting on the front page. Quickly, she let herself out of the flat and into the fresh air. An hour later she found an empty seat on the train and began to read.

CHAPTER 6

Coventry, 14 November 1940

Frances blinked, shading her eyes from the blinding glare that stretched across the horizon. In all her fourteen years she had never seen anything like it.

'It's the Jerries – quick, get into the cellar,' Mum yelled, her voice taut with fear.

'Do as your mother says, girl.' It was Dad's turn now. 'You're not too old for a hiding. *Get down here with your brother before it's too late.*'

But Frances wasn't listening. Down the stairs she ran, out into the night, oblivious to the wailing sirens and the smell of raw fear that hung in the air. She scrambled through the garden and along the back alley, the evening frost glittering on the ground. The street signs had long since gone, but Frances knew the city like the back of her hand. Mesmerised, she headed for the light.

Perhaps the Germans hadn't come to kill them, she told

herself as she approached the city centre. Maybe it was... Just as the next thought crossed her mind a strange whining noise filled her head. A policeman blew his whistle, waved his hands in the air and shouted like a man possessed. 'Get off the streets, get under cover NOW!' Ahead of her stood the Regal Cinema, its doors open for the next showing. She ducked into the foyer, shut her eyes and covered her head with her hands.

The blast blew her to the ground.

Frances lifted her head. The world had gone black and yet she knew she was still alive: all she could hear was the screams and moans of the injured. She leaned forward and began to crawl on her knees away from the commotion.

'You all right, Miss?' A man wearing a uniform, his right arm gashed open, stood above her, shining a torch into her eyes.

'I think so.' She sat back, bewildered, feeling her head with her hand.

Her hair was matted with blood and covered with shards of glass. 'What's happened?'

'The cinema's taken a hit, but it's still upright, thank God. Stay where you are, the ambulances are on their way.' The man took off his jacket, a policeman's jacket she saw now, and draped it round her shoulders. 'Here – take this. And keep your head back so the blood runs away from your face.'

Frances shot him a grateful smile and leaned back against the wall. 'Look out!' The policeman's head jerked upwards as the ceiling above them began to cave in.

'Sorry, Mum,' she muttered, holding her hands together in

prayer. 'If I die, remember I love you.'

The policeman lifted her up as if she were made of paper, the gash on his arm forgotten. Ducking his head, he scrambled out of the building. She hung on tightly as they raced through the smoke-filled streets, shielding her eyes from the chaos and confusion.

'Where're you from?' he shouted as they passed a huge black crater that had appeared in the middle of the street. A car had fallen into it, tilted at a crazy angle with its paintwork eerily unmarked.

'Brunswick Terrace. I ran off tonight when I heard the air-raid sirens. I wanted to see what was happening. Mum and Dad will be furious I didn't take Bobby to the cellar.'

'Never mind, I'm sure they'll forgive you. Just tell them you've had a night out at the cinema.' He turned and grinned, his eyes bright underneath the black soot that covered his face. 'Let's get you into the shelter.'

'Watch out!' Frances waved her arms in front of her. A yellow slick was creeping towards them through the debris, like a stream of oil, and somewhere she could smell cooking. People were panicking, slipping in its path, grabbing hold of each other in an attempt to stay on their feet.

'My God, it's the butter factory,' the policeman yelled, almost dropping her in his haste. It must've have taken a direct hit. I need to get over there and help. Hold on. The shelter's over there.'

Within seconds they reached the air-raid shelter, bombs still whining all around them. Impulsively, she lifted her head – a clear sky and full moon had led the enemy straight to their target.

'I'll leave you now, Miss.' The policeman placed her gently on the ground. 'They'll look after you here.'

She turned to thank him, but he had already disappeared.

'If it isn't young Franny,' a voice boomed behind her. 'Bless my soul – what the dickens are you doing so far from home?' Old Tom from the grocery store was beaming broadly and her heart lifted at the sight of a familiar face.

'I got caught in the raid, I'm afraid. Have you seen Mum and Dad anywhere? I left them at home, but –'

'They'll be safe enough, don't you worry. Good solid house, you've got there – it'd take more'un a few Jerries to knock the hell out of it – pardon my language. Get your head cleaned up first, then find yourself a place to bed down. We're going to be here a good while, I shouldn't wonder.'

Frances gazed around her. The shelter was in the basement of a huge building full of large storage boxes which were being pushed in all directions to make way for more people. The injured and elderly were huddled together at the far end of the room where someone was setting up a makeshift nurses' station. At the other end, a group of mums and young children were singing Christmas carols. She edged towards them, humming under her breath. Anything was better than the sound of people sobbing.

'Here, let me look at that cut for you, me duck.' The red-haired woman who approached, smiling broadly, had a pixie-like face covered in freckles.

'It's nothing, really.' Frances clenched her fists to stop her hands shaking. 'Just a few pieces of glass.'

'It's not all right.' The woman grinned. The name's Gracie. I was born with my hair this colour, but you've obviously had some help from the Jerries.' She produced a sweet from her pocket. 'Suck this while I clean up the wound for you, there's a good girl – then you can come and help out with the youngsters. I hope you've got a good singing voice.'

'I'm in the school choir,' Frances managed a smile. 'And thanks, but I'll save the sweet for the children.'

Frances spent the rest of the night with her mind in a haze. She'd been in air-raid shelters before, but never one as big as this. And never one so full of injured people. She was far too nervous to sleep, so she followed Gracie and helped in any way she could. She didn't know then that the enemy had destroyed their city. Or that her childhood had gone forever.

'How old are you, Frances?'

'Fourteen, Matron. Well, almost fifteen.' She stared determinedly at the neat rows of hospital beds that stretched down the ward.

'And how are you feeling now?'

'My head's a bit sore, but I'll be fine. I'm ready to go home. Have you heard anything from Mum and Dad?'

The older woman shook her head, turning to pull the curtains round the bed.

Frances shivered. 'What is it, what's wrong?' The words came out in a high-pitched squeak.

'I'll pour you a glass of water, my dear. When you hear what I have to say you must be very brave.'

'It's Mum, isn't it?' The room began to sway. 'Something's happened to her! Please tell me she's not dead. Dad will be so angry with me for running away like that. I know I should have brought Bobby down and sheltered from the bombs, but I wanted to see what was happening. The sky was so bright and –'

'The whole street was bombed, I'm afraid.' Matron's voice dropped to a whisper. 'Your house took the full force of the blast. It was *very quick*. I doubt they'll have felt anything at the end.'

'You're wrong, Matron. You see they were hiding under the stairs when the bombs came. It's me who should be dead, don't you see? Me who disobeyed them. What about Bobby? *What about my brother?*'

The matron shook her head. 'The air-raid wardens are still searching for missing people. It will be a while before we... well, before we know for sure.'

'Let me go, let me go and find them. I'm sure they'll be there. Please, Matron?'

'It will only upset you more, my dear. Your home is gone, your family too, God rest their souls. Do you have any other relatives?'

Frances shook her head. Both sets of grandparents had died when she was a baby and there was no one else. 'Can't I stay here until we find them? I know my mum will come looking for me as soon as she can.'

Matron frowned. 'The almoner will be coming to see you this afternoon and she'll help you to find somewhere to live. In the meantime, please try to get some rest.'

Frances didn't move. Her parents were alive, of course they were. The stupid old woman didn't know what she was talking about. Anyway, she'd seen the state of the city centre when they took her into the ambulance: buildings in tatters, craters everywhere, roads blocked by debris. It was bound to take a while to find everyone. Her father was probably out there now helping the injured. He'd insisted on being an air-raid warden and her mother had sat up many a night waiting for him to come back home.

Frances got out of bed and made her way to the lavatories. A workman was replacing one of the windows with a makeshift panel and an arrow pointed her to the next cubicle. She hung around for several minutes as an idea began to form in her mind.

'What are you doing there?' The nurse frowned as she passed by with arms full of dirty linen.

'I just wanted some fresh air.' Frances managed a weak smile.

'Well, hurry up and get back to your bed.'

When the workman stopped for his tea she dashed into the cubicle, stood on the lavatory and with hardly an inch to spare, climbed out of the window.

Landing awkwardly on her ankle, Frances ran out of the sprawling hospital building and onto the street, glancing over her shoulder every now and then to make sure no one was following her. She pulled the old cardigan tighter round her chest; she'd stolen it from a peg outside the lavatories, and her mum would be horrified, but she'd be sure to return it once she got sorted. Gasping for breath, she ran in the direction of home, ignoring the devastation all around her: buildings collapsed into piles of bricks, people with their heads bowed down, desperately searching through the rubble. She stopped. She had no idea where she was, yet she'd always known the city inside out. Just then a large white van appeared in the distance, a loudspeaker perched on the roof. She couldn't hear what it was saying, but it sounded like bad news.

Spying an air-raid warden, she shouted, 'Can you tell me how to get to Brunswick Terrace please? I can't seem to get my bearings.'

The middle-aged man stopped tearing at the rubble and looked up. 'Do you know someone there? Because, if you do –'

'I live there at number seventy-four, with my mum and dad, and my brother, Bobby.' She raised her voice again to make sure he could hear her.

The man looked up at her, scratching his head. 'That's a pretty big bandage you have on your head, Miss. Shouldn't you be in hospital?'

'I was, but they've discharged me.' Why didn't he just show her the way?

'Well now – do you have any relatives you could go to instead?'

'No, I don't, and I'm not going back to that awful hospital,' she said, pulling a face. 'I just want to go home.'

'Look,' he said, more kindly now. 'Haven't they told you what went on? A bomb dropped on Brunswick Terrace. There's not much left of it now. Your ma and pa, well mebbe they could've been out when it 'appened? Try the police station. D'you want me to show you the way?'

Frances shook her head. So it was true. They were dead, all of them.

She turned and stumbled back, past the tobacconist's with its front wall blown off, the owner still stoically serving customers, past the soldiers as they searched through the rubble for bodies, past the burnt-out cars and the children with dirty faces playing in the smoking ruins. The next thing she knew everything went black.

The hospital almoner had mid-length grey hair fashioned in orderly waves, like sea rippling over sand. She wore a dark blue wool suit and carried a clip board which gave her an authoritative air.

'You seem a bit brighter today,' she said. 'It's a good job that air-raid warden found you when he did. Now then,' she put on her spectacles and stared at the file in front of her, 'we have found a job for you at an orphanage in Leicester. You will have your own room and be expected to help with the younger children. Then, when you reach the age of fifteen, and if your work is up to standard, they will consider making you permanent.'

Frances covered her face with her hands. Nothing could be worse than that. 'No, please, don't make me go. I couldn't bear it. I'm fourteen – I don't need an orphanage.'

The older woman shook her head. 'I see you have no relatives? No next of kin? You've had a big shock, my dear. I've given it a great deal of consideration. This will give you time to get used to –'

'Please?' Frances raised her chin into the air, gulping back the tears. She mustn't appear weak. 'Mum and Dad, they wouldn't have wanted to see me in a place like that. I can get a proper job, I know I can – please?'

The almoner stood up. 'I'm sorry, my dear. I had hoped you would be grateful that we've found you a place to live.' There was a note of irritation in her voice. 'I'm afraid it's not up to your parents now.'

'They haven't found the bodies though, have they? They might still be alive. One day they might come back and all of this will be just some terrible nightmare.'

'I'll leave you on your own for a while.' The woman sounded resigned now. 'When you're ready, come and find me in Matron's office.'

CHAPTER 7

The first thing Frances saw as they approached the orphanage was an old oak tree, at least thirty or forty feet high, with gnarled branches spewing out at each side. It looked, she thought, like a clumsy giant fighting its way through the undergrowth. Behind the tree stood an ugly red brick building covered almost completely in ivy, its roof dotted with chimneys in different shapes and sizes. A wide stone driveway led up to the main entrance flanked by huge weathered stone pillars. The front door was a dirty shade of blue, with a shiny brass bell, which the grey-waved almoner pressed firmly.

'Now, Frances,' the almoner said sternly, 'I want you to be on your best behaviour. It's important that you make a good impression.'

Clutching the borrowed suitcase to her chest, Frances nodded and swallowed hard. This was the moment she'd been dreading.

The middle-aged woman who opened the door had dull

brown hair scraped back from her face, unnaturally thin lips and startling blue eyes.

'Ah – you must be our new arrival. I've been expecting you. I'm the matron here. My name is Geraldine Hampton, but the children all call me Mum. '

'How do you do, Mrs, er, Hampton.' Frances stumbled over the words. No one and nothing would ever make her call this stranger Mum. She turned to thank her chaperone, but the grey-waved lady was already on her way back down the drive.

'I don't normally answer the door, you understand, but we're short staffed today.' Mrs Hampton shook her head. 'Now come along and I will show you where to put your things.'

The high-ceilinged hall was full of clutter: an oak dresser covered in photographs of smiling children, a bookcase full of well-worn books and magazines, an umbrella stand, a box full of gas masks and an assortment of boots and shoes in a large cardboard box.

'Leave your case at the bottom of the stairs,' said Matron, 'and you can take it up later. To start with you'll be sleeping in the dormitory with the other girls.'

Frances did as she was told. A smell of overcooked cabbage pervaded the air and she could hear shrieks from what sounded like a game of hockey somewhere in the distance. Mrs Hampton's office was directly off the main hall. It, too, was filled with clutter that lined every inch of the wood panelled walls. In the centre stood an enormous oak desk, complete with an old-fashioned quill pen and ink pot that looked like a relic from the last century. Endless manila files were scattered all over the desk.

'You can sit down,' Matron waved towards a bentwood chair that had clearly seen better days. 'I'm not going to bite.' She looked the new arrival up and down. 'I think it would be wise to braid your hair. It's very thick and might get in the way of your work. You're a pretty girl, you know, and if you smiled a bit more, I'm sure you'd be an asset here.'

Frances nodded politely. She couldn't remember the last time she'd even glanced in a mirror. She knew she had the look of her mother – deep brown eyes, rosy cheeks and neat bow lips that had passed from generation to generation. But right now that was just too much to bear.

'Now to business.' Mrs Hampton seemed keen to move on. 'As you're only a few months away from your fifteenth birthday, you would not normally be eligible to stay at The Oaks. However, Mr Hampton and I have been looking for extra help for some time. We have forty-four girls in all, so we've decided you can stay on as a paid house assistant once you have completed your trial.That is, of course, if your work is satisfactory. Do you understand?'

'I do.' Frances bit her lip. She felt as if she had lost her tongue. 'I understand, yes, but maybe, er ...' her voice trailed.

'Come on, my dear, you needn't be afraid of me. What is it you're trying to say?'

'Surely one of the older girls would be more suitable for the job?'

'You must not concern yourself with such things. Some of

our residents have been in care since they were very small and they need, how shall we say, a change of direction once they are old enough to work. Now then,' she flipped opened the file on top of the pile, 'have you any experience of looking after young children?'

'Oh yes, Mrs Hampton, I have. I was five when my brother Bobby was born. I changed his nappies, fed him when Mum was poorly, and then, when he started crawling, well he got into everything, so we had to –' She stopped. It was the first time she'd talked of her brother in the months since the Blitz. The truth was she'd just blotted him out of her mind. It was far too painful knowing that she would never see his cheeky face again. Maybe her brother had obeyed Mum and Dad and sheltered from the bombs, and a fat lot of good that had done them all. Frances took out a handkerchief and blew her nose.

'Would you like a drink?' Geraldine Hampton reached for the water jug. 'We could add some orange juice, as it's your first day.'

'Thank you, but water will be fine.' Frances wiped her eyes with the back of her hand. She'd rather die than let Matron see her cry.

The following morning Frances woke to see sunshine pouring through the window. Rubbing her eyes, she sat up and stared round the dormitory. The walls were painted a dull shade of green to match the regulation eiderdowns, which were almost threadbare. The lino was dark brown and curled at the edges and the only touches of colour came from framed pictures of the girls' own handiwork with their names and ages written underneath.

'Come on, lazy bones!' The girl in the next bed threw a pillow in Frances' direction. 'It's six o'clock. Everyone else is up and dressed.'

'What time's breakfast, er –?'

'The name's Edith. We don't have breakfast, at least not until we've fed the little ones. And at this rate, they'll soon be starving.'

Frances followed Edith into the washroom, where the girls went about their ablutions without saying a word. Her teeth chattered as the cold water stung her cheeks like a hard slap across the face. Every girl wore the same grey blouse and navy blue skirt with the ugliest grey socks Frances had ever seen. 'How will I know which are mine?' she asked when they eventually sat down to bread, margarine and hot milk.

'You don't need to,' Edith replied airily. 'Everything goes into the laundry on Friday and is collected at six o'clock prompt on Monday morning. It's a case of first come, first served, I'm afraid.'

'Everything?' Frances looked askance. 'Including our undergarments?'

'Yes, I'm afraid you have to share your knickers, too. Nothing's your own here so you'd better get used to it. If you don't get a move on you'll miss out on cook's porridge. It's best cut with a knife.'

After breakfast the older girls cleared the tables, wiped them down and set them again for lunch, all without speaking. Maybe, Frances thought, they had taken a vow of silence. To her amazement, everyone went everywhere in single file – the 'crocodile walk' they called it – and it never seemed to occur to them to do any different. All the orphans had a grovelling approach to their elders, whatever their rank, whether teachers, nurses or helpers. Even the cook was treated with the utmost respect. When Mum Hampton walked into the room the girls straightened their backs, as if they were about to be interrogated. 'Good morning, Mrs Hampton,' they would chant, in perfect unison, and then the owner would nod graciously and say good morning back. As for Mr Hampton, he was a mystery, though Frances had heard he was away on business. No doubt she'd meet him soon enough.

The day disappeared in a whirl of tasks and lessons punctuated by mealtimes which, Frances thought, only the starving could relish. She thought longingly of her mother's delicious Woolton pies made of carrots, turnips and a moist coating of pastry, but then that only made her want to cry. She hated wearing the uniform – it was stiff and itchy – and she couldn't believe these were the only clothes the orphans had ever known.

After supper the older girls helped put the little ones to bed, tying their day clothes into bundles in case they had to leave at the sound of the air-raid sirens. Half an hour's recreation followed before prayer time.

Now, as the moonlight spread its silvery fingers across the bare walls of the dormitory, Frances pulled the sheet over her head and shut her eyes. She stuck her thumb in her mouth, a childhood habit that had come back to haunt her, and began to count backwards from two hundred. Much later, her muffled sobs gave way to troubled sleep.

The following morning after breakfast Frances set out for a walk in the wooded grounds. She'd washed and dressed her two young charges, organised breakfast and then helped with the washing up. At the far end of the grounds she came upon a potting shed and a neat row of bushes in a small clearing beyond the trees. A man was burning twigs and leaves, the smell of wood smoke filling the air. He had a head of dark unruly hair which had once probably been brushed off his face, but now fell over his eyes and ears, making him look like a tramp. He had strong arms covered with masses of dark hair and every now and then he tugged his leather braces with his thumbs. He reminded her of the convict Magwitch, from *Great Expectations*, and she shivered despite the winter sun.

Turning to go, she heard a loud yell. 'Hey – you girl! What you staring at?' She swung round. 'Nothing sir, sorry. It's my second day here and I'm just having a look round.'

'A look round was you? Ain't you got summat better to do?'

'Well yes, but as it's Saturday –'

'Never mind Saturday. We don't stop fer 'olidays round 'ere. Ave you any idea who I am?'

'Er... well, no, sir. Are you the gardener?'

The loud guffaw that followed could doubtless be heard in Matron's office but the man's eyes were not smiling. I'm Cedric 'Ampton, I'll 'ave you know, and I'm the man of the 'ouse. What's your name, eh?'

'Frances. Frances Wainwright.'

'Well, Miss *Wainwright*, you can bow your 'ead every time you see me from now on. That should learn yer some manners – do yer 'ear me?'

She could feel the blood rushing to her cheeks. 'Yes, Mr Hampton'.

'And if I ever catch yer spying on me again then you'll get the back of me hand, you will. Gardener indeed! Go 'n wash ya mouth out with soap or, believe you me, I'll do it fer you.'

Frances turned and ran as fast as her legs could carry her, scraping her knees on the brambles as she fled. Surely that awful man couldn't be Mrs Hampton's husband? He must have just said that to frighten her off. She was shaking when she arrived at the back door.

'Whatever's the matter girl?' The cook was emptying tea leaves onto the soil in the kitchen garden. 'You look as if you've seen a ghost.'

'I saw a bumble bee,' the word's tumbled out of Frances's mouth. 'I thought it was going to sting me'.

'A bee in winter? You're a strange girl, Frances Wainwright. Let's hope this place will knock a bit of sense into you. Now run along and get your hat and coat. It's time for the morning walk.'

On Saturdays, after a breakfast of dry toast and watery jam, the girls took a walk, crocodile-style, through Abbey Park.

'What do you think of Mr Hampton, Edith?' Frances whispered.

Edith was a year or so younger than Frances and at least four inches taller. Her dark curly hair was scraped off her face and held in place with a metal slide.

'I'm not sure.'

'He's a bully,' the other girl hissed over her shoulder. 'Just keep out of his way and you'll be all right.'

Frances felt her heart sink. It was a bit late for that. 'What does he do apart from weed the garden?'

'He's in charge, the same as Mum. We're supposed to call him Dad, and we do, well to his face, that is. You'll discover his nickname soon enough.'

'Thanks for the warning.' Frances shivered, desperate to block the man's evil face from her mind. 'How long have you been at the Oaks, Edith?' She raised her voice above the strengthening wind.

'All my life really. Didn't I tell you? Someone left me on the doorstep when I was a baby and then ran away.'

'So you've never known your mother or father?'

'Oh no, but don't feel sorry for me. I'm out of here in a year's time and then you won't see me for dust. Which reminds me – aren't you a bit old for all of this?' She kicked a stone with her right foot, yelling as it shot back and hit her on the shin.

'Will you two girls at the back get moving or it's no tea for either of you tonight!'

Edith jumped to attention. 'Yes Miss Campbell.' Cupping her hands she whispered, 'I'll fill you in at bedtime.' Then she winked and walked on ahead.

'Ahh, Frances.' Mrs Hampton beckoned her into the office. 'I want you to meet my husband, Mr Cedric Hampton. If you do join the staff here you'll be taking your orders from him as well as me, so it's important that you understand our rules.'

Cedric Hampton turned from the window, eyeing Frances up and down. 'She'll soon learn my rules, won't you my girl? A full grown woman from the look of it, ain't you now?'

Frances blushed, praying he wouldn't mention their meeting in the garden. 'I'm fifteen in a few weeks' time, Mr Hampton. That's why I've been promised a job here.' She could feel her heart crashing against her ribs.

'So I've heard.' His eyes went back to the window. 'You've got to prove yourself first, though, you mark my words.'

'Right then Frances,' Mrs Hampton's voice turned businesslike. 'The little ones want a story and there's plenty of darning to do. I dare say there's more holes than socks these days. You may go.'

Frances ran down the corridor, blocking the awful vision from her mind. What could anyone possibly see in a man like that, let alone the kindly Geraldine Hampton? She arrived, breathless, at the nursery where the little ones were getting ready for bed.

'Ahh – there you are.' The nurse threw her a disapproving look. 'We've been waiting for you for ten minutes. Right, children. Miss Wainwright is going to read you a story now.'

Picking up the Brer Rabbit book, Frances sat down in front of the circle of eager faces. Though the words seemed comfortably familiar, she couldn't concentrate on the story. Cedric Hampton was out to get her. She'd never been more sure of anything.

CHAPTER 8

'So, Frances – you said you wanted to know about Dad Hampton.' Edith was lying on her bed, hips aloft, making cycling movements with her legs. 'I would've thought it was obvious to anyone.'

'What was?'

'That he's a pervert.'

'What do you mean?'

'You know, stupid – a dirty old man.'

Frances gasped. 'Oh I see. Does Mrs Hampton know?'

'Of course she doesn't know. He'd be out on his ear if she did. We girls keep it our little secret.'

'But that's terrible.' Frances wanted to be sick. 'Why doesn't someone say something?'

Edith stopped in mid-air and turned her head. 'You really are naïve, aren't you? Where have you been for the last fourteen years? Do you honestly think anyone would believe us? It would be his word against ours and that'd be the end of it. We'd be down as troublemakers and never get a job.'

'But that's terrible. How do you know all this?'

'Let's just say he can't keep his hands to himself. Anyway, I'm rather busy at the moment – can't you see I'm doing my exercises? They're all the rage in Europe, you know. What's good for the body is good for the mind, that's what Herr Hitler says.'

Anger ricocheted through Frances's veins, her own loss still an open wound. 'How can you even *speak* that man's name after he's killed so many innocent people?'

'That wouldn't include your folks by any chance would it?'

'Why, you –' Frances jumped up, fists clenched and before she knew it she'd punched the other girl in the face.

Startled, Edith let out a yelp like the sound of a wounded animal. She leapt off the bed, blood pouring from her nose, and wiped her face with the back of her hand. 'You won't get away with this,' she sneered, 'I'm telling you that now. Think you're teacher's pet don't you? Full of yourself just 'cus you're going to be one of them. Well, not if I have anything to do with it, you won't.'

Frances grabbed a handkerchief and held it out. 'I'm sorry,' she said, biting her lip. 'I don't know what came over me. It's just that –'

'Just that what?'

'I don't know why I'm here. I don't fit into the place at all.'

'Well at least that's *something* we agree on.' Edith lay back on the bed. 'You'll get your comeuppance, Frances Wainwright, just you wait and see.'

'Shall I get you a flannel?' Frances was panicking now. 'My mum swore a cold water compress stopped a nosebleed.'

'Oh really? Did she punch you in the face, first?' Edith was almost hysterical now. 'God, you're pathetic, Frances Wainwright. Of course you don't fit in here and why should you? You think you're better than us because you had a real mum and dad. Oh, and a brother too, from what I've heard. Well now you've joined the real world, so you'd just better get used to it. For God's sake, leave me alone before I report you to Mum Hampton.'

'Don't move. I'll go and get someone to help.' Frances ran through the dormitory and down the long flight of stairs, crouching outside the nurse's room till her breathing subsided. Then she raised her hand and knocked hard on the door.

The winter of 1940 was the longest Frances had ever known. Despite her protestations, in March she joined the staff of The Oaks as a lowly nursery maid, swapping the dormitory for a tiny shared room at the top of the house. Nowadays she wore the regulation issue uniform: a grey dress made of coarse cotton, black shoes and a freshly starched white apron. The episode with Edith, thankfully, never surfaced again, though the younger girl still used it as a threat whenever she needed a favour. As for Cedric Hampton, Frances knew she couldn't avoid him forever.

One morning, when winter had finally turned to spring, she was pegging out washing in the garden, the last of the daffodils bowing their heads in the cool breeze.

'Pardon me, Missy, are these yours?'

Frances swung round. 'Mr Hampton!'

He was clutching a handful of wooden pegs, his face so close she could feel his breath on her neck.

'Oh, *Mr* Hampton now, is it?' His voice was mocking. 'Still on your high horse, are yer? Too good to call me Dad?'

'I don't know what you mean.' She bent down and pretended to sort the washing in the basket. 'I work here now, so it wouldn't be right to call you Dad.'

'It wouldn't be right because you don't think of me as your dad, do you, dear little Franny? I'm a man to you, aren't I? A big, strong powerful man who knows a thing or two about women.' He reached out with his hairy hand and pinched her cheek. 'I bet you think about men, don't you, behind that prim look – pretty little thing you are. I bet you can't wait to feel my hands on your –'

'*Fraaances*,' the cook's voice echoed from the back door of the big house. 'Hurry up now. I need some help in the kitchen.'

'I'll be with you right away,' Frances shouted back, relief surging through her body. Abandoning the rest of the washing, she ran inside.

'Are you all right, me duck?' Cook eyed her curiously. 'Not sickening for somatt are you?'

'It's just a sore throat, it's nothing.'

'Then it's cod liver oil you'll be needing,' the old woman said, reaching into the kitchen cupboard for a sinister-looking bottle. She grabbed a spoon. 'Now do as I say and hold your nose.'

Frances did as she was told. Anything was preferable to Cedric Hampton.

At five thirty the following morning, Frances received a note instructing her to present herself at the main office. Dear Lord, what had she done wrong now? Hastily smoothing her hair, she trembled as she knocked on the door.

'Hello, Frances, come in.' Mrs Hampton frowned. 'We've some urgent business to discuss. You may sit down.' She waved her hand in front of her. 'Firstly I want you to know that in my opinion your work here has been extremely satisfactory. Since you joined the staff everyone has found you to be helpful, polite and more than willing to do your duty. Except,' she stood up and folded her arms together in front of her chest, 'except, that is, for Mr Hampton who has, on more than one occasion, described your manner as "extremely rude".'

'Rude?' Frances' hands flew to her face. 'But I don't understand?'

'Yes, I'm afraid, those were his exact words.' She stared straight at Frances. 'I believe he spoke to you yesterday, when you were pegging out the washing, and you responded in an insolent manner. What you have to say for yourself?'

So this was how he planned to get his own back! 'I was a bit startled when he appeared so suddenly behind me, Mrs Hampton, but I can assure you that I was not impolite.'

'What did he say to you?'

Frances felt like a rabbit caught in a trap. 'He handed me some pegs.'

'So he tried to help you and you responded with contempt. Is that what I am to believe?'

Francis shook her head. The room was airless.

'Well I'm sorry, but my husband's not the one who's lying. I don't know what brought on this behaviour, but I am prepared to give you one more chance. You will apologise to Mr Hampton, and at the end of the month we will review your position. That is all.'

The day dragged on. Frances went about her duties, speaking scarcely a word to anyone, too shocked to understand what had happened. Whatever she had done to upset Cedric Hampton, he clearly wanted her to pay for it. What's more, all the girls were talking about her and she couldn't even enter a room without someone bursting into a fit of giggles. It had to be Edith's fault. No one else knew how she felt about that dreadful man, and besides, Edith had an axe to grind. Frances felt a sharp stab of pain under her ribs. Damn and blast this awful war. If her mum was alive things would be very different now.

Frances had grown fond of Geraldine Hampton these last few months and wished she could tell her the truth, but that was out of the question. The older woman wouldn't hear a bad word said against her husband and would no doubt blame Frances for making the whole thing up. No, she would have to run away and that's all there was to it. Over the last few days she'd been collecting odd bits of food – an apple or maybe a biscuit or two. It was difficult because everything was still on ration. Still, she'd put by what little money she earned each week for a deposit on a room in a lodging house, and soon she'd be out of this wretched place forever.

When Frances looked in the mirror she saw a very different person from the one who'd left home on the night of the Blitz. She'd lost weight, her chin was more defined and her dark curly hair had grown over her shoulders. Though she kept it tied back at all times, she knew it would help to make her look older when she tried to find a job. They were desperately short of people in the munitions factories and she could always say she'd lost her papers when the bombs came. One thing was certain: she wouldn't miss the sight of that dreadful uniform, though at least she had her own cotton drawers nowadays, instead of sharing everyone else's. She shuddered. No, that was something she wouldn't miss at all.

By the time she was ready for bed Frances had set her plan in motion. The kitchen girls she shared with were giggling about a new lad at the farm across the road as she stuffed her meagre belongings inside an old shawl. She said her prayers – a habit her mother had taught her and one she would never break. Then, faking a loud yawn, she got into bed and pretended to fall sleep.

The following morning while it was still dark, Frances slipped out into the garden. Rumours were rife about her and Cedric Hampton and people hardly spoke to her these days. She could easily leave without being noticed. She was fifteen now, old enough to look after herself, and they could get some other mug to do their stupid chores. She held her breath. A few more minutes and she'd be out of this wretched place forever.

She ambled towards the old oak tree, breathing in the early morning dew whilst trying to appear nonchalant. Hearing the trees rustle behind her she let out a long sigh.

'Come here, you slut.' His arm came round her chest in an iron grip, the other hand clasped across her mouth. 'Come to say sorry for giving me a bad name, have yer? I can think of a perfect way to start.'

She wriggled under his grasp but the lack of air made her want to retch. Instead she tried to knee him in the groin.

'Oh, too clever for our own good, are we now,' he said, neatly stepping aside. 'It's a bit late for that.' He thrust his free hand inside her blouse and tugged at her chemise, grasping at her nipple until she winced with pain. With a strength born of degradation, she pushed him away, her screams resonating across the empty grounds.

'I'd rather die than apologise to you,' she screeched. 'You're a wicked, evil man.'

'Shut up, you little bitch, you always did have a mouth on ya.' He twisted his arm round her neck.

'I'll tell Mrs Hampton what you've done.' She could smell his beery breath.

'Oh. I'd like to be a fly on the wall when ya do that. D'ya think she'd believe a word you said? You'd be thrown out on yer ears.'

'Then I'll call the police.' She was desperate now and he

knew it.

'Why don't ya? You could ask 'em for tea while you're at it. Mrs Hampton's thick as thieves with the sergeant down at the station.'

Frances grasped at his hands, fighting the tears that were burning the back of her eyes. He was right. Who would believe her word against his? She'd be branded a troublemaker and no-one would ever employ her again. Steeling herself, she lashed out with her right leg and this time found her target.

'Bastard!' He let out a yelp and crumpled forward.

Slipping his grasp she grabbed her bag and set off down the drive, faster than she'd ever run in her life.

CHAPTER 9
March 1969

'It was awful, Steve. The place wasn't fit to live in. How could I have let this happen?'

It was gone eleven on Tuesday night when he picked her up from the station.

'You didn't let it happen. Your mother threw you out, remember?'

Sophie shook her head, grasping a lock of hair and winding it round her fingers as she slowly recounted the story.

Stopping the car, Steve took hold of her hand, taking care to release her tangled hair. 'She's still alive, that's what matters, isn't it? She'll recover, surely? You said she was only in her forties.'

'She could be brain damaged. They just don't know the extent of it. Her liver's already diseased from the alcohol –'

'Let me take this up for you,' Steve grabbed hold of her case. 'You get yourself in to the warm. You think Frances really did have something to tell you?'

'That's the scary thing. I know she did. Whoever my father was, he probably died before I was born, but Mum believed he was still alive. She never stopped talking about the day he would come home.'

'It must've been hard, you know, being on her own at the end of the war, when all the lads were coming back. Having to face life as an unmarried mother.'

'No, it's more than that. Something happened when I was a child, I'm sure of it. She didn't want me, that's obvious, so why would she keep a bootee from when I was a baby? And what happened to the other one? It doesn't make any sense.'

Sophie opened her flat door, flicking on the hall light. Should she tell Steve about the notebook? It seemed so very personal somehow, like a private diary, and it would feel like betraying her mother all over again. Out loud she said, 'Come in and help yourself to a drink. You'll find emergency rations in the cupboard under the sink.'

'Thanks, Frigi... I mean Sophie.' Steve pulled out a large white handkerchief. 'I think you could do with this.' Disappearing into the kitchen, he returned seconds later with a bottle of pale ale in each hand. 'Will you join me?' He flipped off the top of one with his teeth.

'No thanks – you go ahead.'

'Look, I've been thinking. You want to know who your father was, don't you? There's a guy I know from school who works as a private dick. Trained as a policeman, but it didn't work out, so he set up his own agency. I could get him to ask some questions for you.'

'Could you?' She bit her lip. 'How much do you think would it cost?'

'Let's just say he owes me a favour. He'd need every bit of information you have, mind you, and a bit more besides.'

'Why are you doing this for me, Steve?'

'Because you're stubborn, loveable, irritating and amazing. And because you *still* refuse to go out with me, Sophie Wainwright.'

'I'd rather stay friends, if that's all right. I won't change my mind.'

'Okay, I believe you. But there's nothing to stop me changing it for you.'

The Miss Harcot competition was run every year by the town council to choose a rose queen for the popular summer pageant. Gasping for breath, Sophie arrived at the hotel venue in the nick of time.

'Good to see you, my dear,' the MC beamed as she entered the crowded room. 'For a minute there I thought you were one of the contestants.'

Sophie smiled back, trying her best to look flattered. 'Thank you. I'm sorry I'm a little late.'

'Don't worry – I've got you the best seat,' the man winked. 'Best seat for the prettiest judge here.' He gestured to a table at the far end of the room where three men in dark suits were talking in animated fashion. If they were her fellow judges then maybe she could see his point.

Sophie slid into the chair and poured herself a glass of water. Pity it wasn't a vodka and lime. The suited men turned round and briefly introduced themselves before resuming their conversation. She recognised one as Harcot's new publicity officer – clearly trying to impress the others who were aldermen from the town council. Glancing at her watch, she wondered if they were getting paid for their services or doing the whole thing out of dedication to duty. Just as this thought crossed her mind the drums started to roll, the lights dimmed and the evening began.

The first two contestants appeared to have stayed up well past their bedtime – teenaged schoolgirls dressed in their Sunday best. The next one, Sophie saw from her notes, was a secretary from a local solicitor's office, a prim looking girl with arched eyebrows that made her look permanently surprised.

'And now to contestant number four,' announced the compere, with a previously unseen flourish. 'Please give a warm welcome to... Miss Pat Harper!' Sophie's eyes swivelled back to see a blonde girl in a bright yellow dress sashaying down the catwalk. This one looked vaguely familiar. Sophie leaned forward and removed her spectacles. To her horror she recognised Julie – the editor's secretary. What on earth was she doing here? The other judges clapped with gusto as Julie gave them a brazen wink and saucily turned on her heels.

'What do you think you're doing?' Sophie hissed at Julie as she passed along the line, shaking the contestants' hands.

'I wanted my photograph in the paper.'

'But you can't do this. You're here under false pretences.'

'They're real, I assure you.' Julie glanced down at her ample chest.

'I'm not in the mood for jokes. It's a good job I marked you down or the *Tribune* could be accused of favouritism. Do you realise we're sponsoring this event?'

'Marked me down? What do you mean?'

'Look, Julie, you can get your picture taken anytime. You're the editor's secretary, for pity's sake.'

'But not by Steve,' the girl pouted. 'I have to do something to make him take notice.'

Sophie shook her head. 'Haven't you heard? Steve couldn't make it tonight. Dave's taking his place. He should be here any minute.'

'You mean the skinny lad with the greasy hair? The new trainee?' Julie looked aghast.

'The very one. And now, I suggest you make yourself scarce before you get us both the sack.'

Arriving home at last, Sophie threw off her clothes and fell into bed. One of the Sunday-best schoolgirls had finally been chosen for the title after the judges had been reminded they were looking for 'the fresh face of youth'. Julie, along with her alter ego, had left in floods of tears. The girl clearly had a massive crush on Steve – as he'd no doubt find out for himself. Sophie sank into the sheets. Thank goodness *she* hadn't made the same mistake.

Sophie was stuffing bank notes into an envelope when she

heard a knock on the door of her flat. She'd decided to pay her mother's rent in cash to buy a bit more time.

Steve stood in front of her, his face unreadable.

'Hi, stranger,' she said brightly. 'What are you doing here on a Friday night?'

He produced some tulips from behind his back. 'I brought these to cheer you up.'

'Thanks,' she smiled. 'Come in.'

'I'm sorry I couldn't make it last night – we had a mix-up in the diary. Did you win the title?'

'Very funny.' She motioned him through to the kitchen. 'You don't know what you missed. Can I get you a cup of tea? There's some left in the pot.'

'If you're not in a hurry, that would be great. So what happened?'

'Let's just say we had a mix-up with the voting – it got sorted in the end.'

Steve sat down, his mind clearly on other things. 'Look, Frigidaire, I know this isn't the best of timing, but I've got an address for you. The private dick I told you about, well, he's found the place where your mother lived when you were born.'

'So soon?' Her hand flew to her mouth. 'But how?'

'It wasn't difficult. It's a former boarding house, apparently, not far from the centre of Leicester.' He pulled out his notebook and flicked through the pages. 'The owner, a Mrs Betty Newby, has lived there since before the war. Her husband died last year.'

Sophie passed him a mug of tea. 'You mean she's still there now?'

'She is, and she's got the house up for sale.' He tore off the page and handed it to her.

'I can't believe it.' She threw her arms impulsively round him.

'Steady on. This is a platonic relationship, on your instructions, remember. You can't change the rules now.'

'Listen to me, please. This woman might know who my father was. Or why my mother hated me so much...' her voice trailed away. 'There's something I need to tell you. I found an old diary with my mother's things, written after her parents were killed in the Blitz.'

'That's great news, but why didn't you tell me before?'

'Because I wanted to read it first, to try to make sense of it all. The almoner found her a job in an orphanage after it happened, but I don't think she ever really got over the shock.'

'Just be careful, that's all. It's one thing looking for answers, but there won't be a happy ending. You must be prepared for that.'

'A happy beginning, at least? Either way, it's too soon to say. There must be some more diaries somewhere. I'm going to the flat again this weekend.'

'Let me come with you, Sophie. I'm sure Angie won't mind.'

'Angie in accounts?'

He nodded. 'I promised to take her to the theatre on Saturday, but this is much more important.'

'Thanks, Steve, but there's really no need to change your

plans. This is something I have to do one my own.'

'Suit yourself, but the offer still stands if you change your mind.' He took a swig of tea. 'Have you been to Leicester before?'

'I was just a baby when we left. I haven't been back since, but I'm curious to see where I was born.'

'It's not a bad city, from what I remember. I saw the Stones once at the De Montfort Hall. They have some amazing bands there – I could take you some time.'

'Thanks – I'd like that.'

He raised his hands. 'Okay, okay, I know when I'm beaten. Just promise you'll keep me posted.'

'Of course. I couldn't have done without you. If anything happens, I promise you'll be the first to know.'

'Good,' he winked. 'And now I must leave you to your chores. I believe it's what you ladies do best.'

Sophie walked through the station foyer and made her way out on to London Road. So this was Leicester. Red brick buildings lined up in front of her, their facades sullied by smoke, and everywhere she looked people scurried by.

The taxi driver doffed his cap. 'Where you off to, Miss?'

'Could you take me to Hastings Place?'

'Up Evington way, me duck?'

'I'm not sure.' She handed him the scrap of paper.

'Righto,' he grinned. 'I can have you there in a jiffy.'

Sophie scrambled into the back seat. Twenty minutes later the driver stopped outside a three-storey building on the outskirts of the city. Number 7 Hastings Place stood at the end of a terrace of four, a sorry sight with its broken gutters, peeling paint and garden full of weeds. Sophie climbed the steps slowly, took a deep breath and knocked on the door.

CHAPTER 10
Leicester, April 1942

Frances stood on the doorstep staring at the middle-aged woman in front of her. 'I'm looking for somewhere to live. I lost my home in the Coventry Blitz.'

'You and the rest of the city, what's left of it. What makes you think I've room?' The landlady leaned back and folded her arms, her dark eyes scanning the newcomer from head to foot.

'They gave me your name, Mrs Newby, down at the Ministry of Labour.' She handed over the letter.

'Did they now – so how old are you then?' she said with a disapproving look.

'I'm sixteen and a half and I've heard they still need more factory people to replace those who... ' Frances faltered.

'God rest their souls.' The woman's face softened as she scanned the note. 'No relatives have you dearie? You'd better come in.'

Frances peered into the tiled vestibule. It was colder than

usual for April and she could feel warm air coming from inside the house. She was filled with an overwhelming longing for home.

'Get yourself in here then, girl, before the wind kills the lot of us.'

She walked through to the high-ceilinged hall from which rose a steep mahogany staircase that seemed to go on forever.

'Up you go, right to the top, I'll be right behind you,' said the older woman, not unkindly.

Frances did as she was told, stopping for a moment at the end of the second flight. There were four doors, three with a number on a wooden plaque and the other in desperate need of a coat of paint; this the landlady thrust open.

'It's very small, mind, more of a trunk room really, but it'll take a bed, at a push, and at least you'll be fed and warm.'

Frances's eyes widened: the room was packed to the ceiling with junk.

'Like I said, it's a trunk room really, but I'll get Arthur to clear it out for you, me duck. He'll soon have it shipshape. Two shillings a week all told with a good breakfast inside you. What do you say?'

Frances's heart thudded underneath the borrowed woollen coat. 'I'll take it please, Mrs –'

'The name's Betty. I live here with my husband and seven lodgers – eight now, including you. Is there anything else you want to know?'

Frances shook her head. She had the urge to run away, but instead she breathed deeply until the panic subsided. 'I'm sure it will be fine, thank you,' she managed at last. 'Do you think I could use the bathroom?'

Later that night as she lay in her makeshift bed, Frances stared at the cobwebs on the ceiling – the ones Mr Newby's duster had left behind. At least she'd escaped from that Godforsaken orphanage. There were no tears left now, just a dull ache where happiness had once been.

'Come along, you lot, gerra move on, don't be shy now.' The factory foreman had a strong Leicester accent, a cigarette seemingly welded to his right hand and a kindly, if somewhat gruff voice.

Frances followed the trail of women, some young, some not so young, all dressed identically in blue cloth dungarees with a turban wrapped round their heads.

'My name's Mick Ford and I'm the gaffer. For them who've ain't done ote like this afore, I'm tellin' yer now it's 'ard graft. If you wanted to keep yer pinnies on, yer should 'ave stayed at 'ome. You'll be mekin' component parts 'ere that you'll never ever see again but I promise they'll 'elp the aircraft stay in the air. And that's all 'at matters. Follow me an' I'll show you 'ow it's done.'

Gazing up at the trusses on the old aircraft hangar, Frances recalled the moments before the Blitz, the night sky above their home emblazoned with light. If only she'd done as she was told. If only she'd listened to her mother.

'All right, me duck? Look a bit peaky if you ask me.' A jolly-looking woman with a loud throaty voice interrupted her thoughts. 'Is this yer first time away from 'ome?'

'Sort of.' Frances nodded.

'And where would that be then?'

'Coventry'

'I'm from Leicester meself. The only one in me family who didn't 'ave an important job. Coventry, did you say? Ooh ya bugger. Does that mean you 'ave no –?' she stopped. 'Opened me mouth again, I did. Never mind, me duck, we'll be family to you now. The name's Irene, Irene Clarke. Folk say I talk too much but don't you believe a word of it. Say what I have to say and that's that. Mind you, it's 'ard not to talk about the war these days, it is, what with bombs going off over our 'eads and folks being killed willy nilly.'

'And I'm Frances, how do you do.' She held out her hand. It was rude to interrupt but she couldn't help it.

'Hurry up you lot!' The foreman's voice boomed out above them. 'There'll be plenty a time for gossiping later on.'

'Aye aye sir,' Irene whispered under her breath. 'Come on Franny – I can call you Franny, carn I? Stick wi' me and you'll soon learn the ropes.'

'So what made you decide to work here?' Frances asked as they sipped their watery tea in the canteen later.

'Wanted to do me bit, that's all. It's chaps' work, but there ain't no chaps around ar' there now?' She winked. 'More's the pity. Lost my Cyril before the war, I did. But we don't want to talk about that now do we? Got to make the bestuva bad job. So what 'appened to you then?'

'After the... well, I went to work in an orphanage.' Frances hesitated. Whatever had made her say such a thing? She never ever wanted to think of that awful man again. 'Left as soon as I could and, well, here I am.'

'Here we both are, me duck, so we'd better make the most of it. But if you ever need any 'elp at all, you can always ask yer Auntie Irene.'

That night Frances climbed, exhausted, into her bed and for the first time since the Blitz, fell into a dreamless sleep.

CHAPTER 11
Leicester, 1969

'Come in my dear,' the old woman smiled as she pulled open the door. Limp grey hair surrounded a lined face, but her eyes had a spark of warmth. 'You must be Miss Jones. The estate agent's running late as usual, so I'll be showing you round. I'm sure I'll make a better job of it anyway.'

'Er yes – Sophie Jones. Pleased to meet you Mrs...'

'Newby. Betty Newby. So what's a slip of a girl like you wanting with a big house like this?'

'It's for me and my mother,' Sophie said with as much conviction as she could muster. 'We've come into a bit of money and we're looking for a place we can turn into flats.'

'Well well well! We used to have it in flats, my Arthur and me. Well, not flats exactly. High-class lodgings if you get my meaning. We were fussy about who we took in back then, only hard-working people with good jobs. None of your riffraff. Anyway, you don't want to know about that now, do you?

Come along, follow me.'

The old woman led Sophie through the high-ceilinged hall into a large sitting room with a deep bay window that covered almost the whole of one wall. Sophie felt as if she'd been transported back in time. Ahead of her, glazed doors opened into an oak-panelled dining room which looked as if it hadn't been decorated for years. She followed in silence. The breakfast room housed a wooden delft rack groaning with colourful crockery, while a stable door led through to the old kitchen at the back of the house. Sophie caught her breath at the sight of the old Belfast sink under the window alongside an ancient outsized Aga oozing warmth; both must have been there in her mother's day.

'Right, then,' Betty Newby grimaced. 'I'll just get my breath back then we can tackle the stairs. It's like climbing Mount Everest when you get to my age.'

The two flights of stairs revealed an assortment of rooms, all cluttered with debris: reference books, old seventy-eights in their record sleeves, clothes, two matching jardinières, a sewing machine, several long-defunct electric fires, crockery, old postcards, carpet samples, a reel-to-reel tape recorder, rolled up lino, a wicker hamper and the biggest collection of toy soldiers that Sophie had ever seen.

'I don't bother with this lot up here,' the old woman said as they finally reached the attic. 'I suppose we were lucky not to be bombed, you know, not like the poor souls in Coventry.'

'What's this?' Sophie gestured at a closed door.

'Nothing – just an old trunk room. No one's been in it for

years.'

A sudden shiver snaked up Sophie's spine. Her mother had come here from Coventry as a young girl, an orphan of the war. How lonely and frightened she must have been. For some reason she felt closer to Frances now than she had done for a very long time.

'You must have been very happy here in this house,' she said, trying to delay the moment when they would have to retrace their steps.

For a moment Betty Newby frowned, then her face broke into a smile. 'Very happy days, they were. When I look back on it, I can see they were the best years of my life. Now, you go on ahead of me, with these old legs it might take me quite a while.'

By the time they arrived back in the entrance hall, Sophie was lost in her own thoughts. There were so many things she needed to know.

'Will you have a cup of tea, my dear, before you go on your way?'

'That's very kind of you, thanks.' She let out a grateful sigh. 'I haven't had a drink since I got on the train.'

Betty Newby smiled. 'It's just that I don't get to talk to many people these days and that estate agent, well, he's always in a hurry, looking at his watch, he is, not like it used to be in my day.'

Sophie sat in the breakfast room, listening as Betty Newby clattered round the kitchen, trying to imagine the house during the war. She could picture her mother now, dark hair tied back from her face, the beauty of her youth still unscarred by drink or sorrow.

'There you are,' the old woman set down a tray, a silver-plated affair with deep sides and ornate handles. A cornflower blue china teapot with matching cups and saucers, milk jug and sugar bowl sat on a hand-embroidered cloth. 'Do things properly here, we do, always have,' she smiled at Sophie.

'So how long have you lived in this house, Mrs Newby?' Sophie accepted the dainty teacup, the shiny spoon resonating on the saucer.

'Let's see now. We bought it before the war, we did. Arthur, my late husband, was left some money by one of his sisters – a spinster – so we set this up as a boarding house. Then when the war started we took in young lads, those waiting for their papers, and girls too, mostly from the munitions factories. We let them each have a room – they couldn't afford any more than that – so we were like one big happy family. Mr Newby, well, he did the heavy work, God rest his soul. He was invalided out of the Great War, you see, but he still wanted to do his bit. Have a biscuit dear. Am I talking too much?'

'Not at all,' Sophie shook her head. 'Please do go on.'

'Well then we had our son, and that changed everything. Came very late in life, you understand, but not too late.' Betty Newby stood up and drew a silver photograph frame from the mantel. 'This is David. A fine-looking boy, even though I say so myself.'

'He is indeed – what does he do?'

'Works for a big electric company in Preston, he does,

something to do with publicity. Went to Grammar School and then to university. Not many lads round here did that you know, at least not back then. Always had his head in a book, never caused us a minute's trouble. Best thing that ever happened to us.'

'Were there many other children around – you know – for your son to play with?' Sophie held her breath.

'He was happy here with us, our David. Liked his books and his model trains, he did. Why should he want anything else?' For a moment, her eyes glazed over. 'Anyhow, that's enough of me. Why don't you tell me about you and your mum?'

Sophie sipped the sweet tea, recounting the story of her life, the fictitious one she saved especially for strangers. However hard she tried she couldn't get Betty Newby to say more about her past.

When she finally left the house Sophie turned back slowly, afraid to let go of the moment. Somehow she knew she would never see it again.

Steve couldn't stop looking at Sophie. 'So the trip was a success?'

'You really should've seen the house,' she nodded, her face animated. 'It was straight out of a black and white film.'

She'd agreed to join him for a drink at the Black Horse after work and so far he hadn't got a word in edgeways. 'So it was the right place – you're sure of it?'

'Oh yes, I'm sure. The dates tally, but it's not just that. Call it sixth sense if you like, but I knew as soon as I set foot in the door it was the place where I was born.'

'I'm pleased for you, really. So what are you going to do next?'

'There's not much point in going to Blackpool. My mother's still in a coma and they've promised to let me know if there's any change. So I've decided to go back to Leicester to do some more research.'

'Is that wise?' He frowned. 'You'd need a pretty good reason to see the old woman again.'

'Don't worry, I'm not going to risk that – and I gave the estate agent a false name anyway. But if Frances lived in that house when I was born, surely someone must remember her? I know it's still frowned upon now, but from what I can gather, illegitimacy was virtually a hanging offence in those days. I want to find a place called Evington, where the US airborne troops were based. I think my mother worked there. Then I can check all the old newspapers in the reference library. You never know, I might find something that could lead me to my father.'

'Slow down, Frigidaire,' Steve ran his hands through his hair. 'You don't give up, do you? I know why you're doing all this. I just don't want you to be hurt, that's all.' He took a swig of his pint, wondering yet again whether he'd been right to find the address for her.

'I need to do this, Steve, don't you see? I need to know who I am.'

'If I didn't, I wouldn't be here, would I? I'd do more, if you'd let me.'

'So come on, it's time you told me what really happened. Like why did your mother throw you out?'

'She was too fond of the drink, and not so fond of me. That's it, really. I was sixteen on the day it happened. When I got back from celebrating she'd all my things on the doorstep. I got a job as a girl Friday at a small printing press down the coast in Lytham St Annes. I think the owners felt sorry for me because they let me stay in the room above the main office. There was no bathroom – I had to use the staff washroom – but it was my own and it felt like heaven. The building was ancient with high ceilings and tiled floors and a big wooden counter at the front where the owner's wife sat every day from morning till night. Most of the time I ran errands, swept up, that sort of thing, but when he was in a good mood the owner let me help set the type. He was a small man with bulging eyes and short, hairy arms and always wore one of those peaked caps, like sub editors in old American movies. I think there must have been a writer in him trying to get out.'

Steve laughed. 'You'll be telling me next you had nothing to wear on your feet.'

She gave him a playful push. 'I didn't feel sorry for myself, that's just it. I thought I was really lucky. There was a chip shop next door and a launderette up the road. What else did I need?'

'So what went wrong?'

'Oh, the owner died and his wife sold up. I took what few belongings I had and moved from place to place: Preston, Chorley, Lancaster, Blackburn – anywhere I could find work.

Funnily enough, the old guy left me twenty pounds in his will. I'll never know why but it felt like a fortune and saved me from starvation a few times.'

He nodded absentmindedly. 'What happened to your mother?'

Sophie lowered her eyes. 'It was difficult. The drinking just got worse. She left the flat we'd lived in, apparently, and moved so many times I doubt I could have kept up with her. In any case, she didn't want me to.'

He looked at her, head held high, green eyes shining with defiance, fighting the urge to wrap her in his arms. Instead he said, 'None of this explains how you came to be in Yorkshire.'

'Oh, that's simple. I entered a short story competition in the *News of the World* – and I won. It was fantasy really, nothing like I'd ever done before. Anyway, I got it printed on the competition page and then a letter came from the editor's secretary sending congratulations. It said I really had talent. That's what gave me the idea to forge a reference from the newspaper and search for a job as a trainee reporter.'

Steve took a gulp of beer and sat back in his chair, oblivious to the steady hum of conversation around them. 'You must have been naïve, or just plain stupid. Anyone could have found out it was a fake, Frigidaire.'

'Well they didn't, did they? I saw an ad for the job at the *Harcot Weekly Tribune*, and applied.'

'You mean Alfred Moulton actually read your reference?'

'He asked me to look him in the eye and say I'd been published in the *News of the World*. And I did, without flinching. It was true after all.'

'Oh, it was true, all right, but why didn't he ask to see the evidence?'

'He did, but the following day head office put a ban on recruitment. It was me or nothing. He didn't have a choice.'

Steve smiled so hard that he thought his mouth would stretch right round his face. 'Good on you, girl – no wonder you're a hard nut to crack.'

'So come on,' she nudged him playfully, 'tell me about your new girlfriend.'

'Right, well, her name's Lizzie. She doesn't work for the paper, you'll be pleased to know.'

'That's good. With any luck, you might even lose your reputation as office Romeo.'

'I doubt it. My reputation precedes me, as you're always so quick to point out. Anyway, you'd like Lizzie; she's training to be a chartered surveyor.'

'That could come in handy when you buy a house!' Glancing at her watch, Sophie added, 'Don't let me keep you. I've got a feature I want to work on tonight. Jo Corcoran's wife finally gave me an interview!'

'Great. That should knock the spots off them, Frigidaire. Get a bit of life into the paper. You don't half know how to stir things up.'

Walking Sophie to her car, Steve cursed under his breath. He'd tried making her jealous, but a fat lot of good that turned out to be. He was seeing Lizzie after being introduced by a mutual friend. They had little in common but he quite liked the idea of dating a 'bluestocking'. Carried away with his thoughts, he didn't see Sophie lean over to give him a hug until it was too late. Dammit – he'd missed his chance.

'Thanks again.' She climbed into the driver's seat. 'You always manage to cheer me up.'

Steve unlocked the door of his Zodiac, and then slammed it shut and made his way back to the pub. What the hell. He could do with another pint.

CHAPTER 12

Sophie dropped her notebook onto the desk and gulped down the dregs of her coffee. An idea had been forming in her head and she couldn't concentrate on anything else. Betty Newby had a son, an upstanding kind of guy from what she'd heard, so what if she tried to find him? He might remember something about Frances from his childhood. Okay, so he didn't look much older than Sophie herself, but at least it was worth a try. David Newby worked in Public Relations for a big electrical company in Preston, so he shouldn't be too hard to track down. She glanced round the office. The men were having a lineage meeting and Moulton hadn't come out of his room all morning. She picked up the phone and asked the operator for directory enquiries.

'Could I speak to David Newby, please?'

'David speaking.'

'Hello. My name's Sophie. I've been given your name by Betty Newby. Do you have a moment to speak?'

'That depends. What can I do for you, Sophie?'

'I'm doing some research into life in Leicester during the last war and was hoping you might be able to help.'

'Bit before my time, I'm afraid. My mother's the best person for that. You know her, I gather?'

'Yes, sort of,' Sophie stuttered. She was making a complete mess of things.

'Well, do you or don't you?' His voice hardened.

'I've met her, briefly.'

'So – what's this about then? Are you a reporter?'

'Yes, I am. But that's not why –'

'Which paper do you work for?'

'The *Harcot Weekly Tribune*, it's a small town near York –'

'I see,' he interrupted. 'If you don't mind, I'm rather busy, Miss, er...'

'Wainwright, Sophie Wainwright. If you could just listen for a moment, please? This is nothing to do with work. I'm a war baby, you see, trying to find my GI father. That's why I went to visit Mrs Newby.'

'I suggest you try the American Embassy. Now, if you'll excuse me, I'm very busy.'

Sophie slammed down the receiver. So much for David Newby. She'd just have to find some other way.

The night phone was ringing as Sophie let herself into the office, but thankfully it stopped as she got to the top of the stairs. After a long day she wanted to send her copy over on the teleprinter and get back home. Ten minutes later the phone rang again.

'Yes?' she barked down the receiver.

'Is Sophie there?' The voice sounded vaguely familiar.

'Who wants to know?'

'It's David, David Newby. You rang me, remember?'

'Oh, yes, hello. I didn't expect to hear from you again.'

'No, well I was a bit abrupt, wasn't I? You caught me unawares. I spoke to one of your colleagues earlier and he said I might catch you there tonight.'

'So what can I do for you?' It was her turn to be abrupt, but she didn't feel up to an argument.

'I'm curious to know why you thought I could help you.'

'It's complicated,' she said, trying to pull her thoughts together. 'A bit difficult to explain over the phone.'

'Try me.'

'I want to trace my father. He may have belonged to an American airborne division based in Leicestershire during the war. I'm sure my mother was lodging with your parents when I was born.'

'Did you tell her all this?'

'No, er, well, I pretended I might want to buy the house.'

A peal of laughter resounded down the phone. 'Oh well, at least you're honest, I'll give you that. I'd like to help, but I'm not sure how I can.'

'Your mother mentioned that you worked in PR. I just thought you might, you know, be able to find something out for me...' her voice trailed off. She knew it sounded lame.

'I'm not a historian, Sophie. And I don't know much about

the Yanks. But I can see it's important to you. Why don't we arrange to meet?'

'Meet?' She was listening hard now. 'I'd love to – if you're sure, that is. Just tell me where and when.'

'I have business next week in York city centre. That's where you live, isn't it?'

'Not far away,' Sophie hesitated. 'Which reminds me, how did you get my number?

'That's easy – my secretary traced your call.'

Sophie scanned the railway platform as the train came to a halt. She didn't know who she was looking for, but she did have a few clues – youngish, between twenty-five and thirty, smart, with a look of sincerity about him. On second thoughts, maybe she should forget the sincerity, that was just being fanciful. He was travelling by train so he could finish a report before the meeting; clearly a man who didn't like to waste his time.

She was waiting where the first-class carriages came to a standstill, wondering if he'd changed his mind. Just then a man came running down the platform, tie flopping over his shoulder, eyes darting backwards and forwards as the train doors closed with a series of heavy clunks. He stopped within inches of her feet.

'David Newby?'

'Yes. How did you guess?' His eyes twinkled.

'It wasn't too difficult.'

'Then you must be Sophie – how do you do?' He dropped

his head in a mock bow. 'I'd no idea we'd got to the station – I must have fallen asleep.'

'Would you like to share a pot of tea?'

He held out his arm. 'I'd be delighted.'

David Newby was younger than she'd expected, with a manner as warm as his smile. Of medium height, he had deep blue eyes, a firm mouth and sandy coloured hair that reached just over his collar.

'Have you anywhere in mind?' he asked, as they walked towards the station entrance.

'I thought you might like to taste a little bit of Yorkshire history.'

'Whatever you say – just lead the way.'

Betty's café was a throwback from the past. With its oak facades, white starched tablecloths and vases of freshly picked flowers, it seemed the epitome of 1920s elegance.

'So this is the famous Betty's,' David smiled. 'Is it your usual haunt?'

'No, but it's where all the tourists come. The place was full of Americans, apparently, in the First World War. They scratched their signatures with a diamond pen on a mirror in the downstairs bar and, well, word soon got round. We can look at it later, if you like.'

He gazed around as they waited to be seated. 'Gee ma'am, I can see the attraction – it sure is swell in here.'

Both were laughing by the time they sat down. They made small talk until afternoon tea was served: smoked salmon and cucumber sandwiches, fluffy fruit scones with strawberry preserve and fancy cakes oozing fresh cream, all presented on a silver stand.

'So come on,' he said at last. 'What made you visit the family pile?'

'I think your mother knows something about my past,' Sophie absentmindedly stirred her sugarless tea. 'But she wouldn't have talked to me if she knew the real reason for my visit.'

'Can you honestly blame her? Pretending you wanted to buy her house? Asking questions about the past?' He grinned. 'It's enough to make anyone mad.'

'I'm sorry.' She lowered her eyes. 'It wasn't very tactful was it?'

His face softened. 'I shouldn't worry. The old lady's not the easiest person to get on with. Mum and I have never had much in common and, well, since Dad died it's been harder still. I'm all she's got and she treats me more like a possession than a son. Anyway, you must know *something* about your past surely?'

Sophie topped up their tea then handed David the milk jug. 'I know the official version. My father, it seems, was an American officer stationed in Leicestershire during the war. Good looking, upstanding, and a pillar of Arizona – or wherever it was he came from – society.'

'I gather he never came back?'

'No.' Sophie sighed. 'It seems he went missing but I suspect that the truth is much more mundane.'

'I'm sorry,' his eyes caught hers for a moment. 'I'd like to help. It matters a lot to you, doesn't it?'

She nodded. 'If only for the closure. When I was small I used to dream my dad would appear at the front door and scoop me up in his arms. He'd bring toys for me, stockings and jewellery for Frances and we'd all be happy ever after.'

'No wonder you wanted to be a writer.'

'A journalist, not a writer. My boss says our job's to report the facts, nothing more.'

'He may be right.' David grinned. 'In PR we tend to specialise in fiction. So what makes you think Frances was lying about your father?'

'Everything, really. My mother's an alcoholic you see, though of course I didn't know it then. She lived in a dream most of the time. I realise now that she was ashamed of being an unmarried mother and built up a world of fantasy to hide behind.'

'But what if your dad is still alive? What if you find him? He might be a huge disappointment.'

Sophie felt her face flush with colour. 'I'm ready for that, of course. I'd rather know the truth and then I can get on with my life.'

'I'm sorry, I didn't mean to sound harsh. I presume you've tried the normal channels – birth records at the time – that sort of thing?'

She nodded. 'As soon as I found your mother's address I wrote to Somerset House. It confirmed my date of birth and my mother's name – nothing more. Frances said she lost my birth certificate but I don't believe that either. She's definitely hiding something.'

David frowned. 'It's unlikely your father's name was on the certificate anyway. I'll have a word with Mum to see what she knows. That's what you want me to do isn't it?'

'Would you?' Sophie smiled, a genuine smile that spread all over her face. 'That would be wonderful. I've written the details down here.' She handed him a slip of paper. 'If my mother *was* in the family way when she lived in Hastings Place, someone must remember her.'

'Okay, I'll do some digging, but don't get your hopes up. My mother's a bit of a prude. Sorry, but I can't imagine her sheltering an unmarried mother.'

'Thanks, David. You've no idea how much this means to me.' She wanted to hug him, but thought better of it. Instead she said, 'By the way, I've been meaning to ask. Do you *really* have business in York today?'

'Of course!' He pulled out his wallet and picked up the bill. 'Why else would I be here?'

CHAPTER 13

Leicester, Spring 1943

'So this is where you live, is it, me duck? I've had pantries bigger'an this.' Irene stared in disbelief at the old trunk room. 'You've been 'ere a year near enough now an 'all. No wonder you 'aven't asked me round before.'

Frances pulled a face. 'And you can't stay, I'm afraid. Mrs Newby will be back before long and she doesn't approve of me having visitors.'

'I'm not surprised. You've nowhere to put 'em.' Irene frowned. 'I'd ask you to live wi' me but, well, I shouldn't be there meself, to tell yer the truth. The landlord took pity on me, you know, after our Cyril... anyhow, that's enough about me. I think it's time you made something of yerself. You've got lovely hair, Franny, and cupid bow lips like the stars in them films. Ain't you ever looked in the mirror?'

Frances blushed. 'I never had time to bother how I looked when I lived with Mum and Dad. I was always out on my bike or helping to look after little Bobby.'

'Did yer mam not tell yer how pretty you was?'

'No, but then, why should she? We never gave a thought to what we looked like. Dad had a butchers shop and Mum used to help out in the shop. We always had best cuts of meat as I remember. Then when the war started, Dad wasn't conscripted. His job was classed as an 'essential occupation', I think that's what they said. Anyway, some of the locals started calling him a coward but none of us took any notice.' Her face broke into a smile. 'The main thing is, we still got our sausages.'

'You was 'appy then, weren't you, me duck?'

'Oh, yes, very happy, though I don't suppose I knew it at the time.'

'Well, we've got to try to mek you 'appy again, so we'll start with a lick of lipstick.' She rifled through her handbag. 'Ere – try this.'

'But I've never worn lipstick,' Frances pulled a face. 'Isn't it a bit –?'

'Common? Is that what you were thinkin'? It's better'an lookin' pasty-faced, any road up.' She pulled out a mirror and rubbed it with the edge of her sleeve. 'Go on then, what are yer waitin' for?'

Frances daubed her lips clumsily, crimson appearing like a slash of blood across her face. 'How do I look?'

'Like yer need more practice. But don't you worry. We'll have you lookin' like a film star in no time at all. You keep it fer now. And tek me make-up mirror, too, I've another at 'ome.' She looked at her watch. 'I'd better be goin' then. Don't want to get yer into trouble now, do we?'

Shutting the door behind her friend at last, Frances unbuttoned her blouse and studied herself in the mirror. Irene was right; she'd grown up without even noticing. She had curves where once the skin stretched scantily over her bones, and the face that stared back at her was no longer that of a child. She was seventeen – old enough to be married and start a family of her own. The girls at work thought she was different, and they were right. All they ever talked about was make-up and men. Only the other day she'd heard that gossip Doris calling her a cissy. So what if she was? Better than being a slut.

Just then she heard a noise. Startled, she put her ear against the wall. It was Bobby calling her just like he used to, from the bottom of the stairs.

'Come on, Franny, come and play hopscotch with me.'

'I'm coming,' she shouted, 'just give me a minute and I'll be there.'

She dare not breathe, eager for his reply, but she heard only silence and the creaking of floorboards on the landing below. Perhaps she'd imagined it after all? After several minutes she crawled onto the bed and covered herself with a shawl. If only she could be like Bobby. He would stay young forever.

CHAPTER 14
Yorkshire, May 1969

Sophie couldn't sleep. The conversation with David Newby kept going round in her head. She'd liked him from the moment they met and couldn't help hoping it might be mutual. He'd been charm itself, more than she deserved since she'd blatantly lied to his mother. In less than an hour they had been chatting like old friends and she'd realised with a jolt that she felt relaxed in his company. She admired his confidence and sense of purpose in contrast to her own life, which was still firmly stuck in the past. She'd wanted to say all this to him over afternoon tea, but he'd probably have thought her quite mad. Sophie smiled to herself as she recalled Steve's reaction to her meeting with David.

'He's a total stranger with a connection so tenuous it doesn't even warrant discussion,' he'd snapped.

'Don't be ridiculous, Steve. He's highly respectable, can't be more than twenty-five and already has a high-powered job.'

'Maybe so, but he could have been an axe murderer.'

'Well he wasn't,' she had replied, her face breaking into smile. 'Quite the opposite, actually.'

Steve had pulled a face. 'So what does he look like and why would he be interested in helping you?'

'Don't tell me you're jealous, Stephen Sibson.'

'You're enjoying this,' Steve had scowled. 'And I'm not jealous. I'm just trying to protect you. You never know when you might need me '

The sound of next door's geyser bursting into life brought Sophie back to the present. She peered at the clock. It was almost two in the morning – why would anyone want a bath at this time? Sliding down the bed she pulled the sheet over her head. At least she could have a lie-in tomorrow. Sunday was her favourite day.

She'd just finished dressing the following morning when she heard a knock at the door. If the guy in the ground floor flat wanted change for the phone he was out of luck. She needed it for the gas meter.

'Hi Steve.' She glanced down the stairs. 'How did you get in?'

'The door was open. I just thought that if you weren't seeing David today you might like to come out for a spin with me.'

'I haven't seen David since that day at Betty's.' She beckoned him in, ignoring the sarcasm. 'I've been too busy sorting out my mother's flat. And anyway, why would I want to come for a ride?'

'Because I've bought a new motor.' He walked over to the window and gestured to where a red open-topped MG sat smugly on the road, its paint shining in the summer sun.

'Okay. You win,' she said, glad of the diversion.

'Is that a yes?'

'Why not? It'll make a nice change from my old jalopy.' Scraping her hair back into a ponytail, she grabbed a headscarf and threw on her cardigan. 'What are we waiting for?'

Once outside Steve gave a mock bow as he opened the car door. 'Can I remind Madame to place her derriere on the seat first, and then swing her legs over? One has to keep one's decorum.'

'Decorum my foot,' Sophie grinned, lowering herself into the plush leather seat. 'I'm wearing jeans, in case you haven't noticed.'

'I wish you didn't always cover your legs, Frigidaire.' He turned the key in the ignition. 'Has anyone ever mentioned you've got a beautiful pair of pins?'

'Are we going for a ride or not?' She looked up at the sky scattered with wisps of rapidly-moving cloud.

Once out on the open road, Sophie let her hair blow loose in the breeze. She enjoyed being with Steve – though she'd never admit it to him – and this was the closest she'd let herself get to anyone. There'd been the occasional boyfriends when she first left home, but it had been fun, a laugh, nothing that even resembled commitment. And now the first time she felt desire, the object of her affections turned out to be the office Romeo. She hadn't intended to fall in love, not with anyone, and especially not Steve.

'A penny for them,' his voice broke into her thoughts. 'Judging by that dreamy look on your face, you must have been thinking of me!'

Sophie blushed hard. 'Don't be ridiculous. I was thinking about Frances. I don't know how long it will be before she recovers.'

'I thought you said she'd improved last time you saw her?'

'It depends what you mean by improved.' Sophie shook her head. 'She's regained consciousness, but she doesn't even recognise me anymore. It's as if we never met.'

'That's tough,' he squeezed her hand before changing gear. 'So what's going to happen now?'

'I'm trying to clear out the flat for when she's ready to go back. A good clean and it should soon be ready.'

'And what if she's not well enough to live on her own?'

'There's talk of putting her in a home.' Sophie raised her chin in defiance. 'But I'm not having that.'

'I'm sorry. This must be difficult for you.'

'I still don't know what she wanted to tell me, Steve, and I'm not giving up until I do.'

A few minutes later Steve pulled the car into a layby and switched off the engine.

'Look, Sophie,' he turned towards her. 'I know it's hard, but it's not as if you've *just* lost your mother, is it? You lost her a long time ago. Maybe it's better this way. Whatever demons there were in her past, they really can't hurt her now.'

'But they're hurting me, Steve, can't you see? No – worse than that – they're haunting me. I have to know the truth about my father, and why Frances hated me so much.'

He leaned forward and touched her cheek with his fingertips. He was so close she could feel his breath on her face. Was he going to kiss her? And would she stop him if he did?

'Sophie – are you all right?' His hand was on her hair now, stroking it slowly, and his eyes bright with longing.

She wanted to lean into the curve of his body, to shut her eyes and wallow in the smell of citrus on his skin. Had Frances once felt that way too? 'I'm fine,' said Sophie, turning her head away, letting the moment go. 'I don't think I'm ready for this, I'm sorry.'

He leaned back in his seat, his face unreadable, and stared up at the sky. 'I'd better get the roof up. Those clouds look as if they might be heading our way.'

'But you can't throw my mother out now,' Sophie's voice rose to a screech. 'She's in hospital, she's *ill*, for heaven's sake.'

'I can do what I like, I'm the landlord.' The scruffy man kicked a cardboard box into the corner.

'I'm still paying the rent, in case you'd forgotten.' She looked on in horror as he swept the rubble into a large sack on the floor. Having arrived in Blackpool on spec on a warm Sunday afternoon, this was the last thing she expected. 'Anyway, it's your fault she's in this mess. The banister's not safe. That's why she fell down the stairs.'

'It's your mother who's not safe.' The landlord grabbed an empty gin bottle and gestured round the room. 'Shall I take this lot downstairs, or will you?'

'Just leave them in the road,' Sophie muttered.

'I haven't had no rent, *and* the place is a pigsty. I could charge you for cleaning it up.'

'But I paid the rent in cash. I put it through your letter box.'

'That's news to me, darlin'. Your word against mine. Now get out of my way before I call the police.'

Sophie sat on the garden wall, surrounded by her mother's belongings. Damn the stupid landlord. She hoped he choked on his words. Right now she had to make a decision, and the options were limited. She'd come to Blackpool by train as the car battery was flat, so she had nowhere to put her mother's things. She could hire a van and take the whole lot back home, though heaven knows how much that would cost. She could ask Steve to help – not a good idea under the circumstances – and besides, he was miles away. Or she could ring David Newby who only lived down the coast in Preston. That was it. David would know what to do.

They were standing in the hallway of David's luxury apartment, Sophie's face infused with colour. 'You didn't have to bring me back here,' she said, aware of how lame she sounded. 'My friend Steve, he would have helped me but he lives so far away and –'

'Don't worry,' David smiled. 'Your stuff will be safe for now. There's plenty of room in the basement.'

As soon as she'd explained the problem, he'd driven the fifteen or so miles to find Sophie outside the flat surrounded by her mother's possessions. Loading the bags and boxes into his boot, he insisted on taking her back to his flat.

She followed him now through to the living area, a huge expanse covered with long-pile carpet and scattered with low-slung Habitat sofas. 'What a beautiful place.'

'The old man left me a bit of money in trust when he died. Heaven knows why as we hardly got on. Sit down and relax, and I'll make us a drink. Coffee okay?'

She nodded, perching on the edge of her seat as he disappeared into the kitchen. Why did he make her feel so vulnerable?

'Take a couple of the boxes to be going on with,' he shouted through the door, 'then when you're up to it, I'll bring the others over. There's no rush.'

'Thanks,' she replied, unsure if he could hear her reply, 'but don't worry, I'll get something sorted out soon.'

He returned with a brown ceramic coffee percolator in one hand and a tray in the other. 'I'm taking you back to Yorkshire, Sophie. I've still got business there and it's no trouble.'

She took the coffee but avoided his eyes, fiddling with the sleeve of her jacket. 'I'm glad we met, David, despite the circumstances. You're the one good thing that's come out of the search for my father.'

'Then let me help you,' he shrugged. 'Two heads are better than one and all that. Why don't we get something to eat and then I'll take you home before that boyfriend of yours gets suspicious again.'

'He's not my –' she stopped before the words were out of her mouth.

'Of course not,' he said, and they both burst out laughing.

Back at her flat Sophie dragged the biggest box on to a dust sheet stretched over the living room floor. Pulling off the string, she winced as the rancid smell assaulted her. There must be another diary, surely, there *had* to be. A frantic search revealed mostly clutter: a collection of trinkets, some well-worn clothes, several used candles and boxes of matches, a hot water bottle and odd pieces of crockery. A search through the second box produced much the same. Bitterly disappointed, she grabbed her keys, let herself out of the door and ran down to the pay phone in the hall. 'Steve, it's me. I just wanted to tell you that my mother's been thrown out of her flat.'

Steve put the phone down and poured himself a whiskey. Strange the way Sophie always rang him when she was in trouble. Anyone would think she really fancied him, instead of pushing him away as she always did whenever he tried to get close. He took a sip of his drink, pulled a face then topped up the glass with dry ginger. It was only six o'clock after all. He thought back to the weekend he'd spent away with Lizzie. Her parents had a holiday cottage in Haworth and they'd lent her the key. She'd been invited to a fancy dress party organised by some of the locals who the family had known for years. The theme was World War Two and Lizzie had bought him a private's uniform that made him look like a boy scout.

When he'd arrived at the cottage Lizzie was dressed as a land girl, her dark hair tied in a turban. She wore white ankle socks and dungarees which made him laugh as soon as he set eyes on her.

'What's so funny?' she'd shot back. 'I thought you might think I looked sexy.' Proud of being upper middle-class, she obviously thought it was hilarious to dress below her station.

One of the party-goers had turned up in an armoured vehicle – heavens knows where he'd got it from – and as they made their way to the pub they saw GIs, Nazi soldiers and RAF pilots mingling on the cobbled streets. Later, by the time the party got under way, she had far too much to drink and insisted on having her photograph taken with a 'spiv' touting nylons from a battered old leather suitcase.

'Come on, Lizzie, let me get you some coffee,' he chided, gently guiding her away.

'Leave me alone, you spoilsport.' She shrugged him off as they fought their way through the a bunch of women dressed in every imaginable outfit – snazzy suits with padded shoulders, mink stoles, cute little hats covered with netting, high heels and the inevitable seamed stockings.

Steve managed to avert his eyes. 'I think you've had enough for one night, Lizzie.'

'Do you now?' she winked. 'Then you'd better make it up to me later.'

That was when he realised she couldn't wait to get him into bed, dressed up as they were like members of Harcot Drama Group. What the hell was wrong with him? There it was being handed to him on a plate and he didn't even want to know.

Pushing this from his mind, he downed the rest of his drink and went in search of another. One thing was certain. If he was in love with Sophie Wainwright he was clearly wasting his time.

CHAPTER 15

The grey-haired lady shuffled backwards and forwards along the lino, her shoulders stooped, her mind locked in another world. Sophie approached the counter where an efficient-looking woman in a starched white cap was talking on the telephone. On seeing Sophie she put her hand over the receiver. 'Can I help you? I'm afraid the receptionist has been called away and we're rather short staffed today.'

'I'm looking for my, er, Mrs Frances Wainwright. Do you know where I can find her, please?'

'She's in the day room right over there.' The woman pointed across the corridor. 'Do ask if you need any more help.'

Sophie tiptoed towards the glazed wooden door, her stomach doing somersaults, the toast she'd had for breakfast threatening to reappear. Why was she so frightened? She'd done her research, had found out everything she could about the mental hospital, and she knew it was the best place for her mother. Anyway, these places weren't called asylums anymore; they were hospitals where people were treated more like residents than patients. They had a ballroom, a library, a chapel and at least two occupational therapy units where painting, sewing and basket weaving were taught several times a week. It could almost have been Butlins, she thought wryly, except at Butlins your time was up after a week.

Gingerly, Sophie pushed open the door of the day room, her knees so weak she could hardly put one foot in front of the other. A strange smell assaulted her – whatever it was had been masked by chlorine – and the silence was punctuated every now and then by a cat-like whimper. Men and women sat motionless in neatly set-out chairs, staring blankly at the air in front of them. Others, those she presumed had not been sedated, paced the room smiling at her with wild, empty smiles that made her want to shrink from view.

Frances was sitting in the far corner by the window, her head drooping forward, arms splayed out either side. Her feet were encased in the same slippers she had seen on the woman in the hall: brown tartan with beige wool flaps at each side and a brown pom-pom in the centre. Sophie approached the chair and gently touched her mother's shoulder. 'Frances? It's me. Sophie.'

Frances's head jerked back. 'Who are you? What do you want?'

'I'm your daughter, remember? I've come to see how you are.'

'Bah – I have no daughter.' The older woman wiped her mouth with the back of her hand. 'I have a son, a fine, upstanding figure of a man. His father was an American captain, you know. My son still comes to see me, of course. Always brings me flowers.'

Sophie nodded in agreement. She'd been told not to contradict anything Frances said. 'How are you feeling?' she attempted to smile, 'you know, after your fall?'

'What's it to you?' The older woman took a handkerchief from her sleeve and rolled it into a ball.

'I want to help, that's all. I've been worried about you.'

Frances's face crumpled. 'Who are you? What are you doing here? I want my son. He's the one who should be looking after me.'

'Tell me about him, please, I'd like to know.' Sophie pulled up a chair and sat down. 'What's his name?'

'I don't know.' She wiped the hankie across her eyes. 'They gave him a different name when they stole him from me.'

'Who were they?'

'They were wicked people. They should have known better.'

Sophie reached out and stroked her mother's blue-veined hand. It felt hot and clammy. 'You've been having a bad dream, that's all. The doctors have brought you here to make you better. Do you remember the old summer house where we played when I was little? We used to have such lovely picnics out on the veranda.'

'Nurse, *Nurse* – take this woman away, she's upsetting me.' Frances's voice rose to a shriek. 'Take her away, now.'

The nurse who came running looked to be still in her teens. 'Your friend's about to leave now,' she gave Sophie an apologetic look. 'Come on, Frances. It's dinner time now.'

Sophie stood up wearily and made her way out of the dayroom, the smell of boiled vegetables vying with the stench of stale urine. Wherever Frances had gone, it seemed she wouldn't be coming back.

Sophie looked at her watch. The library was closing in five minutes and she'd arranged to meet David back at her flat. She'd spent most of her free time recently in the reference section finding out about Leicester during the war. Returning her book to the shelf, she smiled at the now-familiar assistant on her way out. She couldn't wait to see David again. For some reason that she couldn't explain, she felt he held the clue to finding her father.

David was holding another box of her mother's belongings when Sophie opened the main door.

'Removal man here.' He grinned.

'Welcome.' Sophie led him up the stairs and through the cramped hall of her flat. 'Go through and put the stuff down. Can I get you a drink?'

'A cup of tea will be fine.' He glanced round the room. 'This is cosy. So how have you been?'

'I got a half-page feature in the *Evening Standard* this week.' She smiled. 'Jane Corcoran on fending off the groupies.'

'The rock singer's wife? I'm impressed. How did you

manage that?'

'I have my contacts.' She tapped her nose. 'My editor wouldn't touch it with a barge pole, but thankfully the *Evening Standard* is a bit more progressive.'

Sophie passed him the newspaper and disappeared into the kitchen. Filling the kettle, she grabbed a match and lit the gas, which flared into life with a loud pop. This usually made her jump, but today she hardly even noticed. Peering surreptitiously at David through the half-open door, she saw the look of concentration on his face. She realised that she didn't know him any better now than she had on the day they met. He was kind, courteous and always acted the gentleman, asking polite questions as if they were on a blind date. She felt drawn to him, somehow, though not in a romantic way. Anyway, he had a girlfriend at home, someone called Jill who was part of his other life, a life that Sophie knew nothing about. But then why should she? She'd approached David in the first place and for whatever reason he'd agreed to help her in her search. Wasn't that enough?

'Ah, just what I need.' David accepted the steaming mug gratefully and set it on the table in front of him. 'Brilliant article. You certainly know your stuff. You'll have all his fans crying into their Babychams.'

'Thanks. That's praise coming from you.' She sat down. 'So what brings you here?'

Reaching into his jacket, he pulled out a photo of an old newspaper cutting and handed it to her. 'You might not like this but it's important you see it, I'm afraid. It's from the

Leicester Mercury, August nineteen forty-four.'

Sophie scanned the headline. "American Soldier Cleared of Assault Surprise Witness Ends Case".

'Where did you get this?' she said.

'It doesn't matter.' He shrugged. 'Just read it.'

"'Corporal Jed Hughes was today cleared of raping an 18-year-old munitions worker whilst at a dance at the American army base in Leicestershire."'

She looked up. 'But what has this got to do with me?'

'Just read on, Sophie, please.'

> *In an unexpected about-turn the girl, named as Frances Wainwright, orphaned in the Coventry Blitz, spoke up for the soldier. Miss Wainwright was summonsed as a witness by Lt Dan Christiano of the 82nd Airborne Division. After swearing on oath she admitted that she was with the accused on the night of the dance.*
>
> *Asked the Lieutenant, "Did he behave inappropriately at any time?"*
>
> *"No" she replied. "I went outside for some fresh air and I believe Corporal Hughes went to the men's room."*
>
> *"Did you see him again after that?"*

"No"

"So what happened next?"

At this point the witness pulled out
a handkerchief and wiped her eyes.

"I was attacked."

The panel were then handed details
of the attack taken from a previous
interview with the witness.

"I'm sorry to have to ask you this,"
the judge said, "but is this
information correct?"

"It is," Miss Wainwright bowed her
head.

"I'm afraid we need to know if you
saw your attacker."

"Yes, I did."

"Was it Corporal Hughes?"

"No"

"You have sworn on the Bible, Miss
Wainwright. Can you repeat your
answer?"

"No, it was not."

Sophie felt as if her stomach had been stabbed with rusty nails. 'I don't know what to say. Does this mean that the attacker was –' she swallowed the bile that had risen to the back of her throat, 'my father?'

'We don't know for sure, but I'm afraid it has to be a

possibility. Whatever happened, your mother must have been severely traumatised.'

Sophie covered her face with her hands, too stunned to cry. 'Would you mind leaving me for a moment? I need some time to think.'

'Of course. I could do with a breath of fresh air, anyway.' She felt his arm on her shoulder. 'I'm sorry. It was a difficult decision to make, but in the end I reckoned you needed to know.'

Sophie nodded, keeping her head bowed until she heard his footsteps on the stairs. She couldn't believe what she'd just read. Her mother had been *raped*. And if it wasn't the court-martialled soldier, who was it? No wonder poor Frances had dreamed up an imaginary suitor – the truth was impossible to bear.

As soon as the door shut behind David, Sophie grabbed a new box of her mother's belongings and tipped them out over the floor. She scrabbled through the contents, like a fox searching for food, until at last she found what she was looking for.

CHAPTER 16
Evington, Leicester, April 1944

'Hey, Franny, take a look at those Yanks.' Irene stopped in her tracks at the sight in front of them. 'Ain't we just lucky to be on the early shift?'

About twenty paratroopers from the American Airborne Division were running down Shady Lane in single file towards them. The Yanks had just set up camp not far from the factory in a rash of tents that appeared like toadstools in the fields overnight. Frances blushed furiously. She'd never seen so much naked flesh in her life. 'Do you think they always get up at this ungodly hour?'

'That's n'ote, believe you me. It's like an 'oliday to 'em. They've been over in Italy fer nine months or more, they 'ave, covered in muck and bullets.' Irene winked.

'How do you know all this?'

'I 'ave my sources,' Irene tapped her nose. 'They're over 'ere now for a rest.'

'I can think of a better way of resting.'

'Well don't think on it now, me duck, or like as not we'll be late. We'll be seeing a lot more of them from now on.'

Frances smiled to herself. It was now two years since she'd arrived at the factory and she finally felt she belonged. Every now and then she would stay overnight with Irene, swapping her trunk room for the dubious pleasure of the older woman's freezing two-roomed flat. She'd grown fond of Irene and felt safe in her company. No older than thirty-five, Irene was like the big sister Frances never had.

The girls were one big family now with Irene at the helm, doing their bit for the war effort and waiting for the lads to come home. As for the American soldiers, she was just going to have to get used to them. The allies were here to help them win the war after all.

'It's time you got a chap of yer own' Irene said, as if reading her thoughts. 'You're eighteen now, me duck, and yer can't keep away from 'em forever. Any road up, I should find meself a chap soon. I've got a job serving in the canteen.'

The GI canteen, which served copious amounts of 'donuts' and Coke, was run by an American Red Cross lady with the help of volunteers from the village.

'But you've already got a job, Irene,' Frances retorted as they reached the factory door. 'Why on earth would you want to volunteer?'

'I've just told you, fer the talent. They've brightened our

lives, when all's said an' done, and we should be showin' them we're grateful. Now get yerself clocked on before I do it for yer meself.'

Doris, the factory gossip, was waiting for Frances when she arrived at her machine. 'Hello, me duck. There's perks to arriving early, Franny, quite a few, if you look close enough.'

Frances tried not to smile. 'I've seen them already, thanks, Doris. Running along Shady Lane this morning.'

'Have you now? Well I can do berra than that.' She reached under her overall. 'Tek a look at this – they gev me some gum, and they've promised me a bit o' candy later on.'

'Candy, gum? Whatever are you thinking? You'll be talking in an American accent next.'

'That'd be swell!' Doris winked, 'Ah well, I s'pose we'd better get on wi' some work afore the master catches us nattering.'

Nicknamed "Baggy Pants", the men of the 82nd Airborne Division soon became a familiar sight around the village. Dressed from head to toe in olive brown fatigues with strange baggy trousers tucked into high regulation boots, the paratroopers made friends with everyone. Canteen lorries from the camp drove around the neighbouring streets, selling doughnuts and hotdogs, usually besieged by every young child within half a mile. Some of the GIs had taken to borrowing bikes from the local lads so they could go on dates with the local girls.

Frances, however, wasn't one of them. Since the day she fled the orphanage she'd never felt at ease in men's company. She liked the Americans, she really did, and she wanted to trust them, but in the end her courage always let her down. When it came to singing the Stars and Stripes though, she joined in willingly with the rest.

By the time August arrived, the factory air was stifling and the girls would sit outside in their break, smoking cigarettes and sunning themselves.

'Have a Lucky Strike, me ducks,' Irene passed round the packet.

'Frances shook her head when it came to her turn. No thanks, I don't smoke,'

'It's high time you had some fun,' Irene winked, flopping down beside her friend. 'There's a dance on at the church hall tomorrow night. It's a long time since... Well, any road up – you can't be in mourning for ever.'

'I'm not sure it's really my thing.' Frances tried hard not to sound ungrateful. 'Who's going?'

'We all are. You're eighteen now, so you've no excuse. What do you say, me duck?'

'That's very kind of you, but well, I don't have a thing to wear, and anyway –'

The older woman snorted, a deep nasal tone that sounded like a foghorn.

'We can soon sort tha'rout for you. I've still got one of me dresses from before the war. Caught the hem, I did, and spoilt it but any road, it's far too big for me now, what with all these rations. I'll find some pins and a needle, and we'll have it fitting you in no time at all.'

'You really don't have to go to all that trouble, Irene. It's not as if I've got anything to celebrate.'

'You've survived so far. That's enough reason, far as I can see. What more d'you want? Right then – that's settled. I'll start straight the way and we'll soon 'ave Cinderella ready for the ball.'

Frances untied the rags from her hair. She'd practised enough times on the girls at the orphanage and she wanted to look like she'd made an effort. She still shuddered when she remembered the conditions at The Oaks: rows of beds, each with one pillow, a single sheet and blanket whatever the weather, cold water to wash in and a regime of unspoken fear. It was no surprise, really. Some of the kids were abandoned as babies and hadn't a clue what family life was like. And then there was that disgusting man...

Shaking herself out of her reverie, she stared in the mirror. The dress Irene had given her was a pretty shade of blue, but it hung shapelessly over her trim figure, despite the well-meaning alterations. Luckily, she'd borrowed an elasticated belt with a golden clasp from one of the girls at the factory, so at least the outfit looked presentable. Frances pulled out the rags and combed her dark hair up into a roll on top, leaving the rest to fall on to her shoulders, before leaning forward to take a closer look at her face. She was lucky to have strong eyebrows that framed her chocolate brown eyes, though her normally pale face was flushed with apprehension. Biting her lips to add some colour, she picked up her coat and bag and made for the door.

The village hall was heaving. She'd never seen so many soldiers together in one place. Leicestershire folk seemed proud that the Yanks were on their side and were obviously keen to do anything to make them feel at home. There were doughnuts and coffee, provided by the Red Cross, and Union flags and stars and stripes hung up side by side. Like all the other girls, Frances had learnt to sing The Star-Spangled Banner and made sure to raise her voice as loud as all the rest.

Irene came over as soon as she saw her. 'You look a picture, Frances – you certainly scrub up well. Now come on, what are you drinking? There's punch over there and I reckon it would pep you up no end.'

'Thanks, Irene, but I don't drink alcohol.'

'You mean, you've never tried. Away with you. Look at that Yank. Hasn't he got gorgeous eyes? I could fall for him straight the way.'

Frances followed the older woman's gaze. 'He must half your age!'

'Well, he won't know the difference when the lights are dim, will he?' She winked and disappeared across the dance floor.

Approaching with a smile, the private appeared head and shoulders above the rest. 'It sure is swell to be here in your town, ma'am,' he said. 'You limeys know how to put on a welcome.'

'Thank you,' Frances replied, 'that's very kind of you to say so.'

'No trouble.' His smile momentarily disappeared. 'May I ask you something, ma'am?'

'Of course.' Though she'd never admit it, she'd talk to anyone rather than be the odd one out.

'How come you English say "thank you" all the time? You sure have mighty good manners.'

'I'd never really noticed it before,' she smiled shyly, 'but, well, thanks for the compliment.' As soon as the words had left her lips they both burst out laughing.

'I'm Jed Hughes,' the soldier said, 'but they call me Lanky. Rhymes with Yankee - geddit?' he grinned. 'Would you like to dance?'

'I'm not very good at dancing, I'm afraid.'

'Nor me. Sounds like we think along the same lines. So how about a drink? I sure am dry.'

'I'll have lemonade,' she said, remembering not to thank him again.

'Nothing stronger, ma'am?'

'I don't really drink alcohol.' She hesitated. 'Lemonade will be fine.'

'Whatever you say. So what's your name?'

'Frances. Frances Wainwright.' To her embarrassment she blushed.

'Well. Stay right there, Miss Wainwright, ma'am, and I'll be right back.'

Frances sat alone on a wooden bench, her eyes scanning the village hall. Someone had put up bunting along three walls and a half-decent combo was playing on a makeshift stage. There was ample food and drink despite the rationing and that, combined with the general air of joviality, made her feel ill at ease. Most of her fellow workers from the factory had found someone to dance with, she observed wryly, and if she wasn't mistaken, she could even hear bossy Doris cackling over the noise from the band. Oh well, at least she'd been lucky enough to meet Jed and didn't have to look like a wallflower. Besides, he seemed harmless enough. Standing over six foot in his boots, he appeared somewhat ungainly which, together with his dark brown hair, reminded her of a huge grizzly bear. But she had found herself a partner and right now that was all that mattered.

Sighing, Frances loosened her white lace collar and fanned her face with her hand, still conscious that the dress didn't suit her. Come to think of it, not much suited her these days: Leicester, (a city so near yet so far from where she had grown up), her lodgings, the landlady Betty Newby who pretended to be pleasant but seemed quite horrid underneath. Looking back, she realised with a stab of longing that she'd changed out of all recognition since the night of the Blitz. She'd lost not just her family and childhood home but the happy, carefree girl she used to be. Even at the Oaks she'd felt different from the other girls.

'Gee, lady, you're looking kinda sad.' Jed placed the lemonade on the table in front of her and took a swig of his beer. 'I hope it's nothing I've said, because, honest, lady I think you're swell.'

Frances felt her face reddening again. She had no idea how to behave with *English* boys, never mind with an American.

'It's just a little warm in here, that's all.' She wafted her face with her free hand.

'Sure is. We have ice cold beer where I come from and this tastes – let's just say it's kinda like drinking weak coffee.'

'At least you know what coffee tastes like,' she smiled. 'You could do worse.'

'Aw, come on.' He grabbed her hand. 'Let's have a dance. We don't have to like it but we sure oughta do it.'

Before she had time to think he was leading her on to the dance floor.

'Where are you from, Jed?' she asked as they moved together in time with the band.

'From Mississippi, Ma'am – my folk grow cotton on a few acres of land out there.'

'I think I've heard of that. Can we stop a minute for me to get my breath?'

He nodded amiably. 'You English girls can't 'alf jitterbug. Everybody's heard of the Mississippi River, I guess, but it's kinda hard to describe how mighty big it is out there. Why, we could drive for hundreds of miles back home and not see a soul.'

'Are you homesick?'

'Not right now, how could I be when I'm with a pretty lady?'

Before she could answer he grabbed her arms and whirled her back on the floor.

Half an hour later Frances sank back into her chair, downing the rest of her lemonade in one. 'That was fun,' she smiled, 'but I think all that twirling has made me dizzy.'

'Don't worry, ma'am, it sure is hot in here. Are you okay?'

'I feel very lightheaded. I don't know what's come over me. I need to go outside for some fresh air.'

'Then I'll come right with you.' He picked up her empty glass and sniffed.

'What's wrong?'

'Nothing.' Jed put his arm gently under her elbow. 'Don't want you coming to no harm, that's all.'

As the fresh air hit her face, Frances felt a bit better but she had a headache coming on and really wanted to be alone. 'I'm fine now really, Jed,' she said, smiling weakly. 'You go back inside.'

'Okay, ma'am, if that's what you want. I do need to use the bathroom. You sure I can't come back for you?'

'No, honestly. I'll be right as rain in a while.'

As soon as he'd gone Frances started to sway on her feet. Something wasn't right. A couple of the girls had brought spirits with them, she noticed, given to them by the Yanks. Had one of them spiked her drink? She'd heard Doris giggling about such things the other day and couldn't imagine why anyone would think it funny. Stumbling forward, she rested her head against a tree.

He came out of the blue, grabbing her from behind with the crook of his arm, his hand clamped over her mouth. A strangely familiar smell assailed her nostrils before she hit the ground with a thud, her wrists forced behind her back. The man had a handkerchief tied around his face, but she could see his eyes staring at her, like a lion approaching its prey. Fear froze her limbs as he pushed his hand up her skirt then a

144

sharp pain snaked up her spine. She tried desperately not to gag. Instead she focused her eyes on the corners of his shirt, counting the stitches as his hands roamed all over her. Her body shrieked out for him to stop but her lips remained silent.

The man's head jerked forward as a shout echoed from the church hall. Cursing under his breath, he rolled from her and wiped his mouth with the back of his sleeve. She struggled to her feet but he lunged towards her, shrieking as if possessed. Ducking out of his grasp, she yelled at the top of her voice and stumbled towards the road. She tripped in the dark and fell, grit gouging the flesh from her hands as she hit the ground. Blinded by the dark, she lay motionless for several minutes listening to the sound of her own breathing.

As the terror began to recede, Frances scrambled to her feet then ran and ran barefoot along the road, the dark night covering her like a black shroud. Time had lost all meaning but she didn't stop, not for a second, until she reached the Newbys' house. Looking back later, she could see that she was in shock; the suddenness of the attack, the searing pain in her belly and the acts of complete degradation – these would stay with her forever.

Gasping for breath, Frances let herself in through the front door and crawled up the stairs on her hands and knees, praying no one would see her. When she reached the communal bathroom she locked the door, tore off her clothes as if they were on fire and rolled them into a ball. She ran five inches of cold water – it was too risky to use the gas geyser – grabbed the loofah and scrubbed herself from head to toe until her skin felt raw. She shivered uncontrollably, oblivious to the soap-scummed bathwater which had turned a grubby pink. She wanted to rid herself of the smell of the man, his breath, his body, his very existence. Most of all, she wanted to scrub away the shame.

Frances stepped out of the bath and dried herself as best she could before inching open the bathroom door. Covering herself with the threadbare towel, she checked out the landing then ran back to her room. She pushed the soiled clothes under the old mattress, pulled on her nightdress, lifted the sheet and crawled underneath.

'Gracious me, Fran, you look a bit peaky,' Irene frowned as she clocked in on Monday morning. 'What 'appened to you at the dance?'

'She went off with that big Yank,' chipped in one of the older girls. 'Mebe they made a night of it.'

'Don't take any notice of her,' Irene put her arm round Frances. 'She's only jealous 'cus you got the handsomest chap. I was a bit worried where you got to, mind. Whatever 'ave you done to yer 'ands?'

Frances dropped her voice to a whisper. 'Can't talk about it now. Won't be able to give you your dress back, I'm afraid, but I'll repay you, of course.'

'Never mind the dress, me duck. It never suited me anyway. I'm more worried about you. If there's ote you want to gerroff your chest, come and find me later. I ain't gonna say a word to no one.'

'Thanks.' She knew her friend meant well, but it was just too risky. If word got out then people might think she'd asked for it. No, this was something she had to keep to herself.

'Are you lot going to gossip all morning?' the foreman's voice boomed out over the factory floor. 'Or d'ya think you might do a bit of work for a change?'

'Sorry, Mr –' Frances jumped as the machine burst into life. It was going to be a very long day.

CHAPTER 17
July 1969

Sophie woke to the sound of someone banging on the door. Rubbing her eyes, she looked at her watch. It was gone eleven o'clock. Struggling to open the latch, she found David on the doorstep, slightly worse for wear.

'What are you doing here? I thought you'd gone home hours ago?'

'I went for a walk, if you remember, to let you take in the idea, well – you know – the newspaper cutting. Can I come in?'

'Oh, sorry, of course.' What idea, she wondered? The fact that her father was a rapist?

'Oh that,' she said, exaggerating a yawn. 'You were only trying to help.'

'So why wouldn't you let me in, Sophie? I've been back three times, worried sick. I thought you'd... well, you know.'

'Thought I'd what, David? I've had a shock, yes, but it's been a long day and I must've fallen asleep. Where have you been all this time?'

'In the pub round the corner.' He had the grace to look sheepish. 'I couldn't go home till I knew you were okay.'

'So what happens now?'

'About your father or the fact that I'm here after dark?'

Sophie managed a smile. 'You can stay the night on the sofa, if you like. That's the best I can offer.'

'So you're not mad with me for being the bearer of bad tidings?'

She sat down and cupped her head in her hands. 'I'm grateful to you for trying to help, though it beats me why you want to. We still don't know the name of my mother's attacker, or if I'm the result of what happened that night.'

'I want some answers too, Sophie. I'm sure my mother knew something about your past. Which reminds me – Mum's found out that I'm seeing you, so I had to tell her who you really were.'

'Oh dear, she won't be too pleased then. Gaining entrance to her home on false pretences.'

'It's not the house she's bothered about. She just doesn't want me getting involved with you.'

Sophie looked away. 'So did you ask her, then? Did you ask her if she remembered me?'

'That's the strange thing. She only remembers your mother very vaguely. Certainly not you. She reckons she had loads of lodgers over the years and couldn't keep track of them all.'

'That's ridiculous.' Sophie's eyes were blazing now. 'I doubt if loads of them had babies.'

'No, I agree, but perhaps you were born after Frances left my mother's place. When's your birthday?'

'May sixth, nineteen forty-five.'

'A couple of weeks before mine. That explains it.'

'Explains what?'

'If my birth was imminent at the time, Mum would've taken a back seat in the business. Women *in the family way* were supposed to rest up in those days. It's no wonder she doesn't remember.'

'Now you're being ridiculous. You can't just forget a pregnant woman and her baby. Your mother doesn't like me, does she? She thinks you're mixing with riffraff. That's what this is all about.'

'Look, Sophie,' David shrugged. 'The old girl came to motherhood quite late. She never had much support from Dad. In fact I think he was scared of her most of the time. Anyway, there's something I wanted to ask. Do you still think your father could have been an American soldier?'

'I don't know what to believe anymore.' She wasn't ready yet to tell him about the diaries. 'But I have to carry on till I know the truth. What else can I do?'

'You could find me a blanket.'

'What? Oh, sorry. I'll do it now. If you're lucky I might even throw in a pillow, too.'

'Thank you, m'lady.' He gave a mock bow. 'Chin up and I'll

BAGGY PANTS AND BOOTEES

see you in the morning.'

Sophie sighed as she left the town hall. The council meeting had dragged on and she still had to send the copy over to head office. After two hours discussing a plan to make Harcot's main shopping street one-way, they'd still not made a decision. Some councillors were worried about the effect on the livelihood of shopkeepers, others believed it would solve congestion into the town. Her watch said ten forty-five p.m. and it would be nearer midnight before she got home.

She looked up as a shadow appeared in front of her.

'Hi, Sophie!'

'Steve! You scared me for a moment. Whatever are you doing here? It's a bit late for taking photographs isn't it, especially without a camera.'

'Sarcasm doesn't suit you,' he pulled a face. 'I'm worried about you, if you must know. And that new man of yours.'

Tossing her hair back over her shoulders, she walked on in front of him. 'Look, Steve, it's not *my* fault you're jealous.'

'Don't be ridiculous. Nothing could be further from the truth. Just try to see it from where I'm standing. You've got your reputation to think about.'

'And why is that?' She swung round. 'What is it I'm supposed to have done?'

'I'd have thought that was obvious. Some strange bloke stays overnight in your flat and you don't care a jot what anyone thinks.'

'Who told you that? No, don't bother. For your information

he is not some strange bloke and he *didn't* stay at my flat – not in the way you mean. And what if he did? This is supposed to be the swinging sixties. I don't see what my private life has got to do with you.'

'No, you don't do you, Sophie, that's your problem.' Steve lit a cigarette, inhaling deeply till the tip glowed red in the dark.

'I'm not the one with a problem.' She was furious now. 'As far as I know we're not going out together, you're not my keeper and I certainly never gave you permission to order me around.'

'But I'm –'

'You're what exactly?' she interrupted, wafting the smoke away from her face. 'You don't even know, do you? You've finally found a woman who doesn't fall at your feet and you can't handle it. Now, if you don't mind I've got to get back to the office.'

Steve glanced at his watch. 'It's almost eleven. Can't it wait till the morning?'

'You know very well it can't. Anyway I got a story tonight, a real story, better than anything on the stupid agenda. Although that's not saying a lot.' She tapped her notebook and winked.

'Another scoop?' He forced a smile.

'Who knows? A well-known someone stands to benefit if the one-way system goes ahead. A sort of exposé – if I can get it passed Mouldy Moulton.'

'Now *that* I'd like to see.'

'Just watch this space.' She frowned. 'Look, Steve, for what it's worth there's nothing going on between me and David. I like him – I like him a lot – and he's helping me to trace my father. But he's already got a girlfriend so we're just friends, that's all.'

'Okay, okay,' Steve held up his hands. 'Maybe I overreacted, but what did you expect me to think? At least let me walk you back to work.'

'Only if you promise not to listen to any more gossip.'

'Right. It's a deal.'

'Oh, and Steve?'

'Yes?' His eyes met hers.

'Nothing.'

Steve got into his car, lit up another cigarette and headed into the city. He'd no intention of going back home just yet. If only he could stop thinking about Sophie, but he couldn't, damn it. At first he'd been intrigued by the way she'd rejected him and, okay, maybe a little bit peeved as well. He'd never had a problem getting his share of pretty girls, but then Sophie wasn't just any pretty girl. She was sparky, determined, ambitious and what his mother would have called 'a bit of a madam'. She knew what she wanted out of life and clearly it wasn't him.

He drove fast, past street lamps reflecting on the wet pavements. It was raining quite heavily now and people were scurrying about, the women in short dresses, their bare arms glistening. He didn't usually drink Scotch but tonight he had an excuse. When Val on switchboard said she'd seen David coming out of Sophie's flat, he'd wanted to wring the stupid man's neck. A fat lot of good that would do him. Pressing harder on the accelerator, Steve roared off down the road. Just before the Minster he parked the car down a side street and made for the nearest club.

Several hours later Steve crawled back into his MG. After several attempts, he located the ignition and waited for the engine to turn over. Reaching down with his right hand, he guided his foot on to the accelerator and revved loudly. So he was drunk? What of it? He wouldn't be the first man to get into a car with a few nips of whisky under his belt and he wouldn't be the last. He'd hoped the drink would take his mind of Sophie, but no such luck. The sight of half-naked women writhing around the stage had made him want to go home. Sod it – he wanted her badly. He didn't care about anyone else.

Letting go of the handbrake he edged backwards, straining his neck to look out for traffic before setting off down the near-deserted street. So Sophie had a tough exterior? That was only to be expected, he supposed. With no father on the horizon and a seriously alcoholic mother, she had every right to be wary of men. Steve put his foot down hard, squirming at the thought of the Lancashire bloke leaving Sophie's flat. 'My friend David,' she called him. A likely story. The anger rose up like bile in the back of his throat. The next thing he heard was a loud bang, and then he passed out.

'Do you know what time it is, Sir?' The policeman was staring down at him, a notebook and pen in his hand.

Steve rubbed his eyes. 'Is it morning?'

'It's five o'clock in the morning to be exact, sir, and you've narrowly missed a brick wall. Have you been drinking?'

'I had a few last night, constable, and then I must have fallen asleep.'

God, what a mess. All hell would break loose at the paper if he lost his licence.

'So you normally sleep in the car, do you?'

'Well, no, but I'm a photographer on the *Standard* and the *Weekly Tribune*. I was on the night shift, felt a bit knackered, if you know what I mean, and well...'

'Name?' The constable raised his pen.

'Steven Sibson. You can check my credentials if you like.' He fumbled unsuccessfully for his press card.

'Well, Mr Sibson. I go off duty in five minutes and I'm damned if I'm going to be held up by having to arrest you. So I suggest you get out of this car and walk back to where you came from pronto. And if I see you so much as parking on a double yellow line for more than ten seconds in the future, I'll throw the book at you. *Is that clear?*'

Steve nodded, relief spreading through his veins like warm treacle. 'I'll call a taxi, right this minute. Good day, constable. And thanks.'

CHAPTER 18

'So what happened to you?' Sophie opened the door, eyeing Steve up and down. 'Have you been in a fight?'

Steve cupped his swollen eye. 'A fight with a brick wall, to be precise.' He glanced at her pyjamas. 'I'm sorry it's so early – can I come in?'

Running her hands through her hair she beckoned him through. 'Never mind early. It's five forty-five in the morning and I need my beauty sleep.'

'That's one thing you don't need. Do you think you could do me a favour?'

'Anything.' She shivered. 'Providing it won't take long.'

'Can I stay here a bit till I've sobered up? The coppers are on the warpath. If it's not too much trouble, of course.'

She managed a faint smile. 'Wait there while I get dressed, then I'll make you a cup of coffee and you can tell me all about it.'

Sophie reappeared in jeans and an old tee shirt, a mug of

coffee in each hand. 'So why didn't you just go home?'

'Yours was nearer.' He attempted a sheepish look. 'And well, I wanted to...' His words disappeared in a yawn.

'Wanted to what?' She opened her mouth to reply, but Steve was already asleep.

An hour later the two left the flat and headed for Sophie's car. They were almost outside the city before Steve broke the silence. 'It's left here, then straight on past the garage. How's your friend David by the way?'

'The Esso garage? Fine thanks. He's come up with new information.'

'Right, er, is that good?'

'It's good and not so good, really.' She swallowed hard. 'I'd tell you about it, Steve, but now's not a good time.'

'Sharp right, take it slowly, turn left at the corner of Gillygate and there's a dead end. I'd be only too happy to listen, you know that.'

The car swung round the corner into the cul-de-sac where Steve had driven his MG into the wall. Sophie pressed hard on the brakes. 'Oh, my God, you're lucky it's still here. Do you want me to wait?'

'Yes, please.' He opened the door and walked over to his car, crouching down on his haunches to inspect the damage.

'Is it bad?'

'Nothing a quick paint job won't fix. I'll just check she starts okay.'

He climbed into the driver's seat. 'How about a drink tonight? On me, of course. Just to say thanks?' The engine purred into life.

Sophie smiled back. 'Okay, why not?'

'Great, I'll pick you up at seven.'

'No – I'll pick *you* up, Mr Sibson. I think it might be safer.'

Reversing the stricken car, Steve waved his hand out of the window and accelerated down the road.

'So that's it, really.' Sophie put her empty glass on the table. It was her third or fourth in less than an hour, not good on an empty stomach. 'You wanted to know about my past and now you do.'

'Jesus, Sophie, I don't know what to say.'

'Why? Because my father's probably a rapist? Or because I'm a little bit tipsy?'

'Both, er, neither. Oh I don't know. God, what an awful blow.' He put his hand on hers.

'It was and it is.' She brushed his hand away. 'Do you think I could be turning into an alcoholic like my mother?'

'Don't be ridiculous.' He grabbed hold of her hand. 'Now, tell me, after all that's happened, do you still want to know your father's name?'

'Part of me does.' She stared at her fingernails. 'Though I've no idea why.'

'I'm sorry. Maybe the guy, whoever he was, didn't mean to –'

'He assaulted my mother.' Sophie almost choked on her drink. 'For God's sake, Steve, whose side are you on?'

'Yours, of course. But if this man really is your father, well, I care about how it makes you feel.' He avoided her eyes. 'What's David's view on this?'

Sophie felt the anger rising up inside her. 'What is it with you and David? He's only trying to help. It's not his fault the news was bad.' She raised her hands in disbelief. 'Steven Sibson! Don't tell me you really are jealous?'

'Me? Don't be daft. I just want to make sure the man's intentions are honourable. You don't really know him, after all.'

'For a start, I'm sure his intentions are a lot more honourable than yours. Secondly, if he was trying to seduce me, then telling me my father was a rapist would hardly be the way to go about it.'

Several people turned to stare but Sophie was past caring.

'Okay, Frigidaire, calm down and let me buy you another drink. I'm only concerned about your safety.'

'Safety? Heaven help me if I was really in danger.' Grabbing her bag, Sophie threw her coat over her shoulders. 'I'm going home now, *on my own*,' the words came out slightly slurred, 'and I would prefer it if you didn't try to stop me.'

'Okay,' Steve's mouth was set, 'but at least let me call you a taxi.'

'No, thanks, I prefer to walk.' With that, she turned and stumbled out of the door.

When she reached her car, Sophie rummaged for the keys. She felt a bit lightheaded and wished she'd had something to eat before leaving home. Opening the door, she spied an old checked blanket lying over the back seat. She snatched it, pulled it over her shoulders and moved round to the passenger side where hopefully no one would see her. Half an hour's sleep and she'd be as right as rain.

CHAPTER 19

When she finally woke, Sophie stretched her arms and gazed lazily at the ceiling. Glancing around her she peered at the unfamiliar décor, the drawers stuffed to overflowing with socks, the piles of records on the floor. Gradually, realisation began to dawn. Fingers of fear ran down her spine. Someone had stolen her bedroom.

'Morning, how are you?' Steve strolled into the room, a cup of tea in his hand. 'I've brought you my dressing gown.'

Staring down at her half-naked chest, Sophie groaned. 'Where are my clothes?'

'I folded them and put them in a neat pile. They're over there, next to mine.'

Sophie winced. He was obviously enjoying every minute.

Grabbing the dressing gown, she pulled it round her then leaned back down on the pillows. 'Steven Sibson. I want you to tell me immediately how I got here.'

'Simple, I found you asleep in the passenger seat about an

hour after you left, and drove you here in your car. Mine's still at the pub. Anyway, I only have the one bed, so –'

'Shut up, this is important. I need to know, did we –?'

'Did we have a good time last night? Yes thanks, fabulous.'

'You know very well what I mean,' she snorted. 'Did we... sleep together?'

'We slept very well as a matter of fact. But not together. And by the way, you snore.'

'How do you know?'

'I heard you. From the couch in the sitting room.'

'You mean –?'

'No. Sophie, I didn't take advantage of you, more's the pity.'

'Thank God for that. Sorry, Steve, but –'

'You don't fancy me, I know.'

'That's not true.'

'Does that mean you do?'

'Yes, I mean, no, I don't know. It's not fair of you to ask.'

'Okay, so would you like a cup of coffee?

'Yes, please.'

'One strong coffee coming up!'

'Right, Sophie, I've got a job for you.' Arthur Moulton sounded unusually harassed. 'I want you to cover the magistrate's court this morning. Tim's phoned in sick. He's broken his hand playing football so you'll have to stand in.'

A surge of excitement rushed through her. 'I'll get there as soon as I can.'

'I hope you know what you're doing. I'm taking a risk, you

know.'

'I've sat in enough times before. I'm sure I can handle it.'

'Good.' He picked up the phone. 'Because I can't afford to send anyone else.'

'Of course I know what I'm doing,' she mumbled to herself as she headed for her car, stuffing a new notebook into her bag. At least she wouldn't bump into Steve at Harcot Magistrates, unless of course they put her on trial for murdering Moulton. How insufferably patronising he could be. Next time she would come back to earth as a man.

'Will the court please rise.'

Court Number One looked at least a hundred years old. Every visible surface seemed to be made of polished oak, the ceilings overrun with dancing cherubs, while photographs of long-dead dignitaries hung at suitably reverent intervals along the walls. Even the "live" magistrates had an air of antiquity about them, Sophie thought wryly.

First up was a divorce case. The press were allowed to sit in on these, but not to report what was said. Sophie sat at the end of the row, biting the end of her pencil. What was it about modern marriage? Everyone seemed to be splitting up these days – it was enough to put her off matrimony for life. She recalled the night she *hadn't* slept with Steve and her face suffused with colour. Deep down she still wondered why he hadn't been *less* of a gentleman. Could she really be that unattractive? Or was he just trying to protect her? If it was meant as a compliment, right now it didn't feel like one.

The clerk's voice interrupted her thoughts. Next up was a youth who'd been arrested for carrying a butcher's knife while walking home at ten o'clock at night. The poor lad looked terrified.

A policeman stood up and read his notes in monotone, saying he'd found the accused with the weapon near a well-known courting spot. There had been a serious assault in the same neighbourhood recently and all possible suspects were being treated with caution. Sophie sighed. The accused looked as if he wouldn't hurt a fly. It turned out he was a chef who had taken a short cut home. The knife was the one he used at work – it had his initials carved on the handle. He was fined for carrying a dangerous weapon and allowed to go.

Next came a woman in her twenties who looked as if she needed a good wash. Her crime was stealing from the electricity meter in her flat. The reason? To feed her four kids, all of them less than five years old. Her 'fiancé' had left six months earlier and she was finding it hard to make ends meet.

Sophie's heart plummeted. This woman needed help, not a criminal record. The chairman of the magistrates, a fat woman in her fifties, peered over horn-rimmed spectacles, her neatly coiffed grey hair resembling a pantomime wig. 'Were you aware that what you did was theft, young lady?'

'Me kids was starving, Mrs. What was I supposed to do?'

'That is no excuse to break the law, I'm afraid. These laws are in place for a reason.' The grey-wig lady conferred with her fellow magistrates then looked up.

'We fine you twenty-five pounds to be paid at a rate of five shillings a week. If we see you before us again, the fine will be much steeper. You may go.'

At the end of a very long morning, Sophie slipped out of her seat and jumped in the nearest telephone box. 'Can you put me through to Mr Moulton, please?'

The editor sounded irritated. 'What is it, Sophie? Have you sent your copy through?'

'I'm about to. It's just that I've got an idea for a story. There's a woman here who's been fined for stealing to feed her kids. The poor thing needs help, not another debt to pay. If I interviewed her now we could maybe get the welfare involved, you know *make* them help her. What do you think?'

The ensuing silence lasted a few seconds but if felt a lot longer. 'I suggest you stop trying to change the world, Miss Wainwright. You're a reporter not a philanthropist. Now get your copy over to the *Standard* and yourself back here pronto, or you might just find yourself out of a job.'

'It's all so wrong,' Sophie complained when she met Steve at the office later. 'We should be helping these people with their problems, not forcing them to steal to make ends meet.'

'I agree,' Steve sighed, 'but it's not that simple. We might record the events, but we don't have the power to change them. I'm here for twelve months to get to grips with the job, and then you won't see me for dust. Look, why don't you join me for a drink after?'

'No thanks, I'm fine.' To her horror she began to blush. She'd still hadn't got over the thought of waking up in his bed.

'Well, if I can't tempt you with alcohol, how about a steak? You look as if you need building up.'

She thought of the tinned soup waiting for her back at the flat and her heart sank. 'It's a deal.'

Sophie watched Steve as he made his way amiably to the bar, singing along to Scaffold who were playing on the jukebox. She liked the way his dark brown curls flicked up at the nape of his neck. Why hadn't she noticed it before? Rummaging in her bag for her compact, she quickly refreshed her lipstick. What on earth was she thinking? All the girls thought he was dishy, but hadn't he said himself he'd soon be moving on? She'd wanted Steve as a friend and that was exactly what she'd got. She had no one to blame but herself. Besides, she had other things on her mind right now.

For several weeks now Sophie had visited her mother regularly but the routine never changed. She would announce herself briefly at reception, take the lift to the first floor and walk along the corridor, keeping her eyes trained on the floor. She still couldn't bring herself to look at the other patients. Seeing them shuffle along, eyes hollow, their faces devoid of humanity, made her want to scream inside. She would make her way through the day room until she reached her mother's chair where the ritual started all over again. 'Who are you?' Frances would ask. 'Why have you come?' The questions, as always, remained unanswered.

'A penny for them.' Steve placed a glass of lemonade in front of her. 'Hope you were somewhere nice.'

'I was thinking about my mother.' Sophie looked up. 'She doesn't know she's lost the flat. I don't suppose she'll ever be able to live on her own again.'

'So what happens next?'

'Some sort of residential care, I suppose. I can't believe it, Steve, she's only forty-three. Far too young for that.'

'Look on the bright side, Frigidaire.' He squeezed her hand. 'There's still time for improvement.'

'I hope you're right. Which reminds me – Betty Newby's been taken ill. I meant to tell you before. She's in hospital with some sort of chest infection.'

Steve gulped down the last of his bitter. 'How do you know that?'

'David rang me early this morning. I thought I might go and visit her. If I explain why I lied to her, maybe she'll be more forthcoming?'

'You don't give up easily, do you?'

'How can I? Anyway, I'd still think she's got something to hide.'

'What could she possibly want to hide from you, Sophie? Maybe she doesn't like to talk about the war? Times were different then, from what I hear. When people were upset, they kept themselves to themselves.'

'Oh, please stop talking in clichés. I deserve better than that. She's a wily old woman, believe me. Upset doesn't come into it.'

'So when are you planning on going?'

'Saturday afternoon. I'd be there sooner if Moulton would let me.'

'Any chance you could just leave things be after that? With the Newbys, I mean?'

'I'll try, I promise.' She was lying and he knew it. 'Ah, here comes the steak. Maybe I will have that glass of wine after all.'

'What are *you* doing here? Come to gloat have you?' Betty Newby lifted her head off the pillow and glared at Sophie.

'I heard you were ill, Mrs Newby, and wanted to bring you these.' Sophie waved the bouquet in the air, like a peace offering.

'And who told you I was ill, eh?' Her voice came out in a rasp. 'Was it that son of mine?'

'Well, David did mention it yes, but I came down here to –'

'Oh, David is it now? He's turned your head, and that's for sure. I should never have let you into my house, you scheming little madam.'

Sophie put the flowers on the bed and took a deep breath. She could easily back off, but something was stopping her. 'I'm sorry you feel like that, Mrs Newby. I came here to apologise for not telling you the truth in the beginning. You see, David's been helping me find my father.'

'What's your father got to do with it? You should both leave well alone. Meddling with the past can be very dangerous.'

'Your son understands me. He's had a stable upbringing so he knows what I missed out on.' She was patronising the old woman now, but she couldn't help it.

'Bah, stable upbringing my foot. Who told you that? I know your sort. Just keep away from him, if you know what's good for you. Keep *right away.*' Her voice rose above the bustle of the ward.

'What's going on here?' The middle-aged nurse looked directly at Sophie. 'Why are you upsetting my patient?'

'I'm sorry,' Sophie kept her voice calm, 'She's very upset, I agree, but I've no idea why.'

'Yes you have, you little madam,' Betty Newby spat out the words. 'You should be dead, by rights. Your mother took you away, but not far enough it seems.'

Sophie gasped. 'What do you mean? I thought you couldn't remember my mother?'

'Come along, Miss,' the nurse took Sophie's arm. 'I think it would be better if you leave now. Mrs Newby has a weak heart and any upset will only make things worse.'

'Go away, will you?' For one so ill the old woman had a strong voice.

'I'm going,' Sophie said wearily.

'Not, you, you stupid girl, I meant the nurse. You came for some home truths, so I'll give them to you. Are you in love with David?'

'In love with him?' Sophie shook her head. 'Whatever made you think that?'

'What else would a woman *like you* want him for. His money?' Her face was crimson now, sweat shining on her brow. 'Go on – say you love him – I want you to, you deserve to suffer. He'd never be bothered with the likes of you anyway.'

A tight band of fear clutched Sophie's chest. What did she mean by *the likes of you*? Did she know Sophie was a rapist's daughter? Out loud she said, 'I have become attached to your son, Mrs Newby, but not in the way you mean.'

'Hah, I knew it. You little whore.' The words spewed out of her mouth now, dribble running down her chin. '*KEEP AWAY FROM HIM. Do you hear me? If you know what's good for you, just keep away.*'

CHAPTER 20

It was early Sunday morning and Steve hadn't slept a wink. Sophie had been in Leicester all weekend which meant one thing: she was with the Newbys, or more precisely, David Newby. However hard he tried he couldn't get the guy out of his mind. Was he jealous? He kept asking himself the same question but didn't want to know the answer. At first he'd thought he'd fancied Sophie because she refused to go out with him. He liked a girl with spirit and, besides, it made the chase more exciting.

But Sophie was different. She had a way of looking at him with those green eyes that made him want to...well, it was a look most guys would find hard to resist. She was keen to make a success of her job and seemed genuinely indifferent to his advances. Advances? He smiled ruefully. This must be the chastest relationship he'd ever had. He hadn't even kissed her yet, for fear of frightening her away, but sometimes the temptation was overwhelming.

Lizzie had finally given him the push. Okay, so she wasn't exactly the love of his life, but they'd been out a few times and the rejection had come as a bit of a shock. The only female on her degree course in estate management, she seemed very headstrong, but he supposed at times that was just what she needed to be. Admittedly he hadn't shown much interest in sex, but so what? There was nothing worse than a girl who slept with you on the first date.

As for him, he'd always wanted to be a photographer, sailing through his A levels in art, French and history before gaining a place at university to study fine arts. Afterwards he'd travelled round Europe making just enough money from freelance work before moving to London to work for an up-and-coming hippy magazine. He'd had his fair share of girlfriends, but nothing ever lasted for long. He'd never two-timed a girl exactly, but somehow there always seemed to be another one on the horizon.

Sliding out of bed, Steve padded into the bathroom and doused his face with cold water. What made him go for strong women? He'd fallen for Sophie Wainwright, that much was obvious, but he wasn't sure how to deal with it. She'd been away in Leicester again this weekend. He only hoped she hadn't been with David.

'Where's Sophie?' Steve peered into the reporters' room first thing on Monday morning. 'Out on a job already?'

'She's not turned in.' Joe Suggins stabbed the typewriter keys with both forefingers. 'Which means more work for the rest of us!'

'Is she ill?'

'How should I know? Look pal, I've got work to do, even if you haven't.'

'Okay, okay.' Steve knew when he wasn't wanted. He'd promised to call in at the grammar school to drop off some proofs and then he was due at the mayor's inauguration. He looked at his watch. If he put his foot down he could just about make it to Sophie's flat first. He raced down the stairs, jumped into his car, reversed out of the car park and roared off down the road.

'Sophie, let me in – I know you're in there.' Steve banged his fists on the door.

'What's all this noise? Can't a girl have a lie-in?' Sophie peered round a crack in the door. 'What do you want?'

'I want to know why you're not at work, that's what.'

'How did you get in?'

'The guy in the next flat was leaving as I arrived. What does it matter? I'm here now and I want to come in.'

After a few seconds the door swung open and he followed her inside.

'You still haven't said why you're not at work.'

'I've rung in sick.'

'But you never do that.'

'Well I have now. Is there anything else?'

'God, you look terrible. Have you been crying?'

'Of course not. I always look like this first thing in the morning.'

Steve's face broke into a grin. He shouldn't tease her but he couldn't help it. 'Well that's not strictly true now is it, Frigidaire? I seem to recall –'

'Is there anything else I can help you with?'

'Yes, as it happens, there is. You can tell me what's wrong with you, then I promise to leave.'

'All right, you win. Anything to get rid of you.' She slumped down on the sofa. 'I need to offload on somebody, so it might as well be you.'

'I understand why you're upset,' he said gently when she'd finished telling him about Betty Newby. 'But you've coped with far worse than this in your life. Why on earth have you let it get to you now?'

'Because there's something she's not telling me, Steve, I know it. I've never been so sure of anything in my life.'

'Have you mentioned this to David?'

'No. Not yet.'

'Okay, listen to me. We find out what this is all about, what the old woman's got against you exactly, and we do it together. This time no arguing.'

'Thanks, I know you mean it.' She took out a handkerchief and blew her nose.

'Someone's got to look after you.' He headed for the door. 'I must go now. I'm late already.'

She looked up at him and smiled weakly. 'Okay, boss, you win.'

Steve looked at his watch. It was almost one in the morning

and he didn't feel like going to bed. He wanted to help Sophie, he really did, but it was much more than that. He wanted to be with her, dammit, deep down he wanted it more than anything and maybe this was the answer.

The shrill of the phone brought him out of his reverie. Who the hell would ring him at this time of night?

'Hi Steve – it's Jerry. How are you, mate?'

'Well, hello, Jerry, long time no see. I'm fine thanks. Is anything wrong?'

'Nah, it's just that I've got a proposition for you.'

'D'you know what time it is over here?'

'Late-ish? Look – how would you like to come over to the States? There's money in it.'

Steve almost dropped the receiver. 'Go on, I'm all ears.'

The two men had met at university in the Home Counties. Jerry had an English father and an American mother but his father wanted him to spend some time in Britain – which he did until Jerry's grandmother died and left him half her fortune, when he promptly hot-footed it back to New York. Nowadays he called himself an 'entrepreneur'.

'Have you heard of Woodstock?' Jerry was still talking.

'No – should I?'

'It doesn't matter. Believe me, you will. Some crazy guys out here are planning the biggest rock concert ever. One of them's filthy rich, which helps, but they're hoping to make a million dollars. If it's as big as I think it's going to be – three days non-stop – I reckon it'll go down in history.'

'So where do I come in?'

'I want a photographic record of the event. One we can wire round the world.'

'Sounds fantastic. But can't you get someone who lives closer? There must be lots of talent in New York State.'

'Stop talking yourself out of a job, man. I want you, no arguments. The festival starts on August fifteen. You'll need to get here a week or two before to really get the scene.'

Steve thought briefly of Sophie. How could he leave England with that David guy still hanging around? 'It's a great offer. Can I let you know?'

'Okay, but don't take too long. The offer ain't going to last forever.'

CHAPTER 21

'Sophie, are you avoiding me?' David's voiced echoed down the phone. 'I know I said I wouldn't ring you at work, but I didn't have much choice.'

Sophie covered the mouthpiece with her hand, glancing round the office. 'I'm sorry I haven't been in touch, it's just that I've been so busy.' It was a lie but it would have to do. 'How's your mother?'

'She's gone. I still can't take it in. That's what I've phoned to tell you. The hospital called half an hour ago.'

'Oh, David, I'm so very sorry.' He was clearly in shock. 'I did go to see her and I meant to tell you but...' her voice trailed away.

'It's okay. We weren't very close, as you know.' He hesitated. 'She didn't like you very much, did she?'

'I can't talk about it now, I'm afraid. This must be a difficult time for you. Do you need any help with, er, the arrangements or anything?'

'No, I can manage thanks. There's something I need to ask, though. Will you come to the funeral?'

'If you want me to, then yes, of course. And now I really must go. I've got a meeting in five minutes. I'll be in touch very soon.' Sophie replaced the receiver and cupped her face in her hands. With Betty Newby gone, she'd probably never know why the poor woman despised her so much. Grabbing some copy paper, she fed it into her typewriter and began to hammer the keys. When, she wondered, had she become so hard?

The horticultural society's annual show was held in Harcot Institute, a few minutes' walk from the office. For once Sophie was glad to have a boring diary job. She didn't know a plant from a weed, and was only there because Porchester fancied the society's new secretary, though right now that was the least of her problems.

Sophie sucked the end of her pen, trying hard to look interested. The dry summer had hit the pumpkin entries, but otherwise the sunshine had increased the takings. A woman in a large floral hat was busy singing the praises of a vase full of huge pink chrysanthemums and behind her a serious-looking man was writing something down on a clipboard. He had a badge on his lapel so she supposed he must be one of the judges.

Frances had always loved chrysanthemums, but then she liked anything that grew without too much attention. When Sophie was a child, mother and daughter had spent hours in the shared garden of their crumbling flat, sitting on the veranda of the disused sun house, long after the sky had turned red.

Sophie ran her hand absentmindedly through her hair. These last few days she had found it difficult to contemplate her mother's past. From what she'd read, Frances had endured more pain in her miserable life than anyone could ever have imagined. No wonder she'd taken to drink. Yet so much of the story still remained a mystery.

Stifling a yawn, Sophie started taking notes. Shorthand came easily – she could almost do it with her eyes shut – and at least it took her mind off her problems for a while. Anyway, she had to write a piece for the *Tribune* if she wanted to keep her job. Glancing down at her wristwatch she realised the judging was about to end. She jotted down the name of the winners and headed for the exit.

Back at the office Sophie bounded up the stairs, colliding head on with the news editor.

'Steady on, girl,' he said irritably. 'Where's your glasses?'

She pulled a face. 'Sorry, look, can I ask a favour? I need the day off on Thursday to go to a funeral.'

'Do you, indeed. Is it someone you know?'

'I'll take it without pay,' she said, ignoring the sarcasm, 'but I really must go. It's, er... a member of the family.'

'You've got a lot of family all of a sudden. You can take it as holiday as long as Mr Moulton agrees.'

She'd no idea why she'd agreed to go. She could make an excuse, she supposed, but it would seem churlish and she'd have to face David eventually.

Patrick handed her a letter. 'Now make something out of this, will you? We're short on news this week.'

Sophie dropped the letter onto her desk and scanned the contents. Someone was complaining about the lack of parking space in the town centre. It was hardly news. She had far more important things to worry about. Grabbing an empty phone booth she dialled through to the photographers.

'Sophie – at last. I thought you'd got lost. Have you rung to ask me out?'

'Listen, Steve, I'm not in the mood for jokes. I need your advice.'

'Sorry Frigidaire. Fire away, I'm listening.'

'Have you got anyone with you?'

Silence followed. 'I've looked round the dark room and I can't see a soul. So go on, what's the problem?'

'Can't you just be serious for once? Look, this is really difficult. You see, David's mother has died and I need to –'

'Oh, I see, it's that sort of problem. I'm very sorry to hear that, of course, but couldn't dear David sort things out himself for a change?'

'I can't believe you're being so disrespectful.' She rolled her eyes to the heavens. 'What did the man ever do to you?'

'Okay, Sophie, what I said was maybe a tad unnecessary. But what has this guy's mother dying got to do with me?'

'He wants me to go to the funeral. I'm not sure whether it's the right thing to do. Last time we spoke you said you wanted to help...' she hesitated.

'Well, I've changed my mind. I'm not your man, I'm sorry. If

I can be of assistance with anything else at all, you know I will. But this boyfriend of yours, well I reckon he can take care of himself. Is there anything else?'

'No, nothing.' Sophie slammed down the receiver. 'Nothing at all.'

Sophie slipped into an empty pew at the back of the church just as the funeral service was starting. St Phillip's Parish Church, with its stained glass windows and towering stone pillars, was the place where Betty and Arthur Newby were married and where years later their son David had been christened.

The tiny funeral party seemed dwarfed by the cavernous nave. David, dressed in an expensive black suit, stared at his mother's coffin, mouth taught, eyes betraying nothing. Already Sophie wished she'd stayed at home.

Listening to the eulogy, Sophie remembered the last time she'd seen Betty Newby, the old woman's eyes full of hatred, her words escaping in a torrent of vitriol. What had made her say such things? Did she really think Sophie was after her son's money? Whatever the reason, it had gone with her to the grave. Sophie thought of her own mother, incarcerated in hospital, the few happy memories they'd shared now out of her grasp. Poor Frances. That was a kind of death, too.

Later, as the mourners filed out of the church, David took her hand and clasped it in his. 'Thank you for coming, Sophie. It means a lot to me.'

'I came for your sake – it's the very least I could do.' She avoided his eyes.

'So, will you come to the wake?'

'No, I'm so sorry. I really have to get back. Maybe we'll meet again soon?'

Before he could answer, a slim woman with a shiny Mary Quant bob caught hold of David's arm. Her pretty face was covered by a lace veil which matched the trim on her charcoal silk suit.

'You must be Sophie,' she said, extending a dainty gloved hand. I'm Jill. David's told me all about you.'

Sophie forced a smile. Jill, at least, seemed genuine. 'I'm sorry we have to meet on such a sad occasion. I hope you'll excuse me if I don't come to the wake but I have to get back to Yorkshire.'

'Of course. And now, if you'll excuse us, we've lots more people to meet.'

The letter was sitting on the mat when she arrived back at the flat. She was so preoccupied with the day's events that she almost stepped over it. Recognising the writing, she slipped off her coat, flopped down onto the settee and scanned the contents.

Dear Sophie

I've decided to take extended leave from the paper and hope you will forgive me for not seeing you before I go. My mate's made me an offer that's too good to miss. I have a bit of money put by and besides, I need to sort my head out. God, if only you knew how stupid I feel for the way I've behaved about David, but it's too late to change any of that now.

Please believe that I love everything about you, from your crazy green eyes and wild blonde hair to the way you bite your lip when you're worried about something you can't change. But then of course, I don't expect you to believe what I'm telling you – why would any girl believe the Office Romeo?

If I could start again I would do it all differently – except for the bit when I nearly drove into you – for that was the very moment when I knew you'd got under my skin.

Wherever I am I'll be thinking about you.

Yours always,

Steve

Sophie sprang off the settee, made straight for the kitchen cupboard and poured herself the remnants of the Christmas sherry. She took a sip, blinking back tears, and then tipped the rest down the sink. Whatever he said, Steve Sibson would soon forget about her. She just wished she could say the same about him.

CHAPTER 22

August 1969

The long-legged girl with the bleached blonde hair appeared right in front of Sophie, almost blocking her path.

'Hello I'm Julie. Remember – the editor's secretary? Have you got a minute?'

Sophie looked at her watch. She had only just left the office and was due at a meeting on the other side of town. 'A minute but that's all. Is it important?'

'It won't take long. I'm looking for Steve Sibson, your boyfriend. Do you know where he is right now?'

'Steve's just a friend, actually, and I've no idea where he is.' This was the last thing she needed right now. 'Why do you ask?'

'Because he's disappeared without telling me. Without telling anyone.'

'I'm sorry. As I said, he's just a friend. I don't keep tags on him. Is it important?'

'It is to me. I have to speak to him.'

'You can't, can you, if he's gone away?'

'Did I say he'd gone away?' The girl leaned closer. 'You do know something, don't you?'

'Look, Julie,' Sophie stretched to her full five feet five. 'I don't know what your problem is, but if there's nothing else? I really do have to be going.'

'Okay. I'm pregnant.'

'I'm sorry? What did you say?'

'I'm expecting a baby and Steve's the father.'

'And what has that got to do with me?' Sophie rummaged in her bag for her glasses. She'd no intention of letting the shock show on her face.

'It's just that he talked about you a lot, most of the time, actually, and I thought he might have confided in you.'

'It's a while since I saw him, I'm afraid.' That, at least, was the truth. 'So, if you'll excuse me –'

'It's very important, Sophie. I have to tell him.'

'Yes, so I gather. But that really is between the two of you. Why don't you ask at work? They may have a forwarding address.'

'So he *has* left home?' Pulling out her handkerchief, Julie dabbed the corner of her eye.

'For the last time, I really have no idea. Look, I don't want to sound unkind but there must be people you can talk to about this – friends, family, maybe?'

'You slept with him, didn't you? I knew it. You slept with the father of my unborn baby. It's because of you that we're not still together.'

Before her row with Steve, Sophie might have been slightly more tolerant, but now the anger exploded inside her. All this time she had tried to ignore her own feelings, telling herself he was just a womaniser, that if she gave way to her emotions she would only get hurt. Now this stupid girl was proving her right. 'You've nobody but yourself to blame.' The words shot out with ferocious speed. 'You should have known better than to sleep with the office Romeo. And please don't call me Sophie. As far as I'm concerned we don't know each other at all.'

With that she threw back her head and walked away.

Sophie spent most of the night wide awake. All the things she had heard about Steve – all the gossip, all the innuendos – now seemed to have substance. He'd gone away to think, so he said, but how would he face the bombshell waiting for him when he came back?

As the sun rose and small shafts of light penetrated the bedroom, all the doubts she'd tried so hard to suppress seemed to surface with the dawn. Was Julie telling the truth? How did she know for sure that it was Steve's baby? Maybe she'd just made the whole thing up to scare her rival away? Whatever the truth, Sophie did not intend to give up on him quite so easily. Swinging her legs over the bed, she reached for her dressing gown, padded across to the window and pulled open the curtains to let the morning in.

'You're looking very secretive, Sophie.' Joe slung his arm around her shoulder as she entered the reporters' room. 'Come on, give us the gen.'

'I may have something up my sleeve, yes,' she shrugged him away. He'd never been this tactile before. 'I can tell you what it's *not* about, if you like? Now let's see – planning applications, one-way traffic, the Farmer's Union annual ball. It's definitely none of those. Is that any help?'

'You're a cheeky one, you are. If it's a good story I might let you in on the freelance stuff, just this once mind, to see how you go.'

'That's very kind of you, but you can keep your lineage pool, thanks very much. As it happens, I have a contact on the *Daily Sketch*.'

'The *Daily Sketch*?' His eyes narrowed. 'How the hell did you do that?'

'I've friends in high places – that's how.' So Jane Corcoran might not actually be a friend, but as a rock star's wife she was useful when it came to name-dropping. And she did have a brother who worked on the *Sketch*, albeit in the post room.

Sophie was beginning to feel uncomfortable. Joe had his arm round her again. Pushing him away she felt a ping between her shoulders. Somehow – God only knows how – he'd managed to undo her bra. Blazing with anger she headed for the cloakroom, Joe's voice ringing in her ears. 'Sorry to hear we've lost your support, young Soph. Let me know if you need a hand.'

Walking to her car a few minutes later, Sophie breathed in

the fresh air. Joe had made a complete fool of her. She'd wanted to slap him in the face for taking liberties, but that would only have made her the centre of attention. She could complain to head office, of course, but where would that get her? For a start, it would be her word against his, then she'd be made a laughing stock within the whole newspaper group and everything she'd been trying to achieve would be wasted. Besides, she knew the script: if women wanted to work alongside men, they had to put up with the flack. No, the only way to get rid of such blatant sexism was to stay here and fight it. She quickened her pace. If Joe wanted a showdown, he'd chosen the wrong girl.

Sophie spent the morning at a public enquiry, glad to be out of Joe's way. Some bigwig wanted to build a new housing estate on the edge of his land and the local residents were up in arms. Now that the Government had been brought in to sort things out, the protesters would get a stay of execution.

Afterwards she made her way down to Harcot's dilapidated engineering works where the men had gone on strike for better pay and conditions. Already the picket line had attracted plenty of attention. Banners and placards filled the road leading up to the factory gates and blacklegs were being pelted with rotten food from the canteen, which had now been closed for more than a week.

Sophie wasn't concerned with the men on strike – their story had an all-too familiar ring – but now that the typing pool had joined the walkout she'd been promised a 'frank' interview.

Gina Guffog was a straight talking spinster in her late thirties with a booming voice and a very large bee in her bonnet.

'There aren't any women in the engineering union.' Sophie came straight to the point. 'So why have you decided to make a stand?'

'You need to do your homework, love.' Gina bared her teeth. 'We're in the Clerical and Administrative Workers Union – UCAW for short – and we have our rights, too.'

'So what are you striking for?'

'The right to *be* in a trade union, that's what. Management've banned overtime for them with union membership. It's criminal if you ask me.'

Sophie scribbled on her pad. 'And are they allowed to do that?'

'They can do what they bloody well like. Why the hell else do you think I'm here?'

'Do you mind having your picture in the paper, Miss, er –?'

'The name's Gina. Course I don't. I'll stand here naked if it'll make a point.'

'There's no need for that, but I'm glad you mean business. It's time women got their voices heard.'

As soon as she left the site, Sophie found the nearest telephone box and dialled head office. 'Photographers please.' She drummed her fingers on the graffiti-strewn phone directory as she waited. 'Hello? It's Sophie. There's a cracking story down here in Harcot.' She explained briefly. 'Who've you got?'

'There's only me here.' The hesitant voice belonged to spotty Dave. 'Will I do?'

'Of course.' Sophie gritted her teeth. 'Get here as quick as you can. I'll be waiting.'

Later that night, as she put the kettle on the stove, Sophie heard a knock on the door. Pulling her dressing gown tightly round her, she lifted the latch and peered through the gap. 'Telephone for you.' The chap from the ground floor flat was already on his way back downstairs.

Sophie slammed the door behind her and followed him down into the lobby. Something must be wrong. No one ever rang her at this time of night. She grabbed the receiver. 'Hello? Who is it?'

'It's me, Julie. Just tell me where he is and I promise I'll get out of your hair.'

'Julie! You gave me such a fright. How on earth did you get my number?'

'Never mind that. We either talk about it now or we can discuss it at work in the morning. Whichever you prefer.'

'I hope that's not a threat. Look, the truth is that Steve's taken a sabbatical and doesn't know when he'll be back. That's all I know.'

'So you *have* spoken to him?'

'Not exactly, no. He wrote me a note. Look, I've told you before, you'll have to sort this out with him yourself. Threatening to make a fuss at work is only going to make you look a lot more stupid than you do already. Am I making myself clear? I hope so because there's nothing more I can do.'

'Yes there is,' Julie started to sob. 'You can leave him alone. He's mine, and that's all there is to it.'

'Believe me – you're welcome to him.' With that Sophie slammed down the phone and ran back up to her flat.

CHAPTER 23

David looked drawn as he approached the table. 'I'm sorry I'm late. Thought this might be a good place as any to meet. I remembered you liked Betty's Café.'

'I do,' Sophie attempted a smile, 'but you didn't drive all this way for a posh cup of tea.'

'No,' he dropped into the chair. 'I had business to attend to in Harrogate. And I thought it was time we had a chat.'

'What about?' She didn't like the sound of his voice.

He shifted awkwardly in his chair. 'It's been quite a week. We had the reading of mother's will.'

'And?'

'It's not what I expected. The old man had quite a bit of money salted away and I just assumed –'

Sophie gasped. 'She's not left you anything?'

'Oh she's left me plenty, all right. To be kept in trust till I reach thirty – providing I'm still unmarried.'

'But that's ridiculous! Why would she want to do that?'

'I confess I don't understand my mother's motives. I thought maybe you might know something?'

'Me?' Sophie pushed back her chair and stood up. 'What has this got to do with me?'

'She changed after she met you. Look, I'm sorry,' David took hold of her arm. 'Don't go. Stay for a bit longer, please. I really didn't mean to offend you.' He motioned to the waitress. 'Let's have some tea and talk about this.'

Sophie sat down, her face crimson with embarrassment. 'It seems I don't have a choice. Everyone in the room's looking at us now.'

They sat in silence for what felt like hours before the waitress took their order.

Finally David spoke. 'Can we start again? I didn't mean to hurt you. I just needed to understand.'

'She hated me – that much was obvious.' Sophie studied her fingernails. 'I don't know what to say. What else is there to understand?'

'Why would she hate you? Not just because you looked round her house, surely? None of this makes sense.'

'I don't know, David, and I'm not even sure I want to. Maybe she thought I was after your money? You've done pretty well for yourself, after all. What about your girlfriend? What does she have to say about all this?'

'Jill? She's not the jealous type, thank God. She's confused, just as I am, just as anyone would be.'

'I'm sorry, it can't be easy for you, but I have to ask – did the two of them get on?'

'Mum and Jill? Yes, Mum liked her a lot. But what's that got to do with it?'

'Maybe she wanted you to marry up? You know, better yourself. What else could it be?'

'You could be right, I suppose.' He frowned.

For a moment Sophie felt sorry for him. She'd never seen him look vulnerable. 'I've changed my mind,' she said, more kindly now. 'While we're here, we might as well make the most of it. I think I might have a cream tea after all.'

CHAPTER 24
Evington, August 1944

'Fraaances.' Betty Newby's voice echoed up the stairs. 'There's a policeman to see you. I've shown him into the drawing room.'

The 'drawing room' was the landlady's name for her front parlour, kept under lock and key unless she was entertaining guests or needed to impress the neighbours.

Frances ran down two flights of stairs, her face already the colour of beetroot. She'd been warned the police would want to see her, but assumed it would be down at the station. Now everyone in the house would know her secret.

The officer had a round, unsmiling face and an ill-fitting suit that looked as if it had been made for someone else. 'Ahh, Miss Wainwright, I'm Detective Constable Green. I need to ask you a few questions.'

She nodded, impatient to get it over with.

'We have reason to believe that you were attacked by an

unknown assailant on the night of...' he took out his notebook, 'July thirtieth, at a dance at Evington village hall. Is that correct?'

'Yes, but I don't want to press charges.'

'It's out of your hands, I'm afraid, Miss. The Division will deal with the matter, but they cannot force you to give evidence in the event of a court martial. In the case of a civilian offence, we have to make our own enquiries.' He fiddled with his cuffs as he spoke. 'Are you sure you can't divulge the name of the perpetrator of this attack?'

'No.' Frances shook her head.

'Is there anything else you can tell me about the night the incident took place?'

'I went outside for some fresh air because I felt slightly dizzy. I think someone may have laced my lemonade with alcohol. The attacker came from behind. I didn't see him coming and had no chance to escape.'

'So you couldn't describe his height, or hear if he had an accent?'

'I'm afraid not. It was dark. He didn't speak.' She gulped back the tears. 'What will happen to me now?'

'It depends on the outcome of the enquiry by the American forces. In the meantime, if you think of anything else, please let us know.'

With that, the officer replaced his hat and let himself out of the door.

'Come in.'

Standing with his hands linked behind his back, the captain spun round as the door opened. 'Hello, please do come in.'

Frances's eyes widened as she scanned the room. The timber hut they were standing in was far bigger than it looked from the outside. Conscious of her lowly position, she bowed her head.

'Miss Wainwright? I'm Captain Ed Trask. Thank you for coming.' He motioned to a chair on the other side of his desk. 'Please sit down.'

She sank down gratefully, her legs giving way to the fear. She'd been summoned here today expecting the worst, yet this man looked nothing like she'd imagined. With thick sandy coloured hair and a tanned face, his deep green eyes were open and friendly. He was dressed, very casually, in a khaki-green blouson jacket and trousers with a brown tie fastened loosely at his neck.

'Are you feeling okay, ma'am?' The captain was looking straight at her now. 'You seem real pale, if you don't mind me saying.'

'I'm fine, honestly.' She searched her mind for something to say. 'I was just thinking that you, er, don't look much like a captain.'

'That's probably for the best,' he said, with a voice that came straight out of an American movie. He sat down and folded his hands in front of him on the desk. 'I'll come straight to the point, Miss Wainwright. You attended a dance in the village hall recently but halfway through the evening it seems you went missing. You were found by one of our boys outside in a distressed state. Is that right?'

She nodded miserably.

'I don't want to upset you, but I must ask if you were attacked while you were outside, ma'am? The men in this division are sworn to a strict code of conduct and breaking it in any way means a court martial.'

'No, no, please don't let that happen.' Frances stared at the photograph of President Roosevelt on the wall behind the captain's desk. 'It wasn't a soldier I assure you, Captain Trask.' She swallowed hard. 'I shouldn't have gone out there. It was my fault, really all my fault.'

Frowning, he walked round the desk and handed her a large white handkerchief. 'If you're trying to protect someone, it isn't a wise decision.'

She took the handkerchief gratefully and blew her nose. She had to tell him something – but what? The last thing she wanted to do was implicate one of his men.

'It was a big night out for us, you see,' she said at last. 'The girls were always teasing me for not drinking alcohol, so I did, just to prove I'm not a cissy.' She was making it up as she went along. 'Only one, mind, but I reckon they added a couple more when I wasn't looking. Anyway, I went out for some fresh air and must've fallen over as the next thing I knew I was flat out on the ground. I looked up and saw someone standing over me.'

'Did you see the man's face – the one that attacked you? Or maybe what kinda clothes he was wearing?'

Frances shook her head. She didn't need to see. She'd known who it was the minute she smelled his breath. *'Don't tell me you're not up for it... I know your type, all smiles and innocence. You asked for this, you little slut...'*

The captain stood up again and turned towards the window. 'Sergeant Winters was sent out to find you. He'd heard you'd left the room with Corporal Hughes. If you're trying to protect someone, ma'am, you're making one helluva mistake.'

'Thought I wouldn't find you didn't you –you stupid whore – but that's where you were wrong...'

'I was not attacked by Corporal Hughes, Captain. That's all I have to say.'

A look of sympathy flashed across his face. 'I'm not trying to force you into a confession, ma'am. But if you remember something – anything – you come to me right away. Is that understood?'

'Yes, thank you, sir,' she said, her voice almost a whisper. She wanted to ask why he was being so kind, why he didn't think she was a slut just like the rest of them. Instead she stood up, held her head in the air, and walked out of the room.

CHAPTER 25

'Okay, sergeant, keep me informed.' Slamming down the receiver, Ed Trask gave a loud sigh. His men might be recuperating after nine months at the front but *he* couldn't afford to slack. What the hell was wrong with him? Okay, so he knew what was wrong, dammit – he couldn't stop thinking about Frances Wainwright. What was it about her that he found so distracting? The truth was she reminded him of Mary-Beth. Not in looks so much, though she *was* stunning, with her dark hair and gently rounded figure. No, this one had spirit just like his wife.

He got up from his desk and frowned. If one of his soldiers had attacked the girl, he'd got a real problem on his hands. He was pretty damn sure it wasn't a paratrooper but he couldn't just rely on intuition. He'd questioned Corporal Hughes twice over and gotten the same response. One of the most popular men on the camp, the corporal had strongly protested his innocence. 'I took her out for some fresh air, captain. The dame came over dizzy. She said she wanted to be left alone, so what was I s'posed to do? Maybe I shouldn't 'ave gone to take a leak, maybe I should've stayed with her, but that's all I'm guilty of, sir.'

Ed lit a Lucky Strike and drew the smoke into his lungs. Hughes had been a hero at Normandy, risking his life to save an injured comrade when they dropped behind enemy lines. Yes, the guy was innocent; he would stake his reputation on it.

Pulling out his hip flask, Ed took a slug of whiskey. He knew what the men called him behind his back: *'Do the task Trask.'* Hey, he kept his eyes and ears open, even when he was asleep.

Born at the start of World War One, in Culver, Indiana, Ed had lost his father when he was two. Though he was too young to remember, his poor mom never got over it. On summer afternoons she used to take him paddling on the banks of Lake Maxinkuckee, just a few yards from their home. Then, as he got older, she bought a little boat which they'd take out on the lake and she even showed him how to ride a horse. He could see her now in her straw hat, hands shading her eyes from the midday sun. By the time he reached ten Ed saw himself as the man of the house. His mom never remarried, though she was a fine looking woman. Even when he left home he'd still be there for her, like he owed her a special duty.

'If you don't do it, it won't get done,' she used to tell him it and that was something he'd never forgotten. Sure, he had a reputation to live up to, so the sooner he got this mess sorted the better.

Ed glanced down at the papers on his desk, some still untouched. What the hell would he do about Frances Wainwright? Someone had to help her, goddammit. Why had he let her get under his skin?

CHAPTER 26

She couldn't get the captain's words out of her head. Frances knew deep down that he believed her and for the first time in years she felt as if someone actually cared about her future. She could picture him now, side cap slung over his cropped hair, smiling eyes that belied his authority. She hadn't meant to lie to him but she had no choice. She only hoped he could sort out this wretched mess.

It was another week before she received a letter from the regiment. The envelope arrived at her lodgings, neatly scripted and stamped with the official crest of the regiment. 'Going up in the world, are we?' the landlady sneered, as she handed it to her. 'Getting too good for the likes of us?'

Frances snatched the letter and bundled it into her bag. 'I'm late for work, I'm afraid, Mrs Newby.' She'd no intention of telling the old witch a single word.

Later, when she arrived at the factory, she opened the envelope carefully, terrified of what it might contain. *Ed*

Trask wanted to see her again. Did that mean he'd found a culprit? Dear God, don't let it be one of his soldiers. If that was the case then she'd have to tell the truth.

'What is it, me duck?' Irene patted her hand. 'You've only just clocked on and yer miles away already. Still worrying about that business at the dance?'

Frances took off her coat and glanced over her shoulder. 'I know you think I should forget it ever happened, but the girls still reckon it's my fault.'

'Don't take no notice of them lot, they've nowt else to think about. Any road up, I thought the Yankee boss was sorting it for you?'

Frances smiled, despite herself. 'The Yankee boss, as you call him, needs to protect his men. I'm sure he's not bothered about what happens to me.'

'Well, one of 'em must've done it, that's for sure.'

'It wasn't a soldier.' The words came out before she could stop them.

'What d'you mean it wasn't a soldier?' Irene was listening intently now.

'It doesn't matter. I've said too much already. Can we just get to work?'

'Whatever you say, Franny my girl, but you've got some explaining to do. Something nasty happened to you at that there dance and if it weren't a solider, then who were it?'

Frances cursed under her breath. Why on earth had she opened her mouth? From now on she must keep mum.

'I've asked to see you again, ma'am, because I have something important to tell you.' The captain turned and looked out of the window. 'Sergeant Jed Hughes has been put on a charge for assault.'

'But he didn't do it. Please, sir, you must believe me.'

'So why are you protecting him?' The captain swung round. 'We know you were assaulted and he was the last one seen with you. He denies it of course, but we need you to give evidence at the court martial.'

'I can't, please don't make me do it.' She covered her face with her hands.

'Well, ma'am, in that case I guess it's time you told me the truth.'

'I don't know what you mean.' She let her head sink on to her chest. 'I'm so sorry but I'm feeling a bit faint.' She hated lying, but she needed time to think.

'Steady on – take it easy.' Ed Trask took a firm hold of her arm and lowered her into a chair. 'Here, have this water, ma'am. I can't make you give evidence but it sure will make it easier if you do. Right now just forget about the court martial and one of my men will take you home.'

'Thank you, captain.' She let out a loud sigh.

'No problem. But I'll have to ask you to come and see me again as soon as you feel ready.'

She nodded gratefully. 'I understand.' Frances watched as he picked up the phone, relief flooding through her. She'd escaped for now, but how long before he found out the truth?

The next time she heard from the captain, Frances was at

work on her machine.

'Telephone call for you, *Miss Wainwright.*' The foreman frowned. 'It ain't allowed, I'll 'ave you know, so don't make an 'abit of it.'

Hands trembling, she picked up the receiver. 'Hello?'

'I'm calling on behalf of Captain Trask, ma'am. Something's come up. He's sending a car for you right now.'

By the time she left the building, Frances was the talk of the factory floor. Word spread like floodwater in a storm till everyone agreed that she must have been arrested.

'Gerron with your work,' Mick Ford's voice boomed across the floor, 'or I'll sack the lot o' yer.'

'She's trouble that girl,' he muttered under his breath, 'nothing but damn trouble.'

The captain nodded at Frances, motioning towards the chair. 'Sit down, ma'am. This won't take long. I hear you were orphaned in the Coventry Blitz?'

'Yes, sir.'

'And then you went to work in an orphanage.'

'That is correct, sir.' How did he know all this? And where was it leading?

'This man whose name has been sent to me,' he glanced at the papers on his desk, 'this, er, Cedric Hampton. He helped with the running of the orphanage. Is that right?'

'Yes, but –'

'Could he be the one who assaulted you?'

Her throat tightened. This was what she'd been dreading all along. 'I'd rather not say, sir.'

'Then I will say it for you, Miss Wainwright. You worked for this man at,' he glanced down again, 'The Oaks Orphanage in Leicester. He went missing four weeks ago and was picked up this morning by the British police. They already had complaints against him and he was seen round the village hall on the night of the dance. But they've no proof. Not yet.'

The captain stood up and looked out of the window. 'If he was the one who carried out this attack, then the British police will get him charged, damn sure they will, and he won't be bothering you again. Do you understand?'

She nodded, biting her lip.

'And do you have anything to say?'

'No, sir.'

'Right. On the other hand, if it was one of my men, we have to protect you until we find him.' He handed her a piece of paper. 'I've arranged a place for you to stay.'

'But this is a hotel?'

'In Hinckley, yes. You'll be a guest of the division.'

'But I'm fine where I am, sir, really. You don't have to –'

'Listen to me. If it was this Hampton guy, like I said, your civilian police will deal with it, but it won't be very pretty and people will talk. The same goes for your work right now. You'll be in real trouble if this gets out.'

'I'll still have to pay my landlady or she'll throw me out.' Frances fiddled with the sleeve of her blouse.

'We're going to take care of it, ma'am, so I thank you to leave it to me.'

She nodded. Everything had been taken out of her control.

Just then the phone burst into life. 'Not now,' the captain barked impatiently. 'Can't it wait?' Slamming down the receiver, he turned to Frances.' Is there anything else you need to ask?'

'Why are you doing this for me, sir?' She'd finally found her voice again.

'I want my men to be trusted round here, that's why. And you don't seem like the kinda girl to go looking for trouble.' His face softened.

'Will that be all, sir?'

He nodded. 'For now. I've arranged transport so you can get your things from the factory. Otherwise stay in the hotel. You'll be hearing from me soon.'

Captain Trask was true to his word. One Saturday, not long after she'd moved into the hotel – a double-fronted red brick house that looked as if it had once belonged to the gentry – Frances was summoned down to reception. There he was, fair hair slicked back, his cap held firmly in one hand, the other extended out to her.

'Captain Trask – what a surprise. Do you have any news?'

He shook his head. 'Not yet, ma'am. I was out this way and thought I'd maybe come and see how you're getting on.'

Now, as he stood in front of her, she didn't know what to say. She hadn't stopped thinking about him since that last day at the camp and now she was completely tongue-tied. She knew he was married – she had seen his wife's photograph on his desk – but whenever he spoke her heart beat so fast she feared he might actually hear it.

'You alright, ma'am?' His words interrupted her thoughts. 'You sure do look pale.'

'I'm fine,' she managed, 'perfectly fine. Can I offer you tea, or something?'

His mouth creased into a grin. 'You English and your tea. How come you reckon it's the cure for everything?'

She smiled back. 'Sometimes, believe it or not, it is.'

'I sure would love to stop,' he looked at his watch, 'but I can't. I'm due back at camp. Maybe next time? Just keep your chin up, as you English say, until this thing's all over.'

Over the next couple of weeks the captain called to see Frances several times. With no prior warning, she would be summoned down to reception where he would politely enquire how she was getting on. Before long he was taking her out into the countryside for 'a taste of fresh air', all the time telling her not to worry about the trial. She soon found herself longing for the next visit.

Once he brought a makeshift picnic with food left over from the canteen. Laying it out on the grass in front of them, he talked of life back home in the States.

'I was born in Indiana, in a place called Culver, which literally means Big Stone Country. There's a lake, a town park, a convenience store and a railroad crossing – everything a young boy could need.'

'Sounds wonderful,' she smiled dreamily. 'Did you have any brothers and sisters?'

'No, ma'am, it was just me, but I sure never was lonely. My mom still owns the same house on East Shore Drive, overlooking the water.'

Did Ed's wife live there too, she wondered?

After they'd eaten, she talked about her own childhood, about life in Coventry before the Blitz, with her parents and her brother Bobby. She wanted to tell him, despite the terrible loss, and felt stronger somehow for doing so. Frances cherished every moment of the time they spent together. She felt like she had known him forever.

Arriving back at the factory to pick up her things, no one, apart from Irene, had spoken a word. As far as they were concerned, she'd 'got a Yank put on charge,' and that was a hanging offence. It never seemed to occur to them that she might not be to blame, so Frances simply put her head down and ignored the dark looks. She was far too happy to care; counting the days till Ed came to see her again.

'Tell me about your wife,' she said one Sunday afternoon, the words finally tumbling out of her mouth. They were sitting under a tree in a sheltered hollow, away from the glare of midday sun. He looked at her for a long time, his deep green eyes unblinking. 'You remind me of her sometimes,' he said carefully. 'Mary-Beth was beautiful and mighty strong, too.'

Frances drew breath. 'She *was*? Oh, no, does that mean −?'

'It means she died in childbirth. Almost five years ago now. We had a son, but he, well, he didn't make it either.'

'I see.' The words sounded lame. She didn't of course. She didn't know what she was doing here, why he was telling her all this. She just knew she wanted him to hold her close until the pain on his face disappeared.

'Maybe one day I'll tell you more, Frances Wainwright.' He stood up and, grabbing hold of her hand, pulled her up from the grass. 'Right now it's time to get you back.'

'You haven't talked about what happened at Normandy,' she said as they set off, desperate to change the subject.

'There's not much to tell. We were dropped behind German lines on the Cherbourg peninsular as back-up to the US invasion force. It was tough and we lost some good men. Morale's still low back at the camp.'

'That's the end of it now, surely?' She bit her lip. 'Those paratroopers can't be expected to do anymore?'

'It just ain't like that, Fran. I've no idea what's coming next, but even if I did, it'd make no difference.'

'I couldn't bear to think of you...'

He pressed his fingers gently to her lips. 'Then don't.'

They walked on in silence, each lost in their own thoughts.

'Before I go I want you to think about the court martial,' he said, his brow creased into a frown. 'All you have to do is stand up and tell the truth. Remember, it's not you, but one of my men who's up there accused.'

'I know I'm not going to win, whatever the outcome.'

'Be strong, that's all, just be strong for me.'

As they approached the hotel, she squeezed his arm. 'I'm sorry, Ed.'

'What for, my little Fran? 'He raised his eyebrows. 'Tell me what for?'

'For everything.'

Frances remembered little about the court martial which was held at the camp on a hot and sticky August morning. As she entered the hut in the centre of the barracks, she could feel every eye resting upon her. Irene had lent her a blue cotton jacket which she'd buttoned up to the neck, despite the oppressive heat, and she'd tied her hair back in a matching ribbon.

She sat passively as the proceedings began, her hands folded in her lap. How had it come to this? If only she'd told them she knew her attacker, then Jed Hughes wouldn't be in this mess. Maybe she should tell the truth now, without implicating anyone else? That would make it right, wouldn't it?

When her time came at last, the questions seemed endless. *Was the accused man known to her as Corporal Jed Hughes? Had she met him on the night of the village dance? Did he accompany her outside to take some air?*

Forcing herself to relay the events of that awful night, she closed her eyes to conjure up the images in her mind. Then she stood upright, head in the air, answering each question with the truth.

'Did you know your attacker, Miss Wainwright?'

'Yes, I did.' A hush descended on the room.

'Was it the man you see here in front of you?'

'No.'

Would the truth be enough to save him? She didn't know the answer. She knew though, that whatever happened, it wouldn't save *her*.

'Ooh ya bugger, the Yank got off then, did he?' Irene threw her arms round her friend. 'And you in this fancy hotel, an'all. Wa'rever will people think?'

'They can think what they like, Irene.' Frances was in no mood for gossip.

The older woman's eyes roamed the hotel room, missing nothing: the matching wardrobe and tallboy, the soft lighting, the single bed covered with a dusky pink counterpane. She whistled under her breath. 'So you don't mind 'im getting away wi'it?'

'I don't want to talk about it. I just want this whole thing to be over.'

'An' I want the war to be over, but it ain't. When are yer coming back to work, any road up? The sooner you put this place behind yer, the better.'

'It won't be long now,' Frances sighed, wondering which was worse – the strange isolation of the hotel or the whispers of the factory girls. 'Just a few more days till all the gossip dies down.'

'They'll gossip if you don't come back, me duck, I'm telling you now. They reckon that Yankee captain's taken a shine to you, they do.'

'That's ridiculous,' she said, flustered by her friend's direct approach. 'Besides, we hardly know each other.'

'Well, if you don't need me, I'd best be off.' Frances stood up. 'I've gotta ger 'ome an' make me tea. You look as if you could do wi' a bit of a fry-up, too. Thin as a rake, you are.'

'I just need some sleep,' Frances forced a smile. 'Thanks for coming to see me, Irene. I'm sorry I'm not much company at the moment but I really don't know what I'd do without you.'

After a long sleepless night, Frances gave in to exhaustion just as the sun began to rise above the hedgerows. She was woken by a sharp knock on the bedroom door. Glancing at the clock, she realised with a start that she'd slept till almost noon. A high pitched voice on the other side of the door summoned her downstairs.

'Give me a minute,' she shouted, falling out of bed, throwing on her clothes and hastily combing her hair. She'd give anything right now to be back in her 'pantry' at Hastings Place.

'Is anything wrong?' she asked, presenting herself at reception.

'You've had a telephone call,' the girl replied without looking up from her work. 'Captain Trask left a message. He will call for you at two thirty. Please make sure you are waiting promptly at the door.'

Frances ran back to her room, her thoughts in turmoil. Why did he want to see her so soon? Had the Yanks changed their minds about the verdict? Still brooding, she bathed and washed her hair, changed into a clean skirt and blouse and stared at the clock till it was time to go.

She knew as soon as she saw him that something was wrong. 'What is it? Are you going away?'

He ushered her out of the hotel door. 'You know I couldn't tell you, even if I wanted to. We have so many false alarms these days; the men don't take any notice half the time. I'm due some free time, that's all. How are you feeling?'

She stepped in beside him. 'Glad it's all over. Glad for you and the regiment. But what'll happen to me now, Ed? How will I ever be able to hold up my head again?'

'You have nothing to be ashamed of,' he took hold of her hand. 'You have to be brave right now. Go back to work and give it your all, just like you did before.'

'Only it's not like before, is it?' She looked up at him.

'For you and me, no, it's different. Everything's changed. Come on, I'll race you to the field.'

Laughing like children they ran down the lane and fell unceremoniously onto the grass, watched by the curious eyes of a handful of grazing cattle.

'You're beautiful, do you know that?' He cupped her face in his hands, moving his thumbs across her cheek. 'My dear little Fran. God only knows how much I think about you.'

She closed her eyes. 'Do you?' she whispered. 'I never dreamt, well... I thought maybe I'd imagined it all.'

'I know,' he said, catching the last of her words with his fingertips. 'I've been fighting it for so long. I love you, Fran,' he muttered, his voice strangely distorted. 'And right now I want you, more than I ever thought possible.'

His lips came down on hers so fast she had no time to resist. At that moment, everything she had borne or lost in her life no longer seemed to matter. She could feel his hands stroking her hair, his breath warm on her face. At last she had found where she wanted to be.

Afterwards, she rested her head on his chest, her heart beating so fast it made her feel dizzy. She clutched him to her, the scent of him filling her soul. 'What will happen to us?'

'Oh, Fran, my little Fran, if only I could give you an answer. I just wish I knew.'

They lay side by side on the grass, cocooned by the heat of the sun, unaware of the clouds rolling in from the distance.

CHAPTER 27
September 1944

The moment she woke, Frances knew for certain that Ed had gone. With no word from him for two whole days there could be no other explanation. Crawling out of bed, she washed, dressed and packed her things before wearily dragging her suitcase down the stairs. She waited till the coast was clear, then, ignoring the haughty receptionist, she slipped out of the entrance to the road.

Creeping into her lodgings, Frances held her breath. The last person she wanted to see right now was Betty Newby. As she reached the top landing, she let out a sigh of relief.

'What are you doing lurking about?' The landlady's face appeared out of nowhere. 'You're not in that fancy hotel now, you know. What's more – your rent's overdue. The Yanks haven't paid it.'

'Sorry, Mrs Newby.' Frances shook her head. 'I didn't realise. Wait a moment please, and I'll get it for you.'

'It's gone up tuppence a week, mind, since no one's seen fit to mention it. Knock on my door when you're ready.' With that, she clattered back down the stairs.

Frances pushed opened the door to her poky room, gasping at the smell of stale air. No one had been in, by the looks of it, since she'd left. She pushed her case into the corner and sank down gratefully on the lumpy bed. Closing her eyes she tried to imagine Ed lying next to her. She could almost hear him whispering in that crazy accent of his. 'It'll work out, my little Fran, just you wait and see. Everything's going to be just fine.'

By the time Frances got to the factory the following day, her heart was playing ball games against her ribs. She'd been off work more than a month whilst waiting for the trial and no doubt there'd been plenty of gossip. Clocking on, she held her chin in the air and walked onto the machine-room floor.

'Welcome back, Franny.' Irene greeted her with open arms. 'It ain't half been borin' wi'out you.'

'I've missed you too,' Frances returned the hug. 'It's good to be back, thanks. Feels like I've been away forever.'

'Were it nice an 'ot on yer 'oliday?' This came from Doris, always first in line for a bit of scandal.

'Lovely, thanks Doris,' Frances replied, a huge smile lighting up her face. 'Sorry I didn't get round to sending you a postcard.'

The other girls tittered.

'That's the spirit,' Irene said, giving her a friendly pat on the back. 'Don't let the buggers grind you down.'

Making her way towards her old machine, Frances vowed to

work as hard as she could. They were here to help the boys win the war and she was glad to be a part of it. What had happened to Ed, she wondered? Had he taken his men on another raid? This time he might not be so lucky. Clearing her mind of dark thoughts, she tried to ignore the fear that forced its way through her gut. Making love was better than anything she ever could have imagined, but should they have used something? She'd heard of rubber johnnies but she'd never seen one in her life. He must have taken care of it. He was far too considerate to do anything else.

CHAPTER 28

October 1944

'Are you alright, me duck?' Irene frowned. 'You look a bit peaky to me.'

'I'm fine, honestly,' Frances prodded her pie with a fork. The canteen was crowded and she had a headache. 'Just feeling a bit tired.'

'It's no wonder wi' all you've had to purrup with, what with that soldier attackin' you an'all. It just ain't right they got the blighter off.'

'I'd rather not talk about it if you don't mind.' She pushed her plate away. Irene had been a good friend to her; more than good, but this was something she had to keep to herself.

'See warra mean? It's put you off yer food, an all, and us on rations, too. If you don't eat 'ote, you'll starve soon enough, you mark my words.'

'I will, I promise,' Frances nodded. She hadn't been unduly worried at first when her monthlies failed to appear; the curse often came and went as it pleased. But this was different. She felt sick all the time and she could hardly find the strength to work on her machine anymore.

As soon as she'd got back to her lodgings after leaving the hotel, the camp had gone into shutdown and no personnel were allowed in or out. Not a word had passed between them so she'd no idea if Ed had gone away or if he would ever come back. Now the fear of losing him had taken seed inside her chest, squeezing her lungs until she could barely breathe. She wanted to say goodbye, to tell him how she felt in case she never got the chance again.

'Bile beans, that's what you need,' Irene was beaming at her now. 'Me mam used to swear by' em, she did. Sort you out, they will, good and proper.'

Frances smiled back weakly. If only it were that simple.

Rising early the following morning, Frances doused her face with cold water, dressed quickly and made her way to the factory. She couldn't stop thinking about Ed. She'd never loved anyone like she loved him, never had the slightest understanding of what being in love meant before now. Waking or sleeping, she couldn't force the image of his face from her mind.

'Frances?' The foreman's booming voice broke into her thoughts. 'What are you doin' here at this hour? Couldn't you sleep, girl?'

'I'm not feeling well, I'm afraid. I thought if I got here earlier I might feel better.'

'You're an hour early, to be exact. And the machine's idle, as you very well know.' He eyed her suspiciously. 'I've heard the camp's on shutdown. Something's in the air, I'm sure of it.' He grinned at his own joke. 'In the air – geddit?'

She swallowed hard. 'What makes you say that?'

'Well, you'd think the lads 'ud deserve a rest after their time in Italy and then Normandy. But no, they want them out fighting again, I swear it, or my uncle's not a home guard.'

'Whatever they do, I'm sure they'll be on the winning side. They're a brave lot, so everyone says.'

'Hmm. And you should know.' The foreman moved closer. 'Seen any more of that captain fella?'

'I don't know what you mean. Which one?'

'Which one, did ya say?' He was leering now. 'You know – the one that got you off the hook.'

'If you mean Captain Trask, he didn't get me *off the hook*.' Frances stared back. 'The corporal was innocent.'

'Don't get on your high horse with me, young lady. Seems the Yank was protecting a bit more'an his men. We all know him 'ad you put up in a hotel, now don't we? Mighty thoughtful of him, don't you think?'

Frances took a step back, colour flooding her cheeks. 'I've no idea what you mean.'

'Of course you don't. Haven't you 'eard his nickname – Do the Task Trask? The lads were always jesting behind his back.' The foreman grinned at his own joke.

'I know he was very particular, if that's what you mean.'

'Oh, very par-tic-u-lar, was he now? Never mind that. I've

got work to do, even if you haven't. Some of us know which side our bread's buttered.'

Frances kept her head down for the rest of the day. Ed had given back her self-worth and nothing could change that. Please let him come home.

'Are you all right me duck?' Irene's face appeared in front of her, eyes full of concern. 'I've never known you so quiet. You sickening for something?'

'I've got a headache, that's all. It must be the noise of the machines.' She glanced up at the clock. Only an hour to go till the end of the shift.

'You can talk to your Auntie Irene, you know. I'm old enough to be your mam, when all's said and done.'

'Thanks. That means a lot.' She'd grown fond of the older woman and would have given anything to confide in her, but she was far too scared to say a word. She had so much to lose, though not as much as Ed. He deserved her loyalty more than anyone.

'I'm fine, honestly, now that I'm back with the Newbys,' she forced a smile, 'though it's not as luxurious as being in a hotel on my own.'

'I'm sure it ain't.' Irene rolled her eyes. 'Now come along wi'me and get yerself some dinner.'

The talk was light-hearted during the meal. Irene had been given some candy by one of the American soldiers and now she couldn't wait to share it.

'He's a nice lad, that Chuck,' she winked. 'If I were a few

years younger I might've fancied him meself.'

'You're terrible, you are.' Frances managed a smile. 'Which reminds me. I haven't seen any of the lads recently. Do you think they've been sent off again somewhere?'

'The lads?' Irene raised her eyes to the sky. 'Heaven only knows what's going on wi'em. If they 'ave, it ain't fair after all they've purrup wi', but then what's fair these days? Anyhow, shutdown doesn't mean they've gone away. They might be training, or summat.'

Doris nodded. 'Franny's right. We haven't seen any of them for days. It's like the whole place has gone to sleep.'

'I hope yer've not got yer heart set on one of 'em, me duck.' Irene pulled a face. 'It'll only end in tears. Anyhow, you know the lads. They like to give the girls a run for their money. A bit of slap and tickle and they're happy – you mark my words.'

Frances nodded. 'They were supposed to be over here for a break. Some break it's turned out to be.'

'I'm sure them troopers can take care of themselves. Which is more'an I can say fer you. Your face is as pale as a corpse. Come on – 'ave a taste o' this.' She opened the packet of candy. 'Pure sugar, me duck. That should get some colour into our cheeks!'

Frances lay awake into the small hours listening to the sound of her own breathing. Should she confide in Irene, or would it be too risky? She knew nothing of US Army rules but she felt sure that Ed would suffer if anyone found out about them. The fuss of the court martial had more or less died down, but her stay in the hotel had prompted a great deal of gossip. Ed had risked a lot by seeing her, but it only made her feelings stronger. At first, she had to admit, she'd been overawed by the interest he'd shown in her. She'd tried to pretend she was simply indebted for all he had done.

Gradually she found herself looking forward more and more to visits and longing to listen to him talk, especially about home. She never tired of that. She'd been horrified to learn of the death of his wife in childbirth and yet this very tragedy had freed her to love him. When it finally happened, the lovemaking had come naturally to her, with a sense of belonging she didn't even know existed. In her head she already felt married to him, ridiculous of course, but nevertheless quite real. Now he'd gone away it felt like bereavement, as if all the people she loved in her life had somehow left her.

The following lunchtime, Frances picked up her tray and followed Irene to a table in the far corner. A couple of the other girls nodded in acknowledgment as they sat down.

'Couldn't you sleep me duck? Don't look much like it to me. If you're not careful, you'll waste away, you will.'

'There is something on my mind, as a matter of fact,' Frances said, glancing across the table, 'but I can't talk about it here.'

'All right. Why don't we walk 'ome insteaduv gettin' the factory bus? Then yer can tell yer Auntie Irene all about it.'

Frances swallowed the last of the tea in one gulp. 'If you're sure you don't mind?'

'I don't mind at all, but I'm a bit older than you, remember, so I might not walk as quick.' Irene let out a loud burp. 'That porridge I 'ad fo' breakfast is still stickin' in me throat. It's a wonder they don't slice it up and lerrus 'ave it for toast.' Still chuckling at her own joke, she pulled herself up from the table and headed back to her machine.

'So come on me duck – what's mekin' you so miserable?' The two women were walking home together along the darkened lane. 'A young chap, is it?'

Frances scowled. 'It's a bit more complicated than that.'

'The Yanks know how to charm the gals, that's for sure. It only teks a glass of the 'ard stuff. Me mam used to call it a shimmy-lifter. Sorry, what did you say?'

Struggling to keep up with her friend, despite her protestations, Frances took a deep breath. 'That's the trouble, you see. He's not such a young chap.'

'Ooh, ya bugger. Is 'e one o' the officers?'

'No, of course not.' The lie slipped out before she could stop it.

'So what then?' The older woman swung round, her bag almost flying off her shoulder. 'Don't tell me yer up the duff?'

Frances stopped dead, her face flushed with anger. 'That's a horrid way to put it.'

'Well, are ya or aren't ya? Wor'am I supposed to say?'

'I think I might be expecting a baby, yes, as a matter of fact. It happened, er... you know, on the night of the dance.' The lies came easily.

'Don't tell me it wer 'im that did it – the Hampton chap? Oh, glory be... you poor little mite. Why didn't you say summat?'

'I didn't know how to, Irene. I'm so confused. Whatever am I going to do?'

For a moment neither of them spoke. Then Irene put her arms round Frances and gave her a motherly hug. 'I'm sorry me duck I really am. You frit me to death, but I'll help you wi'it, course I will, now I've got over the shock. You're a good girl, not like some of 'em I could mention round 'ere. It's just not right, it aint – this 'appening to you.'

Frances let out a crazed laugh. 'For a minute there I thought you were going to disown me. I wanted to explain, but I just didn't know how.' She blinked back the tears.

'We'll 'ave a lot more explaining to do if we don't get a move on. Now keep your chin up and best foot forward. That way we might just make it home before blackout.'

Irene shook her head, her grey eyes misting over. 'Are you sure you want to do this, Franny?' Sometimes she was glad of the blackout.

'I've no choice, have I? And if you won't help I'll find someone who will.' She turned her head and stared out of the window, hardly trusting herself to speak.

'Aw, come on me duck, don't get yourself all upset. I'll help if that's what you really want. But I wouldn't wish it on nobody, and that's the truth. It ain't safe or legal when all's said an' done.' She wiped her hand across her brow.

'So you'll get me the name of someone?' Frances felt her stomach lurch again. How could she even think about getting rid of Ed's baby? But then how could she keep it? It would ruin his career if anyone found out, then he'd be sent home and she'd never see him again. She hated lying but if Irene believed Hampton was the child's father, she'd be on her side.

'There's summat else we can try first.' Irene was still shaking her head. 'I've never seen it done, mind, but I've heard it works.'

'Another way? I don't understand.'

'Well, you need a bath full of very hot water and a bottle of gin.'

'What on earth do you mean? I've never put gin in the bath before. How can that help?'

'You don't put it *in* the bath, you daft ha'p'orth. You drink it.'

'Drink a bottle of gin? Me? Never.'

'Look here – I know it ain't your fault you're in this mess, but I know you're the only one as can get yerself out of it.'

Frances felt the panic rising from somewhere deep inside her. 'But we're only allowed five inches of water,' she protested. 'It's wartime, remember.'

Irene looked at her watch. 'I've got to go now or I'll be late for my shift. Think about it and let me know.'

Frances watched the older woman disappear down the street, her generous hips swaying from side to side. She was a good friend and, come to think of it, the only real friend Frances had ever had. Some of the factory girls were gossiping behind her back, but they never came out and said anything to her face. 'Wanking a Yank,' she'd heard them snigger, even though the case against Jed had been dropped. Meanwhile she got on with her work and ignored them.

At least Cedric Hampton was now safely behind bars – the only good thing to come out of this mess. The police had got him on several other charges. In a strange way she almost felt grateful to the dreadful man. If it hadn't been for Hampton she'd never have met Ed.

'I want a word with you, young lady.' Betty Newby's voice resounded through the stairwell.

Frances froze. 'I've just got in from work, Mrs Newby. Could we make it a bit later?'

'No – come down now, I tell you, before I drag you down myself.'

'I'll be there in a jiffy,' Frances tried to disguise the fear in her voice. She'd expected this, of course, but had no idea how to deal with it. Taking a deep breath, she made her way slowly back down the two flights of stairs.

The landlady ushered Frances into her quarters, shutting the door firmly behind them. 'There's no point beating about the bush. I heard you being sick again this morning. Are you in the family way?'

Frances stared at the photograph on the wall above the mantel. An old man with a whiskered face was gazing into the camera, his hands resting on a walking stick with a handle carved into the head of a sheep.

'Are you listening to me, girl?'

'Yes, I'm listening, Mrs Newby, and yes, I am expecting a baby.' There was no point in lying now.

'Is that it? Is that all you've got to say for yourself? What's the world coming to? Well, I've got something to tell you, my girl. We don't allow babies here, as you know, and we *certainly* wouldn't entertain the idea of an unmarried mother. This is a high-class establishment.'

'Do you mind if I sit down?' Francis would have preferred to stand, but she needed time to think.

'See what I mean?' Betty Newby motioned towards the sofa. 'Special dispensation already.'

Frances cursed under her breath.

'What was that? You're mumbling girl, speak up.'

'They'll sack me from work soon enough. Please, Mrs Newby, don't throw me out or I'll end up on the streets.'

'I'll end up on the streets…' The older woman mocked. 'You should've thought about that before you got yourself into this mess. Even supposing I did let you stay – how would you pay your rent?'

'I could cook, clean, do the paperwork. My mother taught me to type when I was ten. I'll do anything at all that'll save you money.'

'The way I see it you'd be costing me money whatever you did, and that's a fact.'

Frances stood up. 'Then there's no more to be said. When do you want me to leave?'

A strange look flashed across Betty Newby's face. 'Just a minute. How far are you along?'

'Ten weeks.'

'We might be able to keep you on for a month or two. I'll

have a word with Arthur tonight. And in the meantime, don't say a word to anybody.'

CHAPTER 29

1969

Sophie almost choked when she answered the phone. The voice on the other end of the line was unmistakable. 'Steve! Where are you?'

'It doesn't matter – I'm out of the way, that's all you need to know. I just wanted to make sure you were all right.'

'Oh, I'm fine.' Sophie couldn't keep the sarcasm out of her voice. 'But your friend Julie is missing you quite a lot.'

'Julie? What's she got to do with anything?'

'Do you really want to know?' She lowered her voice, glancing round the deserted office. 'You might find all your sins have come back to haunt you.'

'Dammit, Sophie, what on earth do you mean? You're talking in riddles.'

She could hear the sound of him feeding more money into the phone. 'Julie came looking for me the other day. She wanted to know where you were. Said she had something to tell you.'

'Like what, for God's sake?'

'Like the fact that she's expecting a baby.'

'So,' he said, 'what's that got to do with me?'

'Funny that,' Sophie was laughing hysterically now. 'I've been wondering the same thing myself.'

'Surely you don't believe for a minute –'

'She says it's yours.'

'Look, my money's running out. I had to wait to be put through to you. Can I ring you later?' The pips cut through his words and then the line went dead.

Sophie slammed down the receiver, unable to contain her anger. It sounded like Steve was on the other side of the world. How dare he ring her at work without telling her where he'd gone? How dare he pretend he hadn't slept with Julie? First he'd gone off in a jealous rage and now he refused to admit to his own shortcomings. Deep down she supposed it served her right. She should never have fallen for him in the first place. She grabbed her handbag and headed for the door just as the news editor appeared at the top of the stairs.

'Ah, Sophie,' he grinned. 'Just the person I need.'

'Can't stop,' she lied. 'Mr Moulton's given me a job.'

The payphone in the hall rang at seven that evening just as Sophie arrived home.

She grabbed the receiver. 'Who is it?' She wasn't in the mood for small talk.

'Thank God I've caught you.' Steve sounded desperate. 'I've

tried several times to book a call. I thought you were never coming back.'

'No one ever answers this phone except me,' she said flatly. 'I hope you've got enough change this time.'

'Listen to me. You must know Julie's lying. I don't know why, but she's made the whole thing up.'

'You mean it's not your baby?'

'I mean that we never had that kind of relationship. I took her out once or twice that's all, but we really had nothing in common. Then she kept phoning me day and night. It was, well, embarrassing.'

'Oh, I bet it was. And it's even more embarrassing now. Have you spoken to her?'

'Hell, no, why would I? That would just give her ammunition. I wanted to talk to you first. I didn't mean to leave without saying goodbye. I just thought if I left Harcot for a while it would give you some space, give you some time to decide what you really wanted, but now it seems I've added to your problems.'

'Well that's where you're wrong.' She spat out the words, surprised at the strength of her own feelings. 'The problems are yours entirely – nothing to do with me. I think you should get in touch with Julie. She's your priority now.'

'I'll talk to her, but it won't make any difference,' he sighed. 'And what about you? Have you sorted things out with David?'

'He's busy with his mother's estate.'

'God, what a mess. Why won't you believe me, Sophie?'

For a moment she almost felt sorry for him. 'This isn't

about me, Steve. I do care what happens to you, but I've got too much to think about just now. Maybe one day.'

'Don't patronise me, please.'

Before she could answer, the line went dead.

CHAPTER 30
November 1944

'Hey, Franny, 'ave you heard what's happened to them Yanks?'

'Which ones?' Frances frowned. Doris was always gossiping.

'Them at the camp. They reckon half of 'em 'ave copped it.'

'How do you know?' The walls seemed to somersault in front of her. 'There's been no news from the front.'

'I have my contacts,' the older woman tapped her nose. 'They went on a secret mission, but not as secret as I don't know about it. They're all gonners, I'm telling you, and that there captain with 'em.'

'You're being ridiculous.' Frances heard the tremor in her own voice. 'Those men are all highly trained.'

'Highly sexed more like.' Irene let out a loud cackle. 'You don't have to believe me, duck, you'll find out soon enough.'

'I'm not listening to you anymore.' Frances put her hands over her ears. 'I've got work to do, even if you haven't.'

'What's going on here?' Mick Ford's voice echoed over the drone of the machines.

'Nothing,' Doris shouted, before hissing under her breath. 'Pity about your Yankee boyfriend.'

Frances tried to swallow the fear that forced its way to the back of her throat. The whole regiment, it seemed, had gone on the latest mission and no one had heard a word. Damn Doris. What did she know? She just made up the gossip as she went along.

As the days passed and she heard nothing, Frances began to fear the worst. Night after night she lay awake listening to the sound of his voice in her head. Late one evening when the house had gone silent she pulled on her coat and let herself out of the front door. It was no good; she had to tell Irene while she still had the courage.

'You all right, me duck?' Irene opened the door of her pokey flat. 'You shouldn't be out 'ere at this time in the blackout. Has summat 'happened?'

'No, it's just...' Frances followed her friend into the living room, her heart like a battering ram against her ribs. 'It's just that I don't think I can do it. You know, with the gin.'

'Don't worry about that right now, just sit yerself down.' Irene gestured towards the threadbare settee. 'You're as white as a cotton sheet.'

'I'm fine, really. I just wanted you to know I'm sorry. I thought it was what I wanted but it's not.'

'No need to be sorry.' The older woman let out a sigh. 'Look at it this way. I weren't very 'appy about it any road up, but

I'm 'ere, wherever you decide. Let me get yer a drink o' water, then when yer feeling better we'll 'ave a proper talk.'

'Thanks, Irene.' Frances smiled weakly. 'I don't know what I'd do without you.'

'Is there anything else you ain't telling me?'

Frances shook her head. 'I just can't bring myself to do it, that's all.' She hated deceiving Irene but she had no choice. If Ed really had gone missing she could never part with his baby. The child could be the only part of him she had left. She didn't care what people thought. She wouldn't be the first girl to have an illegitimate child with an American soldier and she'd never survive the rest of the war without some hope to hold on to.

'Whatever you decide, I'll 'elp, you know that,' Irene was still talking. 'Now why don't you sleep 'ere tonight? You look worn out and, any road up, I can mek sure you 'av a proper breakfast in the morning.'

'Thanks, Irene.' Frances looked longingly at the sofa, the faded brown moquette covered with a bright patchwork blanket. 'I might just take you up on that.'

Later that evening, after a cup of warm milk, a feeling of calm descended upon her, like she'd been wrapped in an invisible shield that kept the rest of the world away. That stupid gossip Doris, the grinning factory girls and the cupboard of a room she called home, all of these seemed unimportant now. As for the future – when Ed came home it would just be the three of them, back in Indiana on the shores of the lake whose name she could never pronounce. Back where they all belonged.

'Come on – one last push. Wait for the next contraction, Mrs Wainwright, and then give it your all.'

'Please don't call me Mrs –' Frances faltered as the pain flooded through her. 'I can't take any more.'

'Of course you can. We're nearly there now.' The midwife's voice rose into a crescendo. 'Good girl! There's the head, now breathe, just like we taught you. That's it, you're doing really well.'

'Is it a boy?' The pain was so intense Frances thought she might explode.

'I don't know.' The midwife attempted a smile. 'It hasn't told us yet. One more push now, Mrs Wainwright, and then we'll all know the answer.'

Please God, for Ed's sake, let it be a son. This was her chance to give him back what he'd lost. Frances heard her mother's voice in the distance... *Come back this minute – do as you're told. Get under the stairs NOW*. The sky lit up the horizon, the glow spreading for miles like a never-ending sunset. Too late she heard the noise exploding in her head and the deafening roar of bombs hitting the ground.

'You have a little girl, Mrs Wainwright. Tiny, very tiny, but perfectly formed all the same.'

A daughter? She didn't understand. How did she have a daughter? She heard a sound like kitten mewing and lifted her head. 'Where is she? Let me see her.'

'She's poorly, I'm afraid, my dear. We need to get her to

hospital. Your aunt's calling the doctor now. Whatever happens, you must try to be very brave.'

'My aunt? But I don't have an aunt. Where am I?' *Very brave, very brave.* She closed her eyes as her head sank back on to the pillow, the horrors of the Blitz rolling back over her. The bombs had killed her family, so the matron had said, but still she must be very brave.

CHAPTER 31
Blackpool, May 1945

Frances pushed the battered pram along the promenade, the late May wind almost whipping her off her feet. She'd heard that Blackpool was breezy, but this felt more like a hurricane. Oh, how she wished she was back in her childhood home. Closing the pram hood, she watched as Sophie slept, the child's face screwed into a bright pink ball.

Frances looked up. How long had she been lost in her thoughts? Ahead of her she saw a serious-looking man, sitting on a wooden bench on the seaward side of the road, trying to light his pipe, one hand covering the wooden bowl while the other clicked in vain at a metal lighter. Her dad used to smoke a pipe when she was a child and she could still smell the cotton wool soaked in petrol in the barrel of his silver lighter. As she passed, the man stood up, doffed his cap and smiled. He was around thirty-five with a mass of brown hair and a square chin, his shoulders buried in a huge woollen overcoat.

'I'm not having much luck,' he said. 'Blasted wind.'

'I'm struggling with it myself,' Frances replied, wondering why she was talking to a complete stranger.

He nodded towards the pram. 'Your first, is it? Or doing a bit of child-minding?'

To her surprise she blushed. Not that he would have noticed, her face being crimson from the exertion. 'Oh no, the baby's mine. I'm older than I look.'

He nodded amicably. 'Boy or girl?'

'A boy.' Did she say that? She'd no idea where the answer came from. 'His name's Simon. His dad's in the American army.' She pushed the pram forward, her hands trembling. 'We've waited a long time for the war to end, but he'll be home soon.'

The man dropped his pipe into his pocket. 'Are you all right? I really didn't mean to upset you.'

'I'm fine, really.' France wiped her eyes with the knuckles of her right hand.

'I'm just not used to this weather, I'm afraid. I'll feel better when summer finally arrives.'

'So you're new around here, then?'

'Yes, I am. How can you tell?'

He chuckled. 'Well, aside from the accent, the wind doesn't change with the seasons round here, I'm afraid. It comes in from the sea – the Irish Sea to be exact – so most times we're just stuck with it.'

'Oh, I'll have to get used to it then, won't I?' Frances looked at her watch. 'Goodness, is that the time? It'll soon be time for the little one's tea, and we've a long walk ahead of us.'

'Then I'll bid you good day. Nice to have made your acquaintance.'

Frances felt his eyes boring into her as she started back along the promenade. What on earth had made her say Sophie was a boy? But then why not? Didn't boys have an easier life? Boys grew up to be respected, revered even, and not downtrodden like women. And Ed's poor wife had given birth to a son. Hadn't he told her so himself?

Turning right into Waterloo Road, Frances stopped at the haberdashery store, an idea beginning to take shape in her mind. When Ed came back to her, he deserved to have a son. Sophie, with her little bald head and sparse eyelashes, could easily be taken for a boy. Why hadn't she thought of it before? Frances opened the shop door, manoeuvring the pram over the shallow step, then shut it firmly behind her.

'Can I help you, my dear?' The owner looked up from her knitting.

'I wondered if you had a spare ball of three-ply wool for my little boy here, please?'

'White or blue?'

'Blue, I think.'

The woman scanned the half-empty shelves, stretching to reach the very top.

'Here we are. Just the thing. That will be sixpence please.'

Frances's face fell. 'Perhaps I could have a think about it?'

'Of course you can. Is it for the little lad?'

'Yes, I just wanted to knit him a bonnet. We've only just

arrived in Blackpool and, well, I'd no idea it would be so windy.'

'You'll get used to it, I'm sure.' She smiled. 'How old is, er –?'

'Simon. His name's Simon. He's seven weeks old but very tiny for his age. He was premature, you see.'

'Hello Simon,' the woman smiled, peering under the blankets. She disappeared to the back of the shop and returned clutching a half-used ball of baby blue wool. 'You can have this for a penny if you like. I was going to put it towards the patchwork blanket I'm knitting, but you take it. I'll throw in some needles, too.'

For the first time in weeks , Frances smiled. 'That's very kind. I really don't know how to thank you.' She rummaged in her pocket and handed over the coin.

'It's a pleasure, my dear. God bless you both.'

Frances made her way back to the flat, a satisfied smile spreading across her face. Sophie was about to start a new life. With a little blue scarf round her neck, and matching hat and mittens, the child would easily pass for a boy. Boys were stronger than girls. Boys didn't feel the pain of childbirth. Boys had a much better life. She'd never wanted a daughter, never mind a weakling, but a son with an American captain as a father - now *that* was something to be proud of.

In the days after Sophie was born, Frances had suffered from hallucinations, sometimes in the middle of the night, but often in the day, too. Whenever she looked at the scrawny child, she saw a baby boy with bright blue eyes and a mass of blonde hair, his chubby fists punching the air. As she took him in her arms, the rain beat down so hard that his features began to blur, his face became contorted and his eyes sank back into his skull. Before she could cry for help he'd dissolved into a pool of water at her feet.

She thought she was going mad. 'Postpartum depression,' the hospital doctor called it. 'It happens sometimes, Mrs Wainwright,' he explained with a patronising smile. 'We don't know why it affects some mothers after such a happy event. The sad feelings will go of their own accord in a few weeks' time.'

A happy event? Sad feelings? Hadn't he listened to a word she'd said? 'I've lost my husband and we've lost our son,' she wanted to scream. 'How am I supposed to get over that?'

But she was too frightened to say anything: frightened that they would lock her away, frightened that they would take Sophie too, and then she would have nothing. She'd tried to love the child, tried with all her heart, but it was no use. She felt nothing, just a great big void where once her future had been. Now, as she let herself back into her flat, she knew she'd found the answer.

The run-down flat formed part of a terrace of houses running parallel to the promenade. Once quite grand with its walled garden and stained glass windows, the place looked unkempt now with broken drainpipes, crumbling brick work and peeling paint. Worn curtains in drab colours were dragged half-heartedly across the windows.

Frances pulled the pram up three stone steps to the front

door. Thank goodness she lived on the ground floor. The tiny front parlour, or living room as the landlord called it, had cracked brown lino and a cast-iron range that hadn't been blacked for years. Someone had covered the wallpaper in dirty brown paint and the room was lit by an upturned glass lampshade suspended on chains from the ceiling like a spaceship coming in to land. From the parlour a door opened onto the scullery, bare apart from a stained Belfast sink with a cold water tap and an ancient green cabinet with a broken glass door.

Sophie and Frances slept in the one small bedroom, sharing the evil-smelling bathroom with several other tenants. Otherwise, thank goodness, no one took any notice of either of them. It had seemed surprisingly easy to escape the system. She never went near the doctor's surgery, relying instead on the local chemist's shop for advice. The war may be over but Blackpool, like many other towns, was still full of nameless people.

Frances took the baby out every day, wrapped up in thick woollen jumpers, sturdy leggings and lace-up boots, bought with the last of her savings, and a checked cap that she perched at an angle on his head. Her son would grow up to be strong, no one would ever take advantage of him, and no one would ever put him down.

The familiar-looking man appeared in front of her and doffed his hat. 'I was hoping I'd see you again. I should have introduced myself before. The name's Brown. Timothy

Brown.'

To her surprise she felt happy to see him. 'Oh, hello, Mr Brown. You may be interested to know that I'm getting used to the wind.'

'That *is* good news. Call me, Timothy, please. I've seen you a few times since that first day, but have not had a chance to make your acquaintance. I brought a little gift for your son, to rectify the situation. I hope you don't mind.'

To her embarrassment, she blushed. 'That's so very kind of you, Mr, er... Timothy. I'm Frances, Frances Wainwright. Pleased to meet you'

He thrust a small parcel into her hands. 'It's nothing really, just a felt toy that once belonged to my wife. I hope you can make some use of it.'

'Thank you,' she took it gingerly and tucked it under the baby's blanket, thinking that Timothy Brown didn't look old enough to be a widow. 'Would you like to join us on our walk?'

Smiling, he stepped in beside her, sheltering the pram from the wind as they walked in silence along the promenade.

'You said the toy *once belonged* to your wife,' she said at last. 'Does that mean –?'

'She was killed by a tram, just before the war. One minute she was there and the next she was gone. My life's been empty ever since.' This, without a trace of self-pity.

'Oh, I'm sorry, that must have been dreadful. I know what it's like to lose someone you love.' She stared down at the sleeping child.

'I could push, if you like,' he said, his eyes smiling.

'Thank you, that would be very kind.'

They strolled along in silence looking for the entire world like a happy family. She told him about her childhood in Coventry, about Mum, Dad and Bobby and how happy she was until the day when it all came to an end.

He nodded thoughtfully, sucking on his empty pipe. 'And your husband? Where is he now?'

'He's missing, presumed dead.' She reached out and took hold of the pram. 'He was an American officer stationed in England. He disappeared after the drop into Holland last September.'

Timothy Brown shook his head. 'Operation Market Garden. We lost a lot of good men.'

'I'm sure he'll come home eventually. He promised he would.'

'May I walk with you again, one day?' he said at last. 'I can see dark clouds coming in from the sea and that can only mean one thing. You need to get home.'

'That would be very nice.' As they parted, she raised her hand in a wave and began to push the pram past the row of hotels and back to her dreary flat.

The next time they met he took her to a little café on Victoria Street with tables covered with mismatched tablecloths and a waitress with flame-coloured hair and red lipstick to match. Parking the pram outside, Timothy helped her carry the baby into the steamy warmth.

As the child slept on her lap they talked, hesitantly at first, and then with the animation of new friends, exchanging the details of their lives. He told her about his wife, May, how she was one of ten children and he fell in love with her the moment they met. She wore a navy blue two-piece and pearl earrings when they married. She reminisced about her brother Bobby and the way the old house used to ring with laughter when they were all together.

By the time he'd walked her home, they were comfortable in each other's company. For the first time in a year, Frances almost felt safe.

CHAPTER 32
March 1945

In the days that followed they met up several times, sometimes in the café, sometimes for a walk in Stanley Park. She knew she ought to think about getting a job – she couldn't live forever on the bit of money her parents had left her, but she didn't want to think about that now. She liked Timothy. He was straightforward, uncomplicated and didn't ask about her past, for which she was grateful.

One spring day as she ventured into town, she saw him walking along Abingdon Street reading a newspaper, oblivious to the world around him.

'Good morning,' he doffed his hat the minute he saw her. 'How are you both today?'

'We're fine, thank you. I was just going to the market to see if I could get some baby clothes. Simon's over three months old now and he's growing out of everything. I never thought he would, you know, being so tiny at birth.' She knew she was rambling but nerves had got the better of her.

'That's good,' he said, politely. 'I won't keep you then.'

She turned to go, angry with herself for lacking the courage to speak her mind. 'I was wondering if you'd you like to come for a meal one day? The flat's very small and it wouldn't be anything fancy but we'd like to see you, wouldn't we?' She stared down at the sleeping baby.

'I'd like that, Frances. I'd really like to see you both again.'

'Pardon?' Her face turned crimson. She wasn't sure she'd heard him straight.

'I was just saying that would be delightful. At your convenience of course. Just let me know when you have a suitable day. And now I must be off. Good day.' He doffed his hat again and disappeared.

The appointed day arrived. Frances splashed her face with cold water then scrubbed it with a flannel, staring at herself in the mirror. At the age of twenty-one her skin was pale and her hair dull and lifeless – however had she got into this state? Fetching the scissors from the kitchen, she cut her hair from her shoulders to a line around her chin to get rid of the uneven ends, then doused it in vinegar – she'd read somewhere that this would make it shine. Sure enough, as it dried, the curls sprang up into a neat bob that framed her face. She rifled through the bits and bobs she kept in a box under the bed till she found the nappy rash cream she'd got from the hospital when the baby was born. This she spread liberally on her face and neck.

She had sewn some scraps of lace onto the only decent

blouse she possessed, brightening up the collar and cuffs. She'd washed and pressed it to go with her blue woollen skirt. That, she told her reflection, was the very best she could do.

'This tastes, delicious, Frances. It was so kind of you to invite me.'

Timothy Brown smiled broadly.

'It's nothing really, just a bit of corned beef hash.'

'It's a long time since I had a home-cooked meal like this – and in such good company. You look very charming today, if I may say.'

Frances nodded shyly, the colour rushing to her face. They were sitting at an old card table, Timothy wearing his Sunday best shirt, Frances in a newly-pressed pinny, while the child played happily on a blanket on the floor.

'So how are you finding life in Blackpool?' he asked. 'Are you getting used to being away from home?'

'We're getting used to it slowly, aren't we, Simon? As for Leicester – I never really thought of it as home. Coventry's where I was born.'

'Ah, Coventry, yes, and a bad do that was. We had our moments though. A school in Freckleton, not far from here, was bombed to smithereens, but nothing at all like that. How is the place now?'

'I don't know, couldn't bring myself to go back. One of these days, maybe.'

Changing the subject, she said, 'You were very lucky to grow up by the sea. We used to go to Hunstanton for day trips when I was a child. As soon as we saw the sea appearing over the horizon, we would cheer, Bobby and me. Then we'd take our buckets and spades on the sand and play for hours while Mum and Dad sat in deckchairs, like lord and lady of the manor. Ooh, if we'd lived near the sea, we'd have thought we were royalty.'

Timothy smiled. 'You do take it for granted, I'm afraid, but it's not all fun, living at the seaside. As you can see, the place is crammed in summer – people are just learning how to enjoy themselves again'

'I'd love to go on the beach, now that the war's over.' She looked down at her plate, the familiar fear gripping her gut. He was dead now, Ed, she was sure of it. If not, why hadn't she heard from him? Why hadn't he tried to find her?

'Don't look so sad,' Timothy's voice cut into her thoughts. 'We'll go – all three of us – and take a picnic. It'll be my way of thanking you for today.'

Frances stared across the crowded beach as waves spilled onto the shore and children shrieked and tumbled into the foam. Simon lay asleep in his pram beside her whilst Timothy – trousers rolled up to his knees – soaked up the early summer sunshine. A flicker of long-forgotten contentment warmed her soul.

The baby stirred, stretching upwards, bringing her back to reality. She had lied to Timothy about Sophie and sooner or later she would have to tell him the truth. A sharp pain pierced her chest. How could she explain her behaviour when she didn't understand it herself? Ed going missing, the trauma of the birth, the need to give the man she loved a son – none of these explained the terrible deceit. She'd been ill, that was it. She'd been ill, delirious, hadn't understood what she was doing. And then once she'd started she didn't know how to stop. Yes, she would tell him, but not now. Not yet. In a few more weeks when they knew each other better, then she would do it. She would say she hadn't meant to deceive him, that she hadn't even meant to deceive herself. She'd remind him about her brother Bobby, who died when she was just thirteen, how she really believed that boys could expect a better future. She would tell him – of course she would – but just not now.

She raised her head. Timothy was looking at her now, shading his eyes from the midday sun.

'A penny for them,' he said. 'Or maybe I should give you a sixpenny-piece for such a serious face.'

'It's nothing,' she said, reaching out for her bag. 'I was just thinking that it's time to eat our sandwiches.'

CHAPTER 33

Frances was changing the baby's nappy when she heard a knock at the door. Running to open it, she was surprised to see Timothy.

'Come in,' she said, beckoning him to follow her back to the parlour.

'Thanks. I meant to say before how cosy you've made this room. I do hope you don't mind me calling without –' He stopped suddenly and drew a deep breath.

'What is it? What's wrong?' She followed his gaze.

'Heavens above! I can't believe my eyes. It's a girl. Little Simon is a girl. What the –' He raised his eyes to the ceiling. 'I don't understand, Frances? Why on earth didn't you tell me?'

Frances kneeled down, folded the napkin and deftly secured it with a pin, scrolling through her jumbled thoughts to find something to say.

'I don't think I have to explain myself to you,' she said at last, not daring to look at him. 'And please don't raise your voice. I'm not used to being spoken to like that.'

'I'm sorry, truly I am. It's just such a shock, that's all.' He started to pace the room. I know it's none of my business, but why, Frances – why? What can you possibly gain from this? You can't keep it a secret for ever. People are bound to find out in the end.'

'As you say, it's none of your business.' She lifted the child into her arms. 'I was stupid to allow you to become my friend. That's all I have to say. My life is mine and no one else's.'

'Have you seen a doctor since you've been here?' he paced the crowded room, absentmindedly running his hand through his hair. 'Maybe you could talk to someone?'

'There's no need for that. There's nothing wrong with me. And there's certainly nothing wrong with the child. Now, if you don't mind, I'd like you to go. Please drop the latch as you leave.'

'Look at me, please.' He was pleading now, panic distorting his normally calm voice. 'There must be something I can do to help? For God's sake, how can you push me away like this?'

Balancing the child on her hip, Frances held out her free hand. 'Goodbye, Mr Brown.'

The sparks from the fire illuminated her face as she stood on the deserted beach, a gentle gust of wind fanning the flames. Frances undid the tiny bundle of clothes and dropped them, one by one, onto the burning wood, watching as they recoiled from the heat then flared brazenly in the dark. She saved the little blue hat till last. 'Goodbye baby Simon,' she whispered, the tears slipping down her pale cheeks and disappearing into the night. Pulling her coat around her shoulders, she turned quickly and walked back up the slipway.

CHAPTER 34

1948

'Frances, please wake up!'

Frances blinked in the half-light. 'What is it, Sophie?' The child was kneeling on the eiderdown tugging at her mother's dressing gown sleeve.

'I don't like it. It's dark. The bogeyman might come and get me.'

Rolling over onto her elbows, Frances sat up. Her head was spinning and she wanted to be sick. 'Don't be a silly girl, there's only you and me here – there's no bogeyman.'

Sophie slid off the bed. 'I'm hungry, Frances.'

'Well. You should have eaten your lunch.'

The three-year old eyed her solemnly. 'I didn't have any lunch. You were asleep and I couldn't reach the cupboard.'

Frances looked at the clock. It was almost half past five. My God – had she really been asleep all afternoon? She threw back the blankets and set her feet down on the bare boards.

'Okay, I'll make us something. Strawberry jam soldiers coming up.'

'Strawberry jam solders,' Sophie repeated slowly. 'Do they have guns?'

'You're too clever for me by half, Sophie Wainwright, but if you ask me, brains are a waste of time. Now then, if you'd been a baby boy things might have been very different.'

'Mummy want a baby boy, Mummy want a baby boy.' Sophie danced round the room.

'Shut up, Sophie – *shut up do you hear me? I told you not to call me Mummy.*'

The child's face crumpled. 'I weed in my drawers, Frances, I didn't mean to.' She cast her eyes down to the floor.

'You naughty girl. What were you thinking of? You're much too big for that now. Go and get your pyjamas and get yourself ready for bed.'

Frances picked up the empty vodka bottle from the dressing table and shuffled through to the galley kitchen. The child could be such a nuisance. Anyway, what was so wrong with drinking in the day? She'd only had a few while Sophie had her afternoon nap; it was not as if she made a habit of it. Beryl, her one and only friend in the world, had brought some gin round earlier for them to share. Beryl only lived two doors down and worked nights scrubbing floors. What else were they supposed to do for entertainment? There wasn't much round here, unless you went into town, of course, and you could hardly go into a pub with a young child.

'I'm a big girl now, Frances.' Sophie's shrill voice

interrupted her thoughts. 'I've got into my jarmers.'

Frances scooped up her daughter, sat her on the sofa and handed her the plate of jam soldiers. Poor Sophie. None of this was her fault. She had tried to love the child, she really had, but she just couldn't.

Trying to make amends, she picked up a book of fairy tales and began to read.

'Once upon a time there were three bears –'

'Frances?' the child interrupted.

'Yes, Sophie?'

'I don't want to go to bed. I might have those nasty dreams again.'

'Off course you won't. Just trust me for once and I'll make all the bad things go away.'

She got up, leaning on the sofa for support. If only she really could.

CHAPTER 35

1950

'Tell me again about Daddy.' Five-year-old Sophie climbed on her mother's knee. 'Jonny at school said I didn't have a dad, but teacher told him off. I have got one haven't I?' She stuck her thumb in her mouth. 'He just got lost, didn't he? But one day he won't be lost and he *will* come back home.'

Frances took a swig of vodka, banging her glass on the table. 'Take that thumb out of your mouth. Of course, you have a dad, Sophie; he just lives a long way away. Your daddy's in America, but when he comes home we're all going to have a big party.'

'That's what I said, but Jonny didn't believe me. He says all the soldiers came home a long time ago.'

'Never mind what Jonny says. One day your daddy will arrive just like Father Christmas, with his arms full of presents for you and me.'

The little girl giggled. 'And what will he look like?

'Father Christmas?' Her mother winked. 'He'll have grey hair and a beard.'

'No, I mean Daddy.'

'Oh, *him*. Well, he's tall and handsome with a lovely suntan and hair the colour of lemon drops!'

'Like mine?' Sophie fingered her curls.

'Just like yours.'

'So *when* will he come then?'

'I don't know when,' Frances snapped, 'so don't keep asking.' Her head was aching and she needed another drink.

'Jonny says he's dead.'

'Of course he's not dead.' She struggled to her feet. 'It's time for bed now, Sophie. Go and have a wash, there's a good girl.'

'Will you come and kiss me goodnight? I don't want the bogeyman to get me.'

'I've told you before, there's no bogeyman. I'll be in with your milk in a minute.' Stumbling into the pokey kitchen, Frances grabbed the milk bottle from the cupboard, poured a glass for herself and a smaller one for her daughter. She topped her own up with the last of the vodka and made her way to her Sophie's bedroom. Tomorrow she would stop drinking. Tomorrow she would be a good mother, tomorrow... She tripped at the bedroom door and watched as the liquid flew into the air and dripped down the walls like frozen rain. Tomorrow she would stop lying.

Later that evening Frances crawled out of bed and put her coat on over her pyjamas. She could hear rain slapping against the leaded windows, but she didn't care. She'd run out of drink. It would only take a few minutes to get to the off sales, as long as she ran all the way. She glanced at Sophie, fast asleep with her thumb in her mouth, then quickly let herself out of the front door.

CHAPTER 36
1956

'Why can't we just stay in the same place?' Sophie looked at her mother with pleading eyes. 'I'm eleven now and I don't think we've ever stayed anywhere longer than a year. Other people don't move around like gypsies.'

Frances took a sip of her gin. 'You're lucky to have a roof over your head, I can tell you. There's still families who haven't got a place to call their own and the war's been over for years now.'

'You've always got an excuse, haven't you? Blackpool hardly got bombed, from what I can gather, and anyway...' Sophie glanced round the shabby room. 'It's awful here – not even worth the pittance we pay for it. Why can't we get somewhere decent for a change?'

'I blame that posh school for your high and mighty ways, Sophie Wainwright. Since you passed the eleven plus you think you're better than the rest of us.'

'That's not fair and you know it. I've just had a chance to see how other people live, and this isn't it!'

Frances lit up a cigarette and poured herself another drink. 'Well, why don't you go and live with one of your fancy friends if you're so ashamed of being here? You're not much use to me these days, anyway. Always got your head in the clouds or buried in a book and never lift a finger round the place.'

Sophie bit back a retort. Her mother was drunk so there was no use arguing. Who did she think cleaned the place when she was sleeping off a hangover? Who emptied the rubbish, took the clothes to the launderette and tried to make meals out of measly leftovers?

Sophie had been to her friends' houses a few times now and while the places weren't all immaculate, they were clean, tidy and above all homely. She hadn't realised till recently what that meant. Last week they had a sleepover at Gillian's house on Lytham Road in South Shore. They spent the afternoon at the Pleasure Beach then walked along the Prom eating fish and chips. Back at the house, Gill's mum and dad set up a row of makeshift beds in the front room and bought fizzy pop, crisps and cake for them to eat at midnight. To her acute embarrassment, Sophie was given a teddy to sleep with – something she'd never had in her entire life. But it felt good being treated like a child for a change and she enjoyed every minute.

The trouble was, it was her turn now to invite friends round and she was running out of excuses. Her mother was a widow who suffered with her health, she explained, and it would be a while before they knew if the medicine had worked. The doctor said she still needed to rest, etc etc...

Frances turned thirty in a few months' time but in truth she looked more like forty. Some of the girls' mothers, thankfully, were quite a bit older than her own, and what she supposed was called respectable, which is why she hadn't been very honest about where she lived. 'Just off the main road at Bispham,' she would say if anyone asked, before quickly changing the subject.

She'd been thrilled when she heard she'd got a place at Blackpool High School for Girls. This was a chance to prove herself and no one was going to take it away from her.

'Get me a cup of tea, will you, Sophie?' her mother's voice interrupted her thoughts. 'I've got a splitting headache.'

'Do you want some toast with it? You haven't eaten all day and, well –'

'I'm drinking too much – is that what you're trying to say? Well, don't bother.'

'It's just that most of our money goes on gin and vodka – some days we can't afford to eat.'

'You have those posh school dinners now, don't you? What more do you want?'

'I'm grateful for them, yes,' she said, though secretly she despised the fact that hers were free, 'but I can't live on them entirely.'

'Well, you'd better get yourself a job, then.'

'I can't because I'm too young – who's going to take me on at my age?'

Frances let out a cackle. 'I'm not asking you to run the country, you know, though heaven knows Anthony Eden could do with some help. You could wash up at one of the cafés in town, if you dolled yourself up a bit.' She opened her bag. 'Here, take this. A bit of red lipstick and you could pass for thirteen. Now get me that tea before I die of thirst.'

Sophie woke to the sound of the flat door slamming. She sat up in bed and peered at the ancient alarm clock: five forty-five and it was still dark. Whatever was Frances doing going out at this time of the morning? Stumbling into the hall, Sophie saw a light under her mother's bedroom door.

'Is anyone there?' she called, her heart thudding wildly.

'Go away,' the words came out in a strangled sob. 'Just leave me alone.'

'What is it? What's happened? Who was that I heard leaving just now?'

'No one – it's nothing to do with you. Just leave me alone, will you, and go back to bed.'

Instinctively Sophie opened the door and switched on the light. The older woman's hands shot to her eyes, but not before Sophie saw the bruising.

'Put out the light, leave me alone.' Her voice rose to a shriek.

'It's Bill, isn't it? You promised you weren't going to see him again. What has he done to you?'

Her mother's boyfriend was a jobless builder with a heavy hand and a raging temper, especially after a few beers.

'He swore he wouldn't touch me again – anyway, what's it to

you?' Frances slumped back down on the bed.

'Let me get you a cold flannel. Your eye will close up if you don't do something.'

'Just put the light out and get me a drink.'

Sophie filled the kettle and put it on the stove, shivering as the cold permeated her feet. She would take Frances a cup of tea and stay with her till she'd drunk it. And if her mother tried to lace the tea with gin she'd find the bottle and pour the rest down the sink.

'He shouldn't be allowed to get away with it,' Sophie frowned at her mother. 'We should call the police.' They were sitting side by side on the threadbare settee, Frances nursing her swollen eye.

'Call the police? Good God, Sophie, you really are more naïve than I thought you were. Where d'you think Bill gets the gin he brings me when he calls round? Not from the corner shop, that's for sure. And where do reckon I found my new dress? Under the pier?'

Sophie tried to block the words from her mind. Frances had got involved with a thief. Did that mean they were they living off stolen goods? One of these days the police would come knocking and then where would they be? She didn't care. The man was a coward – he deserved what was coming to him.

Out loud she said, 'We'll all end up behind bars at this rate. Whatever were you thinking? Will he come back, do you think?'

'Not if he knows what's good for him. He's a brute, and you're right for once, I should've ditched him long ago.

Anyway, you'll have to get a job now or we'll both starve. Have you done anything about it yet?'

'None of the girls at school has a job.' Sophie frowned.

'No, but I bet they've got dads, haven't they? Dads who work, dads who hand over their pay packets every Friday.'

Susan's dad's a bank manager, Sophie wanted to say. *I doubt he gets his money from a weekly pay packet.* Instead she stood her ground. 'It's not my fault I haven't got a dad. When I was little you said he was coming back, but he never did, did he? A fine American officer he turned out to be. It wouldn't surprise me if he never existed at all.'

Sophie winced as the back of her mother's hand caught the side her face. 'What was that for? I'm only saying what I feel. Have you any idea how much I wanted him to come home? I used to wait by the window every night, and all for nothing. God, how stupid I must have looked.' The anger she'd buried for so many years spilled out in a torrent of home truths.

'You wanted a son, didn't you – you always wanted a son. I was never good enough. I can hear you now saying it over and over again. *If only you had been a boy, Sophie, life would have been so different.'*

'That was years ago.'

'Do you think I don't remember? When I started school and we said our prayers, I used to ask God if he would turn me into a boy. Then I thought you would be proud of me. Then you would get your brother Bobby back. I really believed that if I behaved he would give me what I asked for. Can you imagine that?' She stopped and looked up. Tears were streaming down her mother's face, dripping over her chin and onto the collar of her blouse.

'What is it? What have I said?' Sophie was frightened now and she could feel a nerve twitching in the back of her neck. 'I'm so sorry, Frances, please don't cry – I'll make it up to you, I promise.'

'And how do you suppose you'll do that, young lady?'

'I don't know but I'll do it somehow.' She fingered the weal on her cheek.

'It's too late for that, far too late. Now go away and leave me alone.'

Over the next few days mother and daughter hardly spoke. Sophie soon found herself a job washing up in one of the many small boarding houses that lined the streets of South Shore. She had chosen this end of town so she wouldn't bump into any of her friends, though the walk there and back was exhausting. Renee Guffog, a tired-looking woman in her late forties with a pinny permanently tied to her ample frame, didn't even ask Sophie's age. Instead she just showed her through to the cramped kitchen where she'd be expected to work.

'You have to do all the pots from the evening meal, but don't use too much hot water, mind. I'm not made of money and the old geyser's playing up. Then I want them dried and put back in the cupboard where they belong before you go home.'

Sophie was paid cash at the end of the week. 'No names, no pack drill,' Mrs Guffog said, tapping her nose, though heaven only knew what that meant. There was no Mr Guffog and the woman seemed to have great trouble running the place on her own. Sometimes Sophie was expected to clean the bedrooms, clear the grate, or bring the coal in from the coal hole for no extra money. By the time she'd walked back home, let herself in the dark flat and finished her homework, she was exhausted.

Sometimes her mother had left out bits of old food, half a loaf of bread or a bag of broken biscuits, but mostly Sophie reheated the leftovers she'd taken from the plates at the boarding house (you couldn't really call it stealing, and what's more, it was much too good to put in the bin). Her friends had stopped asking if they could come round, becoming more distant as the weeks passed. There were only so many lies you could expect people to believe. On the days she wasn't working, Sophie would go straight from school to the town's Central Library, where every daily newspaper was available to read, from the *Times* and the *Manchester Guardian* to the *Daily Mirror* and the *Sketch*. Reading these was her secret pleasure – she drowned herself in crime stories, cartoons, and reports from foreign countries – and when she was in this other world she didn't feel quite so alone.

It was on one of these nights, arriving home after six, that Sophie sensed something was not quite right. Her mother was nowhere to be seen and her bedroom door, usually wide open, was firmly shut. Thrusting open the door, she stared at the empty bed, rumpled sheets spilling on to the floor.

'Frances? Where are you?' Running towards the window, she looked down at the floor and let out a terrified scream.

Her mother's feet were poking out from under the blanket.

Sophie stood still, unable to move her limbs. Her mother must have died. There was no other explanation. Finally, propelled by fear, she ran out of the door and down the road faster than she'd ever done in her life. A man jumped out of the telephone box as soon as he saw her coming. She grabbed the receiver and rang 999.

'Your mother has been very lucky, young lady.' The doctor shook his head. 'If you hadn't arrived home when you did, the outcome could've been very different.'

'What's happened to her?' Sophie words came out in a high-pitched squeak. 'Is she going to be all right?'

'It's not straightforward I'm afraid, my dear. Your mother has what we call alcohol poisoning. She is, I take it, quite fond of a drink?'

'Too fond! I can't make her stop, though heaven knows I've tried. Can you give her something for it?'

'The only cure is to stop drinking, I'm afraid. Is there...,' he looked down at his file, 'a Mr Wainwright?'

'My father died before I was born.'

'I understand. Well, we'll keep her in hospital and give her complete bed rest. After that, it's up to your mother. In the meantime, have you a relative you can stay with?'

Sophie nodded. Lying had become second nature. Just then a nurse appeared and shot her a sympathetic smile. 'Perhaps you could bring in some toiletries and a nightgown?'

'Oh yes – of course.' Did her mother have such things? She

wasn't sure.

By the time Sophie reached the guest house where she worked, the landlady was fuming. 'Where the hell have you been, you stupid girl? I've had to do all the pots myself. And you? You couldn't even be bothered to make a phone call. I've heard you trying to impress me with your 'Yes, Mrs Guffog, no Mrs Guffog,' while all the time you're trying to skive off behind my back. What have you got to say for yourself?'

'I'm very sorry. My mother was rushed to hospital today. I found her in the bedroom and had to call an ambulance.'

'A likely story! That woman's pickled by drink, nothing that a sober life wouldn't put right. Anyhow, I said I'd give you a chance and I have done, so gone on, hoppit!'

Sophie ran down the front path and out into the street, banging the front gate behind her. Stupid woman. She clearly didn't want to hear the truth, just as long as she could get out of paying a week's wages. Well, she could keep her dirty dishes and her kitchen that reeked of stale cabbage. She, Sophie, had better things to do with her life. One day she would have a proper job and people would respect her for who she was.

CHAPTER 37

1969

'So, who exactly have you written to?' asked Sophie.

David opened the file in front of him and pulled out a carbon copy. 'The National Archives and Records Administration in Washington DC.'

'Sounds very grand, but what do you think they can tell us?'

'Well, we have two premises. Your father was a either a drunken lecherous gardener who helped run a children's home, or an officer in the American Army. First of all we need to find out if your mother actually knew this Ed Trask.'

'But his name's in the newspaper cutting – the one you found about the trial?'

'I know, Sophie, but he could just have been an officer involved in the court martial. Who's to say he would even remember her? But even if he did, it doesn't mean Frances had an affair with him, does it?'

Sophie frowned. 'You're saying she could have imagined the

BAGGY PANTS AND BOOTEES

whole thing?'

'I'm afraid so. To put it bluntly, your dad could be any one of the Yanks stationed in Leicestershire at the time.'

She threw him a dark look. 'So, if this Trask guy is still alive, we have to find him.'

'Yes, though, naturally, he might not be too keen to help. The GIs left a lot of broken hearts behind – and a lot of children they were never destined to know. This sort of enquiry is common twenty or so years on. Kids get curious.' David shuffled the papers in front of him. 'Some of the men did send for their sweethearts, of course. But a lot of them were already married. I'm sorry, Sophie, it's not easy for me to say.'

'Don't worry. I know you're only being honest. But how do you know all this?'

He snapped the file shut, conscious he'd said too much. 'My contact was extremely forthcoming. But then, from what I can gather, most Americans are.'

'You think my dad's still alive, don't you?'

'I think there's a good chance. A captain in the US Army would have been, what, thirty – thirty-five at the most?'

'So he could be around fifty now?'

'Yep, with a wife and grown-up family. Probably never given the past another thought.'

Sophie rubbed her eyes with the back of her hand. 'I hate to think of Frances being seduced by an older man.'

'Come on Sophie, chin up!' David rested his hand on her shoulder. 'Anything's better than the gardener. In any case, these things are always handled sensitively, so I'm told.'

'So what happens now?'

'Well, you write a discreet letter saying you're trying to find some distant American relatives, then wait for the response.'

'I see, of course,' she said, trying to take it all in. 'We don't want to cause any trouble...' her voice trailed off.

'You're just making enquiries at this stage, that's all. Be polite and don't forget to include your date of birth.'

'Frances must have gone through hell and I just watched it happen.' Sophie cupped her face in her hands. 'I just had no idea.'

'And what could you have done if you had known the truth?' He pulled a handkerchief from his jacket. 'Here you go. Now dry those eyes and get writing. It's what you're good at after all.'

Dear Mr Trask

I hope you don't mind me writing to you like this, but I have recently found your name amongst my family papers and understand that you were extremely kind to my mother when you were stationed in the Midlands during the war.

As she is unwell at the moment, I have taken it upon myself to make contact with you as I would love to have the opportunity to thank you after all these years.

I am not sure if you will remember my mother after all this time: her name is Frances Wainwright and she worked at the Huntingdon Aircraft Factory in Copmanthorpe, close to where the US Airborne were stationed in Leicestershire in 1944.

She was born in Coventry and her parents were killed in the Blitz in 1940 after which she went to work in a children's home in Leicester. If you do not remember her, then I hope you will forgive me for the intrusion and wish you and your family all the very best for the future.

Yours sincerely

Sophie Wainwright

As the days passed the two of them fell into routine. David would receive a letter back from America, detailing the name and current whereabouts of a former member of the 82nd Airborne Division, which they painstakingly checked out, then subsequently dismissed, each line of enquiry taking them further away from their goal.

Sophie spent the occasional weekend when she wasn't on call, at David's flat. Sometimes when Jill, a biologist who worked for a vaccine manufacturer, was working abroad, David would drive over to York. If Jill ever had any doubts about the situation, she didn't say; she seemed genuinely interested in the search for Sophie's father and the three of them gradually became good, if rather unlikely, friends.

'What's happened to that boyfriend of yours?' David asked one Sunday evening when they were sifting through yet more correspondence at Sophie's flat.

'You mean Steve?' She kept her eyes focused on the letter in front of her.

'Who else would I mean?'

'He's back, I believe, but I haven't seen him. He had some

things to sort out.' She tried her best to sound casual. 'Besides, everyone at the *Tribune* thinks *you're* my new boyfriend.'

'Don't change the subject, Sophie. I know you're missing him. Did you tell him about us?'

'I mentioned that you were helping me find my father, if that's what you mean.'

'And he didn't believe you?'

She shook her head.' I don't know what he believed. Before I had a chance to explain, he disappeared.'

David shook his head. 'No wonder the poor guy's confused'.

'Guilty, more like. He accused you of being my lover.'

'Oh, well that's all right then,' he raised his eyes to the ceiling. 'I'd hate to think *I* might be the cause of your troubles.'

'There's no need to be sarcastic,' she swiped him with a cushion, her face breaking into a smile at last. 'Besides, it'll do him good to feel jealous. He's far too used to having things his own way.'

'Don't tell me that you *do* fancy him, Sophie Wainwright, under all that bravado.'

'I don't need to,' she waved her hands in the air. 'He fancies himself enough already.'

'That's a yes, then?'

'Look David. The only thing that matters to me right now is finding my father. Now stop asking awkward questions and let's get back to work.'

Sophie sat up in bed, her eyes wide open, her heart beating so loudly it seemed to echo around the room. It was dark except for a sliver of moonlight making its way across the old-fashioned counterpane. The nightmare was always the same: the man approached her grinning wickedly, his chapped lips displaying a row of rotting teeth. His clothes were dirty and his fingernails covered in grime. Grabbing her by the hair, he lifted her off the ground. *'I'm your dad, me girl, and you're just going' to 'ave to get used to it.'* he leered. Then she woke up.

Throwing off the blankets, Sophie padded across the room and flung open the curtains. She grabbed her dressing gown from the back of the bedroom door and made her way into the tiny kitchen. Then, picking up the letter that had arrived that morning, she turned it over and over in her hands. In the past few weeks she and David had identified several Ed or Edward Trasks all over the United States, but none fitted the profile exactly. They had written to each one and it would be months before they'd eliminate them all. Then came the breakthrough. An Edward George Trask, formerly a captain with the US Airborne Division based in Leicestershire in the lead up to the Normandy landings, had been found living in Atlanta, Georgia.

She opened the letter and scanned the contents, though she'd already learnt them off by heart.

Dear Sophie Wainwright

I was real surprised to receive your letter but now I've gotten used to it, I sure am glad you got in touch. I do recall a lady of the name of Frances Wainwright who worked at the aircraft factory in Copmanthorpe near where I was based during the war.

She was a bright girl who found herself in difficult circumstances that were not her own fault and she sure did her best to deal with them. As Captain of the 82nd US Airborne Division it was my duty to see to it that Miss Wainwright was fairly treated. I only knew her for a few short months after I took my men into Holland, where, despite Allied successes, I was taken as a prisoner of war. Sadly, for me and many of our men, we were never able to go back to Leicestershire to thank the good people who supported us through those times.

I am sorry to hear that your mother's in poor health. I'm amazed that she should remember me after all these years and hope that her health improves real soon.

You have nothing to thank me for; the debt lays the other way round.

Yours,

Ed Trask.

'We've found him, we've definitely found him!' Sophie waved frantically as David arrived at the gates of the building where he worked.

'Sophie? What are you doing in Preston?' David looked at his watch. 'Shouldn't you be at work?'

'It's my day off so I drove straight over. I've been standing here for at least twenty minutes. I've got a reply, can you believe it? From Ed Trask.'

'Calm down, and talk slowly.' He grabbed her arm and marched a few yards down the road towards a transport café. 'This might not be the best place but it's warm and dry.'

Without another word he sat her down at a table near the fire and returned shortly with two steaming mugs of tea. She took her drink gratefully.

'Look, Sophie, just because the man's replied, it doesn't mean –'

'He remembers her, that's the point. *He remembers Frances.*'

'He said that?' David was listening intently now.

'Yes – see for yourself.' She took the blue airmail letter out of her pocket and spread it over the table. 'Just read it. Please?'

David's eyes scanned the page. He handed the letter back to Sophie and took a gulp of tea. 'He's put his address on the top of the letter, and it's not the one we wrote to, so it must have been forwarded on to him. Which means he didn't mind being found.'

'Exactly. We've got the right man. The name, the place, the timing – everything fits.'

'But that doesn't make him your dad. Maybe he wouldn't be quite so forthcoming if he knew what you were angling after?'

'He had an affair with her, I'm sure of it. You can tell by the way he talks about her – look.'

David burst out laughing. 'That's the writer in you, and the romantic, if you don't mind me saying. This is the beginning of the seventies, Sophie. We're not starring in a forties romance.'

'I'm going with my gut feeling, that's all. Do you think he lied about the prisoner of war camp?' she persisted, ignoring the sarcasm.

'I don't know. That's the whole point. He could have been unaware that Frances was pregnant and simply gone back home to his wife when the war ended.

'Believe me, I know it's no fairy story, but if he did feel something for my mother, I reckon he must've had a good reason for leaving her behind.'

'Look, Sophie,' David put his hand on top of hers, 'most of these GIs – officers or not – expected to have their heads blown off. Getting your end away was par for the course.'

Instinctively, she removed her hand. 'What a delightful way to put it.'

'I'm sorry, but it's true. He might have loved her, he might not, but these men were fighting for their lives on the other side of the world. They probably couldn't wait to get home.'

'Well, whatever you say, I'm going to write back. I'll be careful, of course, before you start trying to warn me off. Aren't you just a little bit excited for me?'

'Of course I am. Why don't you stay over? It's Saturday tomorrow and I'm sure Jill won't mind.'

'Thanks. I could call at the flat and make a few phone calls, if that's all right with you, but I probably won't stay over as I've brought nothing with me.'

'Dinner tonight then? All three of us. I insist.'

'It's a deal.'

'So, did you have a good weekend?' Val took off her headset and grinned.

'Yes thanks,' Sophie nodded. 'Nothing special.'

'That's not what I heard.'

'Have you been gossiping again?' Sophie picked a pile of mail from the counter and began sorting through it.

'Nothing escapes me; you should know that by now. You've had a dirty weekend with that new boyfriend of yours.'

Sophie looked over her shoulder and pulled a face. 'For heaven's sake, don't say that, someone might hear you. David's just a friend, nothing more.'

'A friend you spend the night with?' Val laughed. 'I could do with a friend like that. So what about lover boy – is he still jealous?'

'If you mean Steve, why don't you find out where he's gone to? Then you can ask him yourself.' With that, she grabbed the rest of the post and headed for the stairs.

Back in editorial, Porchester was his usual Monday morning self.

'What time do you call this, Miss Wainwright,' he asked, glancing at the clock.

'One minute past nine,' she retorted, eyes flashing. 'You can deduct it from my unpaid overtime.'

'Less of your cheek, if you please.' He slapped a scribbled note on top of her desk. 'A lead's come in and I want you to chase it straight away. So what are you waiting for? Get to it girl.'

She flopped down at her desk. 'Yes Patrick. Right away, Patrick.'

The news editor was a hard taskmaster, everyone knew that, but for some reason he had a real grudge against Sophie. All the reporters did two night jobs a week, but Patrick often gave her three without a word of explanation. The town council meetings she didn't mind – they usually produced some good copy – but amateur dramatics and long-winded committee meetings of the townswomen's guild were always assigned to her when the reports could so easily have been sent in afterwards. Still, she'd had a long weekend and it'd been good to meet up with Jill again.

Thank goodness David's girlfriend wasn't the jealous type. What a pity that Steve hadn't reacted in the same way. She still hadn't heard a word since he left and whatever the reason for his 'sabbatical', it was clearly taking up all his time.

Fortunately Sophie was far too busy for the rest of the day to think about Steve. When everyone had gone home she put the lid on her typewriter, pulled out Ed Trask's letter and began to write a reply.

'Call yourself a writer?' she muttered, an hour or so later, screwing up another draft and throwing it into the waste bin where it joined a dozen others. Every single one started *Dear Mr Trask* followed by a list of reasons why she thought he might want to keep in touch. Was she reading too much into his letter? Maybe he simply wanted to be polite? But why would he admit he'd known her mother? It would've been so much easier to deny all knowledge. Or better still, not to have answered at all. The more she thought about it the more she knew she had to do something.

Her agony came to an abrupt end the following morning with the arrival of a second letter from America.

Dear Miss Wainwright

Have you ever been to Nice? Every year, at the beginning of June, I go on a European cruise which takes in several Mediterranean countries. The ship will be stopping in the South of France on August 12. Maybe you could fly over to meet me? Don't worry if this is too short notice but if you can make it, I'd be mighty glad to see you. Here's my plan...

Sophie glanced down at the itinerary. Her hands were shaking and she'd no idea whether to laugh hysterically or cry her heart out. Ed Trask wanted to meet her. That could only mean one thing.

'I'm coming with you, Sophie.' David's voice shrilled down the phone. 'Your precious Steve seems to have vanished off the face earth and you're not doing this on your own.'

'But why? We still don't know each other that well, and then there's Jill. How would she take it?'

'Never mind Jill, she trusts me. Besides, for some reason I feel like I've known you for years. Now – give me the dates and I'll get my secretary to book the flights. With your permission, of course.'

Sophie put down the receiver, her mind racing. She'd grown fond of David, though she'd never admit it to anyone, and having him with her in Nice would make the whole thing so much easier. If only Steve hadn't taken off so suddenly. If only they'd had more time to talk.

She stood up and ran her hands distractedly through her hair. She'd just had a letter from the man who might be her father and all she could think about was Steve. Straightening her skirt, she made for the door. She'd better get the meeting with Moulton over with. Not that it mattered. She was having this holiday whether he liked it or not.

CHAPTER 38
September 1969

Sophie stared out of the taxi window at the towering palm trees lining the Promenade des Anglais. Reaching out towards the sun, they looked more exotic than anything she'd seen in the travel books. She and David had caught the early morning flight and now the day stretched ahead of them. Normally she'd be excited to discover a place she'd only read about, but she was so frightened of meeting Ed Trask she could hardly speak.

'You all right, Sophie?' David squeezed her arm.

'Just nervous,' she forced a smile. 'I want to get it over with.'

'I am too, believe it or not, though God only knows why.'

She glanced at her watch. Ed Trask's ship docked in less than three hours and by the time they'd booked into the apartment and had something to eat, he would be waiting for them. On second thoughts, maybe she would skip the meal. The very idea of food at a time like this made her stomach churn. What would he look like? What on earth would she say? What if he didn't believe her story?

'A penny for them.' David's voice broke into her thoughts. 'You were obviously miles away.'

'I was just looking at the ocean. It's so blue – just as it is in photos only so much better somehow.'

'Is it hot enough for you?' He grinned.

'It's like being in an oven. I've never been so hot in my life.'

'Don't worry. The hottest time of the year is over now. Anyway, the flat's much cooler.'

The taxi turned left off the promenade and drove through the musicians' quarter, stopping outside a three-storey stone building with balconied windows and an enormous wooden front door opening onto the street.

David paid the taxi driver and produced an old fashioned key from the pocket of his waistcoat. 'Wait till you see this.'

She nodded appreciatively as they stepped into the ornate entrance hall. 'It's good of your friend to let us stay here.'

'He owes me a favour,' David winked, carrying their bags in each hand.

The ancient lift, with its black wrought iron gates and walnut interior, looked like the setting from a Hercule Poirot novel, Sophie mused, as it clunked and clanked its way to the first floor.

The high-ceilinged hall of the apartment led through to a magnificent living room, dominated by a huge white marble fireplace. At the far end two shuttered windows opened on to juliet balconies, which overlooked the busy street. There were two bedrooms, one single, one double, both scattered with fresh flowers.

Pulling her case into the smaller room, she sat down on the bed. 'What's the name of the place where we're meeting?' she called out.

'Hotel Negresco. It's one of the most famous in the world.'

'Do you think he knew that when he chose it?'

'I suspect so. Americans like to show off their money.'

Sophie swung round to see him grinning broadly.

'Just trying to wind you up. Relax. I'm sure he's a genuine guy.'

She picked up a copy of *Le Monde* from the bed and aimed it in his direction. 'Well I'm not going into a posh bar. I'm nervous enough already.'

'Don't worry, I'll see if I can steer him somewhere a bit less swanky. Now come on, put the kettle on. I could murder a cup of café noir.'

He was standing outside the magnificent hotel entrance, studying a map. Dressed in cream linen trousers with a matching casual jacket and colourful shirt, he wore dark glasses and a panama hat that almost hid his face. Sophie looked at her watch: two minutes before noon.

'That's him.' She grabbed David's arm. 'It's Ed, I know it is.'

'Okay,' he pushed her gently forward. 'Come on – head up and *smile*.'

'Mr Trask?' Her voice came out in a high pitched squeak.

The man looked up and held out his hand, his tanned face breaking into a smile. 'You must be Sophie?'

Nodding, she proffered a clammy palm. 'And this is my friend, David.'

'Pleased to meet you.' David's handshake was firm. 'I trust you are enjoying your trip?'

'Sure am. Good of you folks to come.'

Sophie stared at him in disbelief. She'd waited for this moment since she was old enough to talk and now she couldn't tear her eyes away.

Now in his mid-fifties, Ed Trask had clearly been good-looking when he was young. Despite the frown lines visible on his forehead, he seemed quite comfortable in his own skin. He took off his sunglasses to reveal definably arched eyebrows over deep green eyes, exact replicas of her own.

'Are you okay?' He was looking straight at her now.

'I'm fine,' she managed, wondering if they were both thinking the same thing.

Thankfully, David came to the rescue. 'There's a bistro further down the promenade where I know they'll make us welcome. Take it from me, the Negresco is just for wealthy tourists.'

Ed Trask burst out laughing. 'Well go on, buddy, I can't argue with that. We'll follow you.'

He fell into step beside Sophie as David led the way. 'You're a fine looking girl if I may say. Your mom must be very proud of you.'

To her embarrassment, she blushed. 'Thank you, Mr Trask.

That's very kind. I've got so many things to ask you, but I don't really know where to start.'

'Call me Ed,' he said amiably, 'and there's no rush. When we've gotten ourselves a table you can ask away as much as you like.'

It was all too correct, she thought, like a scene from a 1940's film. *So, did you love my mum? Do you think you could be my dad?* The words tumbled round inside her head. Why was he making small talk? Why didn't he just tell her the truth? From what she'd heard that was more the American way. She tried to keep walking at the same pace as the two men, her body taut with uncertainty.

At last they found themselves in a shaded bar on the edge of the beach. The table was covered with a white linen cloth neatly clamped underneath, she noted, to protect it from the breeze. Fresh flowers in vibrant colours adorned the centre, while overhead canopies in shades of white and beige protected them from the heat of the sun.

The waiter poured cold Chinon into Ed's glass. The older man took a sip and nodded his approval. Glancing around, he held up the glass. 'The views here are spectacular.'

After they'd placed their order, Ed turned at last to Sophie. 'I was a young man, no more than thirty when I first met your mom, and she was only just nineteen. She was beautiful, a picture, with dark wavy hair and cupid bow lips, like she'd just stepped out of the movies. She didn't know it of course, didn't rate her own looks, seeing as she'd been treated so bad...' he hesitated. 'You know she was in some kinda kids' home when she was a girl?'

Sophie nodded, scared that if she spoke he might stop.

'I was a captain at the time, serving in Leicester. Fran worked in the munitions factory across the fields. My men had come back to England for a rest – they'd had a pretty rough time out in Italy. Some rest it turned out to be, so many of 'em killed at Normandy. We'd never have met, your mom and me, if it hadn't been for....' he took a long sip of his wine.

'Don't worry,' David interrupted. 'We know about the court martial.'

'Yes, well, it's something I'd rather forget. None of it was Fran's fault. I wanted to make sure she was looked after, you know, she seemed kinda vulnerable. Look, I knew my men, but I had to be sure that none of them had stepped out of line... and if they had... well, I needed to fix it.'

'But they hadn't, had they?' Sophie's voice trembled. 'They hadn't stepped out of line?'

'No, ma'am. It was some guy from outside the camp. He got what he deserved. The division stood by your mom, had her stay in a hotel, made damn sure she got the best care.'

'Some guy?' David interrupted. 'Who was he?'

'It's not for me to say.'

'So who *is* going to say it?' David was getting angry now. 'Who's going to tell us the truth?'

Sophie leaned forward, unable to keep quiet any longer. 'Were you married at the time you knew my mother?'

Ed pushed his hands through his thick fair hair, now showing streaks of grey.

'Well now, I'd been a widow for about three years. My wife died in childbirth and our son soon after. I'm not making excuses for what I did. I guess I was lonely and your mom was the first woman I'd looked at since.'

'I'm sorry, that must have been awful for you.' To her surprise, Sophie meant it.

'There were times when I wanted to give up,' he shook his head. 'Fran gave me hope again.'

'But there's something I need to know.' Sophie held her breath. 'Did you feel the same way about Frances as she did about you?'

'Did I love her, is that what you mean? Yes, I did, very much. But you have to remember we're talking about a very different time. I was worried about my men. They'd arrived in England for a break but I knew they had much worse to come. We suffered quite heavy losses in Normandy, then just a couple o'months later we were back in Holland. Operation Market Garden was even bigger than Normandy, though we didn't know it at the time. I'd no idea if any of us would ever be coming back.'

'Nor had Frances.' Sophie could hear the accusation in her voice. 'But she waited. She waited for you, believe me. You've no idea for how long.'

Ed reached out and touched her arm. 'I always intended to go back for her, believe me, but I didn't know about the... hell, Sophie, I didn't know about you.'

'So what happened?'

'I dropped in Holland with my men. Most of them reached

their targets, but I was captured and sent to a POW camp. We had no way of communicating with the rest of the world, but I wrote to Fran all the same. Somehow I thought I could show her the letters after it was all over. As soon as I got back to Indiana and got myself fit again, I flew back to England. But by the time I got to Leicester, Fran had moved from the area. Nobody knew where she'd gone, or if she was even alive. It was as if she had just disappeared.'

Sophie felt light-headed. She knew more than ever now that this man was her father. She could still feel the heat on her skin where his hand had first touched her arm. He'd come thousands of miles to tell her what she'd waited her whole life to hear, but in the end he was still a stranger. He was still talking but, she realised with a jolt, she'd stopped listening. 'I'm sorry?'

'I was asking if your mom ever married.'

'Oh, no. I think she had the chance a few times, but she never wanted to. She always reminded me that my father was a US army officer. "One day," she'd say, "he'll come back to England and scoop us in his arms and we'll all be one big happy family. We'd go back to his homeland, and live on a great big ranch. When you're a child you just want to believe it."'

'It's sure as hell what I wanted.' Ed leaned back in his chair. 'Look, Sophie, there is something else I guess I should tell you, though it's going to be real hard.'

'I've come to Nice to hear what you've got to say.' She looked straight ahead, not daring to catch David's eye. 'Go on.'

'When I came back in forty-six to find Fran, I guessed there was a chance she'd still be waiting. I chased up the records from the Evington camp. It took time but I still had some clout back then so they let me have her address. It was what you English call a boarding house, in Leicester city, run by some mighty strange folk.

'You went there?' David's eyes narrowed. 'To Hastings Place? Why didn't you say so before?'

'I was waiting for the right moment.' Ed beckoned to the waiter. 'I found it, yes, but I wasn't made welcome. The lady said Fran had gone away, and she sure as hell wouldn't be coming back. Reckoned she hadn't paid her rent for weeks, had left in the middle of the night owing them money.'

Sophie held her breath. 'Did you believe her?'

'I guess I didn't know what to believe. The dame didn't like me, that was obvious. I thought she was maybe trying to protect Fran from me. A Yank – more than ten years older than your mom. She couldn't get rid of me quick enough.'

'But what about me? I must have been a year old by then. Surely the landlady mentioned a child?'

'Not a word, I swear.'

'What else did this woman tell you?' David interjected

'Aw, nothing. I didn't believe it, anyhow, not about Fran. She was so sweet, so young, like she never wanted to grow up.'

'What didn't you believe?' David would not be put off.

Ed paused as the waiter poured their drinks, clearly glad of the distraction. 'She said she'd found another guy after I left. Reckoned it was a waste of time waiting for a GI who ain't never gonna come back.'

Sophie froze. This proved that Betty Newby had lied about the past. But why? What had Frances done to make the old woman hate her so much? None of it made sense. Ed Trask believed that she, Sophie, was his daughter – why else would he come halfway across the world to meet her? And she knew it too. She had inherited his eyes, his sandy-coloured hair and his air of defiance that had become her shield against the world.

'Thank you for telling me,' she said, breaking the silence. Longing to ask more, she turned instead to David. 'Shall we order now?'

'Go ahead.' His anger was palpable and she wondered if Ed could sense it, too.

'Tell me about your childhood,' Ed asked amiably. 'It's a credit to your mom that you've grown into such a fine woman.'

She told him what she could, skating over the poverty and the nature of Frances's illness. The poor man seemed to have suffered enough.

To her surprise, David said little, his eyes lost in the distance. Why had his mother lied? He clearly didn't know the answer.

'What will you do now, Ed?' Sophie asked when they finally finished the meal. He seemed to hesitate, as if wondering for a moment what she meant.

'I will carry on to Naples,' he said, smiling, 'glad that I got to meet you at last. You sure have got your mom's spirit.'

'Forgive me. I need to go to the powder room.' Gulping back the tears, Sophie pushed back her chair and left the table.

As soon as she was out of earshot, Ed Trask's face clouded over. 'You're a good friend to Sophie – right?'

David nodded. He was still trying to absorb the fact that his mother had lied.

'Planning on getting hitched, are you?'

'Oh, no – nothing like that. I have a girlfriend back in England.'

'You could do worse you know, son.'

'It's not going to happen, I'm afraid.' *What was wrong with everyone? Why did they keep trying to push the two of them together?*

'Pity. Either way, I have to tell you that I'm too old for this, godammit. It's too late for me to add to my family now. I thought one hell of a lot of her mother, but it was a long time ago and I'm a different guy now. My wife and I split up a few years ago. We have three grown daughters and, who knows, maybe some grandkids soon.'

'So that's what you came all this way to say?' David's anger flared again and this time he didn't mind showing it. 'Sophie doesn't want anything from you, if that's what you're thinking.'

'Hell no, I don't think she's after my money. She's a swell girl and I meant it when I said she's just like her mom. But I reckon she'd be best to go home and forget all about me.'

'You say you have daughters back home? Would it have made any difference if Sophie had been a boy?' It was cruel but he had to say it.

For a moment neither of them spoke.

'I can see why you think that, David, but I lost my son a long time ago, and either way I wouldn't be looking to replace him. Does that answer your question?'

David donned his sunglasses and stared out to sea. 'I appreciate your honesty. I'll try to explain to Sophie how you feel, but it won't be easy. That's what you want me to do, isn't it?'

The other man nodded. 'It's hard for you to believe right now, but it's for the best.'

'Will you keep in touch?'

'Maybe. Who knows? She's a great girl, David. Seems to me she kinda needs a man to look after her. I reckon I can rely on you.'

'I'll do my best, sir.' His anger was abating now, a tight band of disappointment squeezing his chest. There was nothing to be gained by prolonging the meeting, especially as Ed Trask did not intend to break the news himself.

'Will you give her something for me?' Ed reached into his inside pocket and brought out an envelope. 'There's a letter in there that I'd kinda like Sophie to read. I've kept it a long time but I guess it's finally gonna find a home.'

Taking the envelope, David stood up. 'I hope we've done the right thing, getting in touch with you after all these years. I just wish it could have been different.'

'Me too, son, me too. You did right, both of you, if that makes this thing any easier.' With that Ed stood up and signalled the waiter. 'Don't forget to give her the letter. Oh, and let me take care of the bill.'

'He doesn't want me, does he? He doesn't want to know.' Sophie faced David full on, her eyes accusing. She'd been so upset when she'd found Ed gone that they'd walked in stony silence back to the apartment. 'I can't believe it. He didn't even wait to say goodbye.'

'Look, it's not that simple. He wouldn't have arranged to meet you if he didn't want to know you. He *is* your father, there's no doubt about it. It's hard for him, that's all...' David's voice trailed away.

'Hard for *him?* Whose side are you on?'

I'm trying to help, but you're not making it easy.' David sighed as she followed him through the heavy front door. He pulled out a sealed envelope. 'Ed gave me this to give to you.'

She snatched it from him and slammed it down on the table. 'So he's gone for good, has he?' Flinging open the wooden shutters, she stepped out on the balcony.

'He thought it was for the best,' David said evenly. 'He just didn't want to prolong the goodbye.'

'The best for him, you mean.' Sophie leaned over the railings as the traffic rushed by beneath her.

'I think it's just all come too late,' he said. 'He's not proud of what happened but his life has moved on. He has three grown-up daughters at home and is looking forward to having grandchildren.'

'How lovely for him.' She turned back to face him, her eyes

swollen with tears. 'I'm sorry, David. That was unnecessary. So what happens now?'

'He's gone back to the ship. They're sailing for Naples tonight. I'd read the contents of the letter if I were you, then you can decide what you want to do.'

Seconds later he was gone.

She picked up the envelope, her hands shaking. A brief note, scribbled on cruise ship notepaper, was attached to the front. So this was how her father planned to say goodbye. She scanned the note, the blood draining from her face. *Dear Sophie I hope this tells you what you want to know. Please forgive me – for everything. Yours, Ed.* Inside the envelope was a single sheet of paper, yellowed with age, the handwriting faded but still legible.

My dearest Fran

I may not get a chance to see you again, my darling, for quite some time. The Jerries got me in the end, but I sure as hell hope I'll be back. So far they haven't treated us too bad. The food goes down OK, though I couldn't half murder a donut right now. Trouble is, we can't get letters in or out, so I've no way of letting you know where I am. But I'm writing this anyway- it makes me feel closer to you.

These last couple of months with you have made me come alive again – something I never thought would happen. I believed that side of me had gone forever when I buried my wife and son.

I love you, Frances Wainwright, and that's why I'm writing to you now. If anything happens to me I hope you will always hold on to these words. I want you to be strong while I'm away, to keep those beautiful brown eyes smiling and think only about the future when I will finally take you back home.

Be brave.

Yours always

Ed XXX.

CHAPTER 39

David boarded the train to Monaco, a trip he usually enjoyed. Sophie deserved some space and he needed time to think about the whole damn mess. To his right, foam-topped waves washed onto beaches the colour of pure gold, to the left hills and mountains rose up over the glorious skyline. Today, though, the views seemed something of a mockery, his mother's cruel actions still crowding his mind. Why would she lie to Ed – a man who'd come halfway round the world to claim his bride? And was his father in on the whole thing, too?

As a child David had never felt close to his mother, but now it seemed he'd never really known her at all. She'd had a grudge against Frances, that much was obvious, and years later she'd shunned Sophie too. What had made her so bitter? If his mother had lied to him all these years then he wanted to know why.

From the moment he'd met Sophie, David felt like they'd always been friends. Why else would he help her, why would he let her into his life? He and Jill had been together for two years now and he knew she trusted him, but how much longer would she put up with the situation? He'd even suggested she come with them to Nice but Jill had politely refused.

Even Ed seemed to assume that he and Sophie were a couple and that made him feel uncomfortable. Maybe he'd been rash to suggest they make the trip together – what if she expected something more from him? She seemed intelligent, feisty, and amazingly strong in many ways. Sophie had grown up without a father and still managed somehow to deal with her alcoholic mother, but underneath he sensed a real vulnerability. However hard he tried, he just couldn't work out what drew him to her.

One day Sophie would make it to the nationals, her innate sense of justice trying to seek out the truth. She cared about the underdog more than anyone he'd ever met. Similar in age to Sophie, David's background couldn't have been more different. While she'd left school at fifteen to earn a living, he'd been head boy of the county's top grammar, reading English at a red-brick university in the south of England. Moving away from Leicester and his doting parents had been the best thing that ever happened to him, and a first class honours degree in fine arts had been his reward. Luck intervened in the shape of his roommate in halls, whose father was a director of GEC, one of the world's largest engineering companies. Offered a lowly job in personnel, David was told,

'If you balls it up, you're out on your ear, there's no room for dimwits here'. He'd moved quickly into the PR department, travelling around the globe, and at twenty-four had been promoted to assistant departmental manager.

Making his way through the streets of Monaco, David felt a twinge of guilt at his own good fortune. His head jerked up as a car horn screeched in protest, the red Ferrari narrowly missing his feet. What the hell was he doing here dwelling on the past? He should be with Sophie right now. In twenty-four hours they'd be back home.

Harcot Magistrates' Court seemed busier than usual when Sophie arrived. Trust Patrick to make her cover court on her first day back. With its lofty ceilings and oak-panelled walls, the stone and brick building buzzed with activity as solicitors, clerks and uniformed police mingled with members of the public.

Both Court One and Court Two had cases that might make a decent story, but as she had no help this morning, Sophie had to make a choice. She stared again at the court lists, absentmindedly sucking the end of her pencil.

'Can I have a quick word?'

Sophie swung round. 'Steve! What on earth are you doing here? I'd no idea you were back.'

'Look, I'm sorry, it won't take a minute but we have to speak. It's really important or I wouldn't have come.'

She looked at her watch. 'I don't even have a minute, I'm sorry – can't it wait?'

'I had to come back, to see Julie. I've been on the other side of the world, or believe me, I would've come sooner.'

'To see Julie?'

'Yes, I owed it to her, and to you.'

Sophie looked up at the sound of the clerk's voice. 'That's Court Number One – I'm sorry – I have to go. Come to the flat after work. Seven o'clock.'

'So what did you have to tell me about Julie that just couldn't wait?'

Steve's face darkened. 'She was lying, Sophie, about the baby. She's admitted it all now.'

'But why? Why would she lie about something so important? I don't understand.'

'Oh, I don't know, she had some sort of crush on me it seems, but I never encouraged her. She just wanted to scare you off.'

Sophie looked at Steve, his hair dishevelled, his chin covered in dark stubble. He looked so vulnerable standing there that she wanted to gather him up in her arms and tell him everything would be all right. But it was much too late for that now. Instead she said, 'Julie came to me for help, or so I thought. She seemed genuinely frightened, like a small child. I told her there was nothing I could do.'

'No, Sophie, you're not listening. She wanted to scare you off and she succeeded, didn't she?'

'Well, it's not as if there was anything between us, was there? Nothing that she could be jealous of?'

'Not if you say so.' He sighed.

'What's more, I already knew she had a crush on you.'

'You did? How?'

'Where do I start?' She told him about the Miss Harcot competition.

Steve listened in amazement, pacing up and down the room. 'So you knew she was barmy? Why didn't you say something?'

'I suppose I thought you got what you deserved.'

'Do you still feel that now?'

'No.' She stood up, breathing in the woody aroma of his aftershave. Resisting him was harder than she'd ever imagined. 'So is that all? It's been a long day and I need something to eat before I expire.'

Steve's face lit up. 'Have you got any eggs?'

'That's about all I have got – why?'

'Scrambled eggs are my speciality. Let me make you some as a peace offering. I use the top of the milk and lots of butter. You won't regret it, I promise.'

'Ok,' she relented, 'but after the eggs, that's it. We part as friends – agreed?

'Agreed.'

'Right, Frigidaire – lead me to the kitchen.'

After they'd eaten Steve poured them each a glass of lager. 'You haven't told me about your trip. That's the other reason I wanted to see you. Did you find your father? Are you now officially a US citizen?' The light-hearted quip belied the serious look on his face.

'Nothing like that, no, but I did meet my father. He came

over to Nice on a cruise.'

'Sounds like more than just a coincidence. Go on.'

She took a sip of her drink. 'Captain Ed Trask, formerly of the US 82nd Airborne Division based in Leicestershire, England is now divorced with three grown-up children. How can I describe him? Very polite, very correct, smart with lots of sandy-coloured hair greying at the temples – what the *Daily Sketch* would probably call *your all-American man*.'

'And he admitted that he knew your mother?'

'Much more than that. Oh, Steve, they had a passionate affair. You should have heard him reminiscing. Fran, he called her, and his face lit up when he talked about their brief time together. At least now I know it wasn't just a fling. He said he intended to marry her after the war.'

'So what happened?'

'He took his men to the Netherlands, Operation Market Garden, I think he called it, or something like that. He was captured and spent the rest of his time in a German prisoner of war camp.'

'Why didn't he keep in touch with Frances?'

'He wrote to her several times apparently, but the Germans sabotaged the mail. Anyway, she never received them.' Sophie stood up and opened the sideboard drawer. 'This is one he never sent.'

Steve scanned the letter, shaking his head as he handed it back to her. 'So he did love her, that much is obvious. How does that make you feel?'

'It makes me feel I *was* wanted after all. At first, I admit I felt rejected, especially as he left without saying goodbye.' She told him what had happened.

'I'm sorry, I'd no idea.'

'Don't be. I've thought about nothing else since. Strangely, I don't despise him for feeling it's too late. I should do but I don't.'

His face softened. 'D'you think you'll ever see him again?'

'Who knows? Maybe one day. But for now I have got the answer to the question I've been asking the whole of my life.'

Steve stood up and walked across to the window. 'And what about David? Where does he fit into all this?'

'He's been very good to me. We still, well, have a lot to talk about.'

'I should have gone with you, Sophie. Why him? Just tell me. Why is he prepared to do so much for you?'

'I don't know. We just seemed to hit it off the minute we met.' She bit her lip. She owed Steve more than that. 'Okay, he reckons his mother was lying when she said she didn't remember me. He's convinced Frances was living in his parents' house when I was born.'

'But why would she lie? What could she possibly have had to gain from it?'

'Exactly. But when my father came back to find Frances after the war, it seems she lied to him too. She said my mother had gone off with another man.'

'That woman caused a lot of trouble. I can see why you and David need some answers.' Steve stood up. 'I'm sorry, Sophie, sorry that I've been so stupid. I wish I'd been around to help.'

'It doesn't matter now. You have helped, just not in the way you imagined. We can catch up again – as friends, of course.'

'Thank you. I'd like that.' He headed for the door.

'Oh, and Steve?'

'Yes?'

'You didn't say where you'd been?'

'The States. A big hippy festival. You'd have loved it.'

CHAPTER 40

November 1944

'Sit down, Arthur, I've something to tell you.'

'All right, I'm coming.' Her husband folded the paper and sank into his chair.

'Our young lodger Frances Wainwright is in the family way.'

'She's what?' He sprang forward. 'Then she'll have to go.'

'Just listen, will you?' Betty Newby laid her hand on his arm. 'I've got an idea.'

'Well, it'd better be a good one. We've built up a reputation here over the years and I don't want it spoiled by some little –'

'She won't be able to keep the baby. She's no money, no home, so it will have to be adopted.'

'That's not our problem. She's lucky we haven't thrown her out already. What's wrong, Bet? Are you losing your grip?'

'There is another solution – that's all I'm saying.'

A strange look came over Arthur's face. 'You're not suggesting that we –?'

'That's exactly what I am suggesting. We let her stay here until the child's born and then she hands over the baby. We give her some money to help her set up home – in the north of England maybe, you've got friends in Blackpool – then adopt the child officially.'

Arthur scratched his head. 'You've really thought this through, haven't you?'

'I've thought about nothing since she told me the news. It's our one chance, Arthur, our only chance. We're both over forty now and we'll never get another opportunity like this.'

'Have you mentioned it to her?'

'Don't be such a fool. Of course I haven't. She thinks she has to leave now that I've discovered her little secret. But she's nowhere to go and she'll lose her job as soon as they find out about the baby. No, I reckon we should offer her free board in exchange for help around the place, cleaning, cooking, that sort of thing. She says she can type so she could maybe help with the books.'

'Oh, I don't know about that.'

'You don't know about much, do you?' Betty snorted. 'We have to be sure she doesn't suspect anything. Then, when the child's born, we'll tell her the employment's come to an end. We'll be doing her a favour in the long run, just you see.'

'Well, I hope you're right. Though I'm not sure she'll see it that way. Do we know who the father is?'

'She's not likely to tell me that now, is she – that's if she even knows. But the child will grow up respectable because we'll make sure it does. A good home, education, manners, that sort of thing. What do you say?'

He considered for a moment. 'Let's offer her a job and see what happens. After all, we don't even know if she's telling us the truth about her condition.'

'Of course we do. I've heard her being sick in the mornings. Besides, women know about these sorts of things. Just leave the details to me. We'll make a father of you yet, Arthur Newby.'

'I'm giving in my notice, Irene.'

'Your notice? How in heaven's name is that going to help?' Irene hit the power button to stop the lathe and turned round, her mouth wide open.

'Come along, stop chatting you two, or I'll make one of ya move on to another machine.' Mick Ford's words echoed across the factory floor.

'They've offered me a job in return for board and lodgings,' Frances hissed. 'Cleaning, cooking, that sort of thing.'

'And why would they do that?'

'I don't know, but I'd be stupid not to take it.'

'I won't tell you again. Now quit it, both of you, will you?'

Irene gestured at the foreman's back and returned to her machine.

It was lunchtime before they got a chance to talk again. The two women were queuing up in the canteen as Glen Miller blared from the loudspeaker.

'What'll 'appen after – you know, me duck?' Irene glanced round to make sure no one was listening.

'I don't know,' said Frances. 'I'll have to worry about it then. But I'd be stupid to turn the job down, don't you see? I won't have to listen to people here gossiping, and they'll throw me out, anyway, won't they, as soon as I show?'

Irene shook her head. 'I dunno. It don't seem right somehow. But you're happy wi'it, I can see that, so I'll give you me blessing. Just mek sure you keep in touch, that's all. You're gonna need some 'elp when the time comes.'

Impulsively, Frances kissed her on the cheek. 'I don't know what I'd do without you.'

'Heyup!' One of the canteen girls was laughing at them now. 'Get yer 'ands off her or you'll put us all off us dinners.'

Several people in the queue turned to look at them, but Irene just pulled a face. 'You'll get me in real trouble one of these days, you will, our Franny. Now get yer food down yer afore it gets cold.'

'Can I have half a bottle of vodka please?'

The barman eyed Frances suspiciously, grabbed a bottle from the shelf behind him and banged it onto the counter. 'Anything else, *Miss*?'

'No, that'll be all, thanks,' she said, ignoring the sarcasm. She handed him a ten shilling note.

'Are you carrying it like that?' He was staring at her burgeoning stomach. 'Or have you got a bag?'

'I can manage thank you very much.' She pulled the

patchwork shopping bag from under her coat – the one Ma Hampton had given to her before she left the orphanage – and deposited her purchase inside.

Leaving the off sales, Frances lifted her chin in defiance. It was impossible to hide her condition any more so she'd better get a curtain ring to wear on her wedding finger. That way she'd feel more at ease with strangers. Decision made, she walked the three or so miles back home, let herself in the front door and mounted the stairs two at a time. Once in her room she opened the bottle, took a gulp of vodka and closed her eyes, waiting for the numbness to take effect.

'I'm sorry baby, really I am. I'll cut down on the drink, I promise.' She stroked the soft mound of her stomach. Would the child be drinking the alcohol too? Could it be born drunk? She must stop, but how else could she get through the day? It had been bad enough at the factory, but since she'd started working for the Newbys several weeks before, life was almost intolerable. Why they had let her stay she would never know. Whatever their reasons, they were certainly getting their money's worth out of her. Every day she cleaned and polished the dining and sitting rooms, did the laundry and helped with the meals, as well as typing out invoices and sorting out ration books.

Gulping down the last of the vodka, she screwed the top on tightly. 'I'm not having you adopted, baby bump, I promise. When the time comes we'll find somewhere to live. No one's going to take you away from me.'

'You're a fair size for your dates, Mrs Wainwright.' The midwife eyed the tape measure wrapped round Frances's stomach. 'You must've been eating a lot of the right things.'

'It's my landlady – she insists on serving me more than everyone else. And it's Miss Wainwright. My fiancé is away fighting for our country. I'm expecting him home soon and then we'll be married.'

The midwife stared at the notes in front of her. 'I'm sure you can't wait, my dear, but in the meantime I'll call you Frances. Now let me listen to baby's heart.'

She wielded a sort of metal trumpet and gently pressed it against the taught skin.

'Loud and clear,' the older woman smiled. 'That's one of the strongest heartbeats I've heard for a long time. Now then dear, just one more thing. Will you be staying with your landlady after the birth?'

'Oh no, Ed and I, we'll be taking the baby back to America. After we're married, of course.'

The midwife stood up. 'I see. In the meantime it's always worth making contingency plans. It stops you being disappointed.'

Frances slipped off the couch and buttoned up her blouse. 'I assure you I won't be disappointed. Ed promised me that he would come home.'

CHAPTER 41

May 1945

'Where's my baby – where's my baby girl?' Frances stared up at the ceiling. Something was wrong. 'Where am I?'

'You're in an ambulance, Mrs Wainwright.' The midwife placed the child, wrapped in a woollen blanket, onto her mother's chest.

'How is she – will she live?'

'She's tiny, very tiny, but perfect all the same. Whatever happens you must try to be very brave.'

Very brave, very brave, the words swam round in her head. Where had she heard those words before?

Leaning forward to stroke the child's head, Frances felt a sharp stab in her stomach. She let out a yelp. 'Please take the baby. I'm still having pains. They feel like contractions. What is it? What's wrong with me?'

'It's all right, Mrs Wainwright,' the midwife's voice was soothing. 'It's only the afterbirth. You'll soon be right as rain.'

Another sharp pain swept over her body and Frances began to shake. 'What's happening? I'm scared.'

'Let me take a little look.' The older woman's brow furrowed. 'That's strange –'

'What is it – tell me?'

'There's no sign of the afterbirth. It's nothing to worry about, Mrs Wainwright, you just need to stay calm.'

Frances shrieked as another wave of pain rolled over her.

'Am I bleeding to death?'

'No, of course not.' The midwife placed the trumpet on Frances's stomach. 'Just stay there, very still. I think I'm going to need some help.'

'But why, if there's nothing wrong?' The pain was sweeping over her again, stronger than before.

'Because I don't think your daughter was alone in there. I think there may be another baby.'

Another baby, another baby, the words whirled round in Frances's head. She heard the ambulance screech to a halt, and she yelled with pain as they lifted her on to a stretcher.

Someone shouted, 'We need the doctor *now.*' Then she heard a man's deep voice uttering a jumble of words *Forceps... breech position... Good God, there's definitely another one... Just breathe deeply for me, Mrs Wainwright. We're doing the best we can.'*

'Arghhhhhhhhh...' This time she could stand it no more.When she came to, she heard the midwife say,

'Congratulations, Mrs Wainwright. You have a healthy baby boy.'

Frances lay back, the sweat pouring from her face. What had happened to her daughter? Did someone say she had a son? She could see Ed now, his face smiling down at her.

'Here we are.' The midwife placed the child in Frances's arms as his eyes blinked open. They were strong blue eyes with long fair lashes, just like his father.

'I don't understand. Another baby? What's happening to me?'

'You've had twins, Mrs Wainwright. This has come as a shock, naturally, and it will take some getting used to. Now just try to rest.'

Frances nodded, her eyelids slowly pulling her down towards sleep. Had she just had a baby, or was it a dream? Nothing seemed to make sense any more. She could hear the cry of a child, so maybe she should stay awake. Ed would be here soon and she had so much to tell him. Soon everything would be all right.

'Mrs Wainwright is asleep at the moment, I'm afraid, Mrs Newby.' Matron looked up from her work. 'She's had a very traumatic time. I take it you are a relative?'

'I'm her adopted auntie,' Betty lied with ease. 'Her poor mother died some years ago. There's no... well, father of the baby, if you know what I mean. I'm all she's got now.'

'I think you'd better sit down, Mrs Newby. This is going to come as a shock.'

'Why?' Her heart missed a beat. 'Has something happened to the baby?'

'No, the baby's fine. In fact they both are.'

'Then, that's good news, isn't it?' Betty felt a surge of relief. 'I thought you were going to tell me something was wrong.'

'When I say they're both fine – I mean both babies.'

'Both babies? You mean – ?'

'Yes. Your niece has had twins. One a healthy boy and the other a sickly girl.'

'But that's impossible. Why didn't anyone know?'

'We don't understand enough about it, I'm afraid, but it seems both babies were conceived at the same time and grew in separate amniotic sacs. What we call fraternal twins. In this case, however, one twin seems to have had more sustenance than the other.'

'So the boy's all right then?' Betty Newby clasped her hands together to stop them trembling.

'He is indeed, but I'm afraid the little girl is very poorly. I doubt if she'll live till the morning. Would you like me to arrange for the hospital chaplain to visit?'

'Oh yes, thank you, that's very kind. But in the meantime my husband and I can look after the boy at home. We've everything ready, and it will give Frances some time alone with her daughter.'

'That's extremely kind of you Mrs Newby. As I said, the little boy is perfectly healthy. There's no need for him to stay in hospital, though the midwife will have to visit you at home first, to check everything's in order. And,' she lowered her voice to a whisper, 'your niece seems rather confused. It's understandable, of course, under the circumstances. She will need complete rest.'

'I see.' Betty Newby arranged her mouth into a sympathetic smile.

'And what about the baby's milk? Will Frances be able to express some milk so that we can take it home?'

'All in good the time. We have the little girl to think of now.' The matron stood up, bringing the meeting to an end. 'As I said, the mother is very tired at the moment. Now if you will excuse me, I must get on.'

Frances woke with a start. She peered through the artificial light at the face of a stranger looming over her. 'Who are you? Where am I?'

'You're in hospital, Mrs Wainwright. I'm Nurse Dawkins on the night shift. Your little girl is very tiny, but she's a fighter. We're doing everything we can.'

'What are you talking about?' Frances forced her head off the pillow. 'I don't have a girl, I have a son. That's what my husband wanted. Where is he? Where is my son?'

'You do have a son, and he's fine. He's being looked after by your relatives. You've had twins, boy and a girl. Isn't that wonderful? It's been quite a shock, I expect.'

'What do you mean my relatives? I don't have any relatives. Where's Edward junior? I want to see him now.'

'Please don't worry,' the nurse smiled. 'You're tired and confused. It's been quite an ordeal. I'm going to give you an injection to make you feel more relaxed. Just stay calm, Mrs Wainwright, and everything will be fine.'

'Will you stop calling me that? My name is Mrs Trask.'

'Yes, of course, Mrs Trask.' Shaking her head, the nurse put out the light.

CHAPTER 42

'Are you sure we'll get away with this?' Arthur Newby followed his wife through to the bedroom. 'What if Frances objects?'

'She's not going to object. She's not in a fit state. Anyway, we're just looking after the little lad for now.'

'I don't know, Betty. I'm just worried, that's all. It doesn't seem right seeing how, you know, the little girl's not expected to survive.'

'Oh, don't trouble yourself with that. When Frances hears what we're offering she'll come round to our way of thinking. What's more, I heard the nurses talking. She's gone a bit funny in the head. She might not be capable of being a mother. You'll soon have a son and heir, mark my words. That's all you need to think about now.'

Arthur scratched his head as a nervous smile emerged from behind his moustache and crept across his face. 'Forty-eight years old and I'm going to be a father. Whoever would have thought it, eh?'

'It's no more than you deserve. We'll be the toast of the neighbourhood for taking him in – you mark my words.'

'So what are we going to call him?'

'I think we should call him David. It's a Bible name and it's what I wanted to call the one we lost.' She pulled out a handkerchief and wiped the corner of her eye. 'And I reckon it suits him, don't you?'

'David Arthur Newby,' said Arthur, as he peered into the wooden crib where the baby was sleeping peacefully. 'Welcome home, son.'

Frances crashed through the front door, marched down the hall and burst into the Newbys' living room.

'What on earth do you think you're –?' Betty Newby stopped, open mouthed, when she saw the intruder.

'Frances, my dear girl what are you doing here?'

'I've come to see my son. You've stolen him from me.'

Betty's flushed cheeks rapidly began to pale. 'There's no need to get upset. We're just looking after Dav... er, the boy, while you get your strength back.'

'While you wait for my daughter to die, more like. You must think I'm stupid. Do you think I don't know what you're up to?'

'You obviously need to concentrate on your daughter just now, so we've offered to help out, that's all.'

'Her name is Sophie and she may be very tiny, but she's a

fighter. She hung on to Ed in the womb and she's certainly not going to leave him now.'

Betty Newby sat down and fanned her face with a newspaper. 'The child has gone for a walk in his pram with his... with Mr Newby, but they'll be back in a moment. It might be better if you speak to my husband.' She frowned. 'And who, may I ask, is Ed?'

'He's my son.' Frances shrieked. 'What have you done with him?' She ran through to the bedroom. 'Where is he? Where's my baby?'

'As I said, Arthur's taken him out for a walk.' The older woman's face softened. 'Now why don't you get yourself back to the hospital? Your daughter must be missing you, poor little mite. Right now she needs her mother.'

'I'm staying here until I see Edward.' Frances sat firmly down firmly on the sofa. 'And there's nothing you can do to stop me.'

Arthur's face paled the minute he walked through the door. 'Frances! My dear girl. What are you doing here? Shouldn't you be in hospital?'

'I've come to see my son.' Frances ran to the pram and swept the baby into her arms. Burying her head in the folds of his shawl, she wept.

'Come, come you poor dear,' Betty's voice was controlled. 'We're looking after him for you, so you've no need to worry. 'When your daughter is,' she hesitated, 'when she's better, we can all talk about what we're going to do.'

'What do you mean, what we're going to do?' Frances

clutched her son tightly to her chest.

'We'll help you, just see if we don't. We'll look after the little lad good and proper. You can have money, to make a new life for yourself.'

'I don't want a new life, you stupid woman.' Frances rocked the child backwards and forwards in her arms. 'You don't know what you're talking about. I want my *son*.'

Arthur's face turned the colour of dead violets. 'How can you look after him when your own daughter's at death's door? You're hardly in a state to look after yourself.' His eyes scanned her slippered feet, the coat thrown hastily over her nightgown.

Frances started to sob, trying to make them see sense, stumbling over her words as the baby grew heavy in her arms. She felt someone tugging at the baby's shawl, pulling him from her till he slipped out of her grasp. Desperate now, she lunged forward and grabbed at the child's feet. A single white bootee came away in her hand. Blindly, she stuffed it into her pocket, screaming, the noise so loud that she thought her head would burst. 'Please, please give him back... please don't take my baby...' Then everything went black.

Over the next few days and weeks, Frances retreated inside her own world, an ethereal world where no one could reach her. Sometimes she thought she heard her brother, Bobby, calling out from heaven. *Come and join us Franny – we're all here. It's not such a bad place. Mum and Dad are missing you and Mum still cries because she thinks you're not happy.*

We're waiting for you, so hurry up and then we can be together again.

Sometimes she could see people crowding in front of her – paratroopers marching together, holding their rifles over their heads. When she looked closer they were heading towards a row of planes, their guns turning into parachutes. One after the other, the men climbed into the planes, keeping their eyes straight ahead. But now Ed was waving at her frantically as his plane taxied down the runway. *Quick, come with me, Fran. Do it now before it's too late.* She ran, faster than she ever thought possible, till her feet left the ground and her body floated into the air. She reached out her arms, stretching out towards the sun's rays, catching hold of them and climbing upwards. But when she looked again, Ed had disappeared into the clouds.

When she finally woke, Frances was back in her hospital bed.

'Thought she'd never come back,' she heard someone whisper.

'Withdrawal symptoms,' said another. 'She's addicted to drink. It's the same as coming off drugs.'

'And what about the twins?'

'They've been having the same symptoms, too. The boy's getting better – he's gone home now – good job his auntie's offered to look after him. But we're worried about the girl. There's still hardly a scrap of weight on her, poor little mite.'

Frances pretended to be asleep. So that was it. The Newbys had been planning it all along. They'd let her stay on at

Hastings Place so that they could steal her son.

As for the girl – it would be better for everyone if she just died. Besides, didn't Ed say he wanted a son? She rolled over and curled herself into a ball. Damn the wretched Newbys. How could she have been so stupid?

'We've got some good news, Mrs Wainwright.' The nurse was smiling broadly.

'Is it about my son?'

'It's your daughter – she's finally responding to treatment. Her breathing's improved and she's managing to keeping down her milk. It may take some time but there's a good chance now that she'll recover.'

Frances raised herself up on the pillows. 'So I can take them both home, is that what you're saying?'

'We need to keep Sophie for a while longer yet. We've arranged for a doctor to see you later this afternoon. You've been quite poorly yourself, Mrs Wainwright, and it might help to talk things through.'

'I don't want to talk to anyone, thanks.'

'That's a pity because you have a visitor. I'll just make you comfortable and then I'll send her in.'

'What are you doing here?' Francis glared at the intruder. 'Have you come to take Sophie as well?'

'Don't be ridiculous.' Betty Newby clutched her handbag in front of her chest. 'We're pleased, me and Arthur, that the little girl is improving, but we have no intention of taking her from you. Quite the opposite, in fact.'

'Please get on with it.' Frances spat out the words. 'What is it you want from me exactly?'

'You do realise, of course, that you cannot continue to live in our home. And without us, your children would be taken away from you.' She shuffled uncomfortably in her chair. 'We're happy to assist you by taking care of your son, providing you agree to leave Leicester and never return. We intend to give you an allowance once we have reached an agreement. Mr Newby has a friend who can find you some rooms in Blackpool. You must go as soon as you are fit and take the girl with you.'

'Allowance? Blood money, more like.' Anger surged from the back of Frances's throat, filling her mouth with the bitter taste of bile.

'There are conditions, yes. You must sign a form to say that David is officially ours.'

David. So they'd given him a name him without telling her.
'And what if I don't?'

'Then you may find it hard to get somewhere to live – or any means of support, ever again.'

Frances covered her face with her hands. 'Why are you doing this to me?'

'The boy will be better with us and he'll have a proper future. You'll be grateful to us one day, just you wait and see'

'And Sophie? What do I tell her when she grows up?' Frances lunged forward. 'That I gave her brother away? Or that he was *stolen* from me?'

Betty Newby stood up. 'You're tired and emotional. Please think very carefully about this. I'll be back tomorrow for your decision.'

CHAPTER 43

November 1969

Sophie stared in the mirror. She'd been up since dawn reading her mother's diary. Leaning forward, she peered at the face in front of her, as if for the first time. Yesterday she knew who she was. Or thought she did. Today she had no idea. All she could think about was David. David who had been so kind to her. David, Betty Newby's son. David, her twin *brother*. She covered her face with her hands and began to sob, the tears sliding down through her fingers and soaking through her nightdress on to her skin. She had to tell him. She owed him that at the very least. But how?

If only they'd never met, if only she'd never made contact. But it was too late for that now. She'd drawn him into this nightmare and now he would have to suffer too. No wonder Betty Newby had been so cruel – she thought Sophie was in love with her own brother! Maybe the old woman had kept it a secret for so long that she finally wanted someone to know the truth? Maybe deep down she despised herself for what she had done and didn't want to take it to the grave.

From the moment they'd met, Sophie had trusted David and he seemed at ease with her too. But as for being her brother, her twin brother at that, why on earth would he believe such a preposterous story? She could hardly believe it herself. Yet here it was in front of her, written in her mother's handwriting and she knew instinctively that it was the truth.

Sophie stood up. She would run herself a bath then go downstairs and make the call. She couldn't put it off any longer.

David picked up the envelope from his desk. He'd done the same thing about twenty times since it came down from the legal department, but still he couldn't bring himself to open it. Whatever the truth, he had hurt Sophie badly and he wasn't sure he would ever be able to make it up to her. Taking a key from the bottom drawer of his desk, he glanced over his shoulder and headed for the drinks cupboard in the corner. It was strictly for entertaining prospective clients and he'd never done this before, but right now he needed the balls to face up to the truth. He pulled open the door, grabbed a bottle of vodka, took a long swig and slammed it back down on the shelf. Then he reached for the phone.

'Jean – can you hold my calls for half an hour please? I'll buzz you as soon as I'm free.'

Reaching for his lighter, he pulled out a packet of Benson and Hedges and leaned back in his chair. As the smoke rose lazily into the air, he grasped the silver letter opener – a present from his mother – and slit through the white vellum.

She could see David at the far end of the bar clutching an empty glass, his shoulders hunched forward. Thankfully, the place was almost deserted. She watched him for a while, rehearsing her words like an actress frozen by stage fright. Just then he turned, his eyes homing in on hers and instinctively she understood. She didn't have to tell him anything at all. She didn't have to tell him because he already knew.

Sophie stared at the piece of paper he put in front of her – a copy from the General Register Office of May 18 1945.

No 386, Time 2.47 Sophie Wainwright

No 386, Time 3.04 David Arthur Wainwright

She turned to look at him. 'So what are you telling me?'

'We were born on the same day, in the same place and have the same reference number in the register. That means, without any doubt, that we were, that we *are* twins.'

'I knew it, David. I knew Frances was telling the truth.'

'You knew? But how could you?'

'I've been reading her diaries. It's all here, just as it happened.' Sophie rummaged in her bag. 'Have a look for yourself.'

'But I don't understand,' he scanned the pages. 'Your mother must have known she was having twins?'

'No, that's just it – she had no idea. Non-identical twins, it seems, come from two separate eggs that are fertilised at the same time. Back then, unless the mother was unnaturally big, there was no way of telling if she was carrying more than one child. I was much smaller than you, so it didn't show.'

'But what about heartbeats? Didn't they have those contraption things to listen to the baby's heart? Surely they would have heard two heartbeats?'

Sophie smiled despite herself. 'Not necessarily. Sometimes the hearts beat in unison. The "contraption", as you call it, was not very good back then.'

He looked at her, a puzzled expression on his face. 'How do you know all this?'

'Because I've been doing some research. I'm struggling to take it all in just as much as you are.'

'So let me get this right – Frances didn't know she was expecting twins until the minute they were born?'

'*We* were born, David. You're talking as if it happened to someone else.'

'That's how it feels.' He pulled a face. 'I'm sorry – go on.'

'Sometimes, one of the twins is much slower to develop. The weak twin is hidden behind the larger baby and appears after the afterbirth of the first. With us, it was even rarer, because it happened the other way round.'

'Hold on, please. You're getting too technical for me now.'

'Put it this way –   I weighed less than two bags of sugar. Does that mean something to you?'

He took hold of her hand, his eyes dangerously bright. 'I was never close to my mother, er, Betty Newby as you know, but the thought that she was prepared to separate us so that she could bring up a child of her own fills me with disgust.'

'Don't blame her for everything, David, we don't know why she –'

'Don't blame her, Sophie? What else can I do? She stole me from your mother, separated me from you and pretended to be the woman who gave birth to me. Why the hell would anyone do that? It makes me feel sick.' He picked up the copy of the register. 'She even faked my birth certificate – registered me under a different name two weeks later.'

'Is that possible?

'Oh yes. A lot of people did it apparently, registered the wrong date of birth because they'd broken the law by leaving it too late. She just decided to give me a new surname as well.'

'She can't have been in her right mind when she did it.'

'And by the time she'd finished, your poor mother wasn't in her right mind, either.'

Sophie nodded thoughtfully. 'I knew there was something strange about my mother almost from the minute I could talk. She seemed to like me one day and hate me the next. She kept saying I should have been a boy. That life would've been so much better if only she'd had a son. Sometimes I had no idea what she really wanted from me and sometimes, as I grew older, I didn't care. I wanted to be part of a family. I wanted a mum and a dad, just like everyone else. Now, at last, the whole thing makes sense.'

Letting go of her hand, David shook his head. 'I just don't know how you can be so gracious when it almost ruined your life.'

I have some answers at last, that's why, which is more than you do. What good would it do to be bitter?'

He shook his head. 'You should be angry with Betty Newby – just as angry as I am. Oh God, I always knew something was not right. I should've faced up to it years ago. Now I'll never get the chance to ask her why.'

For several moments they stared at each other, the rain slamming noisily against the windows.

Sophie was the first to speak. 'Will you come with me to see her?'

'See who?'

'Frances – our mother – I think we both owe her that.'

'But she doesn't even know *you* these days, Sophie, so what good would it do to see me?'

'I can't answer that, but somehow I know it's the right thing to do. Will you?'

He shuffled uncomfortably before bringing his eyes back to rest on hers. 'I'll do it for you, though heaven knows why you want me to.'

'My God – you're scared aren't you? Scared of what you might see? Scared that the truth will be worse than the sad reality of your own suppressed childhood?'

David's hand flew to his face. For a moment she thought he was going to hit her. 'You think I'm a coward, don't you, Sophie?'

'I think you're afraid to face the truth, but the truth won't disappear just because you ignore it. You've accepted me as your sister, haven't you?'

'Of course I have – you must know that.'

'Then accept Frances as your mother too. She wasn't always like this.' Sophie reached into her pocket and pulled out a faded black and white photo. The pretty young woman sitting in a deckchair had a mass of curly brown hair pulled back from her face in the fashion of the forties, her bow lips stretched into a brilliant smile.

David took the photo from her. 'She looks so young, so full of life.'

'And some of the time she was. Maybe if she'd been allowed to keep you she wouldn't have had her demons. That's one thing we'll never know.'

'You really do think this is about me now, don't you?'

'I'm sorry, David, but yes. I do.'

'No wonder she resented you for being a girl. It must have been awful for you.'

She nodded. 'I confess I didn't understand it at all. I spent most of my childhood trying to be the kind of person she wanted me to be. Now I know that I couldn't, and more importantly, that none of it was her fault.'

'But it wasn't yours, either.'

Sophie looked up at him. She knew he was trying to protect her and it made her feel safe. But she couldn't let the moment go. '*Will* you come to see Frances with me?'

'I will, if you answer me one question. Why did you never call her Mum? It's something I've often wondered.'

'It wasn't because I didn't want to, if that's what you're thinking. She was very young to be a mother and, well, making me use her Christian name, it sort of camouflaged things, I suppose. In a lot of ways she was very forward thinking.'

'And now she's losing her mind? That must be very hard to accept.'

'Yes, but she'll still my mother.'

'And mine, too, is that what you're trying to say?'

Sophie nodded. The barman was staring at them now, obviously convinced they were having a lovers' tiff. 'Shall we go for a walk?'

He forced a smile. 'Okay, sis. Follow me. I'll lead the way.'

'Are you ready, David?' Sophie squeezed his arm.

He shot her a brief smile, perspiration forming in tiny globules above his top lip. 'Ready as I'll ever be.'

Frances was sitting in her chair, arms folded in front of her, her once dark hair now streaked with grey. Her eyes stared past them into some vast abyss.

'I've brought someone to see you, Frances.' Sophie took hold of her mother's hand.

'Hello, dear,' Frances managed a polite smile. 'Visiting again are you? It's very kind, but there's really no need.' She let go of her daughter's hand. 'Just remind me, will you, who are you again?'

'It's me, Sophie, and this is David, a very good friend of mine.'

'Pleased to meet you, Mrs Wainwright.' David held out his hand but she made no move to take it.

'Are you indeed?' A faint smile stretched over the older woman's face. 'And why would that be?'

'Because I've heard a lot about you.' Good God. Was that the best he could do?

'Is anyone coming with the tea?' Frances stared round the room. 'We always have tea when visitors arrive, you know. But then nobody comes to see me these days. Who is this man you've brought with you?'

Sophie grabbed hold of her brother's arm, clearly afraid he might leave. 'Are you all right, David? Why don't you just sit down for a minute?'

'I prefer to stand.' He knew it sounded lame but the place was stifling.

Frances picked up her handbag and began to rifle through it. 'Now where have I put my purse?'

'You don't need it now,' Sophie chided. 'Why don't you talk to David? He's come here specially to see you.'

'I'm sorry, dear, but we always have tea when visitors come. I must pay for mine. You can't expect anything for nothing nowadays.' She was looking directly at David now. 'Do *you* have any children?'

'Er, no, Frances. I'm not married.'

'Since when did that matter, my boy?' She let out a loud cackle that sounded more like a sob. Her eyes glazed over and he thought for a moment that she would cry.

'I had a son once, you know.' Frances pulled out a handkerchief and twisted it round her fingers till it made red weals on her skin. 'Just like his father, he was, blue eyes,

338

lovely blonde hair, always laughing and giggling.' Her eyes glazed over. 'He used to wait by the door each day for his dad to come home, always looking, always waiting, but you see he just never came.'

'You had a son then, as well as a daughter?'

Sophie shot David a threatening look.

'Of course I had a son, didn't I just tell you? Dressed him all in blue, I did. His father would have been so proud of him.'

'What was his father's name?'

'David, stop it, please.' Sophie's voice rose to a shriek.

'Captain Ed Trask. Loveliest man you could ever wish to meet. Now, if you'll excuse me, it's Monday and I've got the washing to do.'

Just then a nurse came running. 'What is it, Mrs Wainwright? Whatever is the matter?'

Sophie leaned forward. 'It's nothing is it, Frances? You're just over-emotional, that's all. It's nothing nurse, I'm sorry.'

Frances stared at the white-clad intruder. 'Go away, you stupid girl, can't you see I'm busy? Ed will be here soon and he'll need to polish his boots.'

'We'll all be going soon, don't you worry,' David said, wiping the sweat from his brow.

Sophie grasped her mother's hand. 'Before we do, I've brought you something I found in your flat. I thought you might like to have it with you.'

'A present for me?'

'Not a present exactly, just something you've kept for a very long time.' Sophie removed the package from her bag, opened the tissue paper and held the contents in the palm of her hand. 'Remember this?'

'It's a baby's bootee,' her mother looked puzzled. 'Why ever would I want that?'

'It's yours, that's why. I thought you might be able to tell me who it belonged to.'

The older woman picked up the scrap of cotton and studied it carefully. For a moment her eyes flickered. She opened her mouth as if to speak, then slumped back into her armchair. 'It's neither use nor ornament without the other one.'

'What happened to the other one, Frances? Where did it go? Who did it belong to?'

Frances shook her head. 'There were never two, don't you see? I only ever had one.'

'I'm not sure I can do this,' David muttered, loosening his tie with his right hand. 'You're obviously busy, Mrs Wainwright, so if you don't mind, I'll say goodbye.'

Once outside in the hospital grounds, David pulled out his cigarettes and chain-smoked nervously till Sophie reappeared.

'I'm sorry,' he said, as soon as he caught sight of her. 'That wasn't my finest hour.'

She stared at him for a moment, her eyes giving little away. 'At least you came. You would have regretted it otherwise. I'm not angry, if that's what you're thinking. I just wish you'd stayed a bit longer, that's all.'

'The trouble is, your mother means nothing to me, ill or well, and I can't hide it from you, or anyone.'

'I see.'

'Do you? I'm not sure you do.' David felt a tug at his gut. He'd just met the woman who'd brought him into the world, yet she was a stranger and always would be. Right now he wished he'd never set eyes on Sophie, never let her get under his skin.

'I think I've messed things up for you.' Sophie bit down on her lip.

'No, don't worry, I did that for myself. I'm beginning to understand how Ed felt after all. Maybe it is too late. Come on, I think it's time to get you home.'

'All right, but there's one more thing I need to know.' Sophie looked at him squarely. 'What are you going to do about Ed?'

'I don't know yet. Part of me wants to see him again. I actually liked the guy, even though he thought you and I were a couple.'

'And so did Betty Newby.' Sophie smiled wryly. 'Which reminds me. Do you think Betty knew who Ed was all along?'

'It's hard to say. Not originally, I'm sure. But when he came back after the war she must have done. She wanted him out of the way so that he couldn't interfere with her plans. It seems she was a very determined woman.'

'Determined to keep you, that's obvious. And to get rid of me,' Sophie said, without a trace of bitterness.

'So, in answer to your question, I would like to see Ed again, one more time at least. He's my father and I reckon I'd always regret it if I didn't.'

'Are you going to tell him?'

'I don't know. Do you honestly think he'd want to keep in

touch with me any more than he did with you?'

'You should at least give him a chance.' She nodded. 'Strange, really. I wonder, perhaps, if he was meant to have a son.'

'He was meant to have us both, Sophie, but it just didn't happen. Do *you* want to see him again?'

'I don't know. My feelings are mixed. After all, he didn't have to tell me he would be in Nice. Or that he really loved my mother. Maybe he just changed his mind when we met.'

'I'm sure that's not true. I think he just felt you'd been hurt enough already.'

'And what about you, David? Would he have felt the same if he'd known you were his son?'

David stood up and walked towards the window. 'You really do think he wanted a son, don't you? That it would have made all the difference?'

'Yes, in a way. I just think you should try again, that's all.'

'Tell me something, Sophie. Why are you being so understanding?'

'Because I got the answer I was looking for in the end. Now I know what really happened, I want to make it up to Frances.'

He turned back to face her. 'And I admire you for that.'

'The only thing I can do now is help her get better. I've applied for a job, one or two jobs actually, around London. There's a pioneering hospital in the Home Counties that specialises in Electric Convulsion Therapy. It's the latest treatment for mental illness.'

'Sounds a bit gruesome. How does it work?'

'They put electric currents through the brain, apparently, to erase memories of the past. The ones the patient would rather forget. Some people have been known to make a good recovery.'

'But what about the drinking? Surely that's still a problem?'

She looked animated now, happier than he'd seen her for a long time. 'The liver's the only organ in the body that can grow new tissue,' she said. 'Mum hasn't touched a drop since her fall, so there's a chance she may be all right.'

David smiled. 'I've never heard you call her Mum before. Just one more thing.'

'And that is?'

'What about Steve? I want to know what's going on between you two.'

Bright spots of crimson suffused Sophie's cheeks. 'Nothing. We haven't spoken much since he came back. I can't see the point.'

'The poor guy's in love with you, that's the point. It's obvious to anyone.'

'He's a womaniser.'

'Rubbish.'

'He likes himself too much.'

'Insecure, more like.'

'And he left when I needed him most.'

'We pushed him away, Sophie, you and me. Does he know I'm your brother?'

'Well, no, but –'

'So tell him. Believe me, it's the only thing to do.'

She reached up and gave him a kiss on the cheek. 'Thanks, David.'

CHAPTER 44

Sophie kept going over David's words. He'd helped her find her father – their father as it turned out – when he'd no idea who she was. He'd supported her, despite Betty Newby's hostility, and she would always be grateful for that. But it was what he'd said about Steve that troubled her most. *The poor guy's in love with you. It's obvious to anyone.* She'd been busy planning her future and it didn't include Steve. She may have wanted it to, but that was another story. Anyway, he'd probably moved on by now. No, her first priority must be Frances.

Pushing Steve to the back of her mind, she buried herself in work. She'd sent some pieces off to a magazine looking for "fresh new writers" as the idea of going freelance really appealed to her. She'd applied for one or two jobs advertised in the *UK Press Gazette*, though she didn't really hold out much hope. After a year on the *Tribune*, Sophie had covered every event in the calendar, from court to council, fêtes to flower shows and she couldn't face the thought of doing it all again. She needed a change and, anyway, Yorkshire held nothing for her now.

She'd seen David a couple of times since meeting Frances at the hospital. He'd got a new girlfriend, an actress called Annie he'd met at the Preston Playhouse. David had introduced Sophie as his sister and she'd smiled and nodded as if it were the most natural thing in the world.

As the weeks passed, Sophie somehow managed to avoid Steve – or maybe he was avoiding her. Either way, it didn't matter. She'd be gone from here for good soon. Strange how he'd shown such an interest in her initially, how he'd appeared to be jealous of David. It seemed so ironic now.

Sophie had been so keen to label Steve a womaniser, so sure she didn't have room in her life for romance, she hadn't seen what was going on right in front of her nose. By the time she did, he'd disappeared from her life. It was too late now to expect him to feel the same, but he'd been good to her since she'd arrived in Harcot and she owed it to him to put things straight. Suppressing her excitement at seeing him again, she grabbed her bag and made for the car.

Steve had a cardboard box in his hand when he opened the front door. 'Sophie, come in – this is a surprise. Where've you been all this time?'

'Where have *I* been? It's *you* who disappeared. Besides, I've been busy – with David. There's so much to tell you I'm not sure how to begin.'

'Try me,' he motioned her to a space on the sofa.

'What are you doing?' She stared in dismay round the half-empty room.

'Packing up.'

'But you've only just come back!'

'Exactly. It made me realise there's nothing left here for me.'

'What did?' Her heart took a dive. He'd just confirmed what she knew all along.

'My trip. I've been to the Woodstock Festival.'

Sophie's mouth dropped open. 'In New York?'

'The very one. Along with half a million others. Mud, nudity, free love, you name it, I saw it. The hippies have started a revolution. Best shots I've taken in my whole life.'

'Oh, I see.' She didn't at all. Visions of naked women throwing their arms round his neck flashed before her eyes; wild carefree women, caked in wet mud. Jealousy stabbed like a knife deep in her stomach. 'That's amazing, really, the chance of a lifetime...' her voice trailed off. 'Did you join in?

'Me? Of course.' He winked. 'Anything to please.'

She studied her fingernails. 'Still hoping to be David Bailey?'

'Something like that. Just wait till you see the results. My mate Jerry's planning to put the lot of them into a hardback book – a coffee table book I believe it's called. This is it, Sophie. This is the start of my career.' He picked her up and twirled her in the air before depositing her gently back on the sofa. 'So, come on, what did you want to tell me?'

She grabbed an old copy of the *Harcot Weekly Tribune* and fanned her face. Being so close to him had set her heart racing. 'I'd almost forgotten why I came. I've decided to forgive my mother. I should have done it long ago.'

'I see. That's good, of course, but why now? After all this time?'

'Because I've read her diaries. If I'd known what she'd been through sooner, it might have brought us together instead of forcing us apart. Maybe we could've had a different kind of life.'

'And what sort of life will she have from now on?' Steve frowned, his face full of concern.

'They're going to give her electric shock treatment. She's young enough so it shouldn't harm her.'

'I've heard of that. Sounds quite drastic, but I suppose anything's worth a try.'

'It's a last resort. There's nothing else they can do. But at least I can be with her while she's going through it.'

'You're just a big softy underneath, Sophie. You wouldn't hurt a fly. I suppose I've know that all along.' His face fell into a frown. 'You still haven't told me everything. How does David fit into all this?'

Sophie opened her bag, pretending to search for her glasses. 'My father seemed to think David would make a very good husband.'

'Don't joke about it, Sophie, please.'

'I'm not joking – that's exactly what he said. He sensed a closeness between us. He was right, of course, he just didn't know how close.'

'Damn your stupid David.' Steve's voice cracked. 'I wish I'd never heard his name. He's the only guy in all my life who's ever made me jealous.'

Sophie's eyes widened. Had she imagined what she'd just heard? 'Did you say jealous?'

'I'm not going to say it again, if that's what you want. Once is definitely enough.'

'That's a shame. I'd quite like to have heard it again, just to be sure I'm not dreaming.' She was standing behind him now, her throat dry, the desire to feel his skin on hers overpowering. 'There's something you need to know about David. I've been wondering how to tell you.'

'Go on.'

'Well, the fact is, he's not just my friend, you see.'

'Really? You do surprise me.'

'No. I've just found out that he's – well – he's –'

'Say, it Sophie.'

'My brother.'

'Your *brother!*' Steve yelled. 'Please don't make fun of me, Sophie. This isn't the time for jokes.'

'Why would I joke about something like that? You have to believe me – I've never been more serious in my life. David's my brother, my twin brother to be exact. I've seen the proof. His so-called mother stole him from mine just after he was born.'

'David's your brother? I can hardly believe it.' His voice broke. *'How long have you known?'*

'Not very long. I haven't really got used to the idea myself.'

Steve threw his arms around her, so tight that she could hardly breathe. 'That's amazing news, that's front page news, the best I've ever heard in years. I'm not really sure I can take it in.'

'Nor me.' She felt quite giddy.

'But I don't understand. How come you've only just found out?'

'I'll tell you the whole story, I promise, but not today.'

'Is there anything else I need to know?' He was staring at her intently now, his hand absentmindedly stroking her hair from her face.

'There is something, now you mention it.' She steadied herself against his shoulders. 'I've been offered a job on the *London Evening Standard*. The letter came this morning.'

'So you're leaving Harcot, Sophie, is that what you're trying to tell me?' He let go of her as if he'd been stung.

'Why ever not? This means everything to me. It's just what I've always dreamed of. I will finally *be* somebody, don't you see?'

'But I thought that now you've found your mother, you'd want to stay around here,' Steve offered lamely. 'To be close to her?'

'Close to her! All my life I've wanted to be close to her.' Sophie's voice shook as the anger unleashed inside her. 'I've never belonged to anyone, can't you see? I may have found my father and a long-lost brother, but the only people they really belong to is Frances. They're locked inside her head, always have been, to the exclusion of everything else – including me. But I'm not going to give up on her, not yet. One day there might be a cure.' She stumbled back, shoulders sagging, as the reality of her own words sunk in.

Steve plunged forward, just in time to break her fall. 'Oh Sophie,' he groaned as his arms closed round her, 'is that why you've always pushed me away – because you're scared of belonging, scared of becoming attached to anyone, scared that you might get hurt?' He smoothed her hair, cupping her face between his palms. 'I want you, I've always wanted you, from the moment I first saw you in the rain. Somehow, you crazy girl, somehow I just thought you knew.'

She reached up and kissed him now, like she'd never kissed anyone, like she knew she'd never kiss anyone else again.

'Besides,' he said, when she'd finally prized herself out of his arms, 'you must take up the job offer. It's what you've always wanted.'

'But what if I'm not up to it? London's a long way away, and I'm not sure the car will get me there in one piece.'

'Mmm, yes, I see what you mean.' Steve's face fell into a frown.

'Do you, now? About me or the car?'

'You know very well I meant the car. I've never doubted *you* for a minute. I tell you what – Jerry used to live in London so I know the city quite well. We could go down for the weekend, see the sights, then scout round some places for Frances. It might help you decide. What do you say?'

'Why not?' Sophie did her best to sound casual. 'It sounds like a great idea.'

'Right.' He stroked her hand. 'I might even move down there myself one of these days. There's not much left for me here now, not without you.'

'Nor me without you.' She licked her lips, her mouth so dry she could hardly speak.

'Do you mean that?'

'I'm a journalist remember – I never say anything I don't mean.'

'Good, because I've thought of another name for you.'

'Anything's better than Frigidaire.'

'You might not like it.'

'Try me.'

'Are you sure?

'Quite sure.'

'How about Sophie Sibson?'

She reached out and fingered the hair that curled around his collar. 'Sophie Sibson?'

'I can see the name now in a by-line. On the front page of the *Evening Standard*.' He leaned forward and kissed her again, then cradled her head in his arms. 'We'll go to London together. Forget that old jalopy of yours – I can give you a lift. What do you say?'

'Yes, please.' She closed her eyes. 'I'd like that very much.'

ACKNOWLEDGMENTS

I would like to thank my husband Les for reading every word several times, Elaine for her amazing role as 'project manager', Diane for believing in me and Amy and Chloe for steadfastly supporting me all the way.

Lightning Source UK Ltd.
Milton Keynes UK
UKOW03f0414080914

238218UK00002B/39/P